Test the Gods

Then

~~ Run Like Hell!

Zeek's Feet Detective Series

Jo Hammers
Paranormal Crossroads & Publishing

Test the Gods

Copyright © 2013 by Jo Hammers

ISBN 978-0-9882412-8-2

www.paranormalcrossroads.com

This work is fiction. All of the characters, organizations, and events portrayed in this novel are either products of the author's imagination or are used fictitiously.

Cover Art by Mindy Blodgett, 2017.

Table of Contents

Test the Gods

Then

~~ Run Like Hell!

Zeek's Feet Detective Series

Jo Hammers
Paranormal Crossroads & Publishing

CHAPTER ONE

Test the Gods and Run

Chester Holly sat at the foot of his grandfather's hospital bed. The oldest member of his family was dying. The nurse had given him a pain killer and he was temporarily dozing. It was November first and Chester was skipping school to sit by his grandfather's side. His parents were busy making a living, and there was no one else to sit with him. Chester didn't mind. School had always been a nightmare experience for him, even though he was a 4.0 student. He was the smelly garbage dump kid that his classmates turned their nose up at.

Chester's Grandfather's hospital room was a double. It housed two patients. In the bed by the window, there was a new patient. Chester surmised that he had arrived sometime the night before. The new man was elderly like his grandfather, possibly eighty years old. There was a straight chair at the end of each bed for visitors to sit in. Chester was quietly sitting in the one at the foot of his Grandfather Holly's bed, lost in thoughts concerning his future. He was a senior and would graduate high school in May. Escaping his dump town of Gardenia was number one in his thoughts. He planned to leave the day after his high school graduation and never return.

The older male patient by the window, who was sitting up and looking out, looked really familiar. Chester couldn't place where he had seen him before. However, he was sure that he knew him. He just couldn't decide where he knew him from. The window bed man looked washed out white, like he was getting over a bad round of flu or other illness. He looked pasty, like a ghost. The white hospital gown he had on didn't help.

"Hey, bud; you wouldn't help me find my nurse's call button would you?" The elderly man asked, turning his attention away from the window to Chester.

"It is on the side of your bed railing." Chester replied rising from his chair and walking over to show the old man where the button was.

"Would you push it for me and then run?" The pasty faced, white haired man asked.

"Run?" Chester asked as he pushed the button for the old man.

"Yeah . . . run! I don't want the nurses to think it has been you pushing their buttons all day. I enjoy annoying them. At my age, how many pretty women do you get a chance to talk to on a daily basis? This hospital stay is a social event for me. I'm testing the goddesses."

Chester smiled. "Maybe this should be a social event for me too! Pretty, nice smelling girls don't seem to find my smell appealing. I live out by the dump. My skin has absorbed its odors. I am a garbage collector's son!"

"You are what you say you are, son. My parents owned a fish market and I was a fish gutter when I was your age. Just like you, nice smelling girls turned their nose up at me. One day a light bulb went on in my head. I wasn't a fish gutter. My parents were wealthy, and in the import and export business. Fish were just what my parent's dealt in. The girls started looking at me differently, because I looked at myself differently."

"That is good thinking. But what did you do about the smell. Fish smell just as bad as garbage. All my classmates say I smell like garbage. I have tried everything to make myself smell less offensive. Nothing seems to work."

"When people see you differently, they will also smell you differently. There are some very expensive after shaves and colognes for men out there that are nasty smelling. They remind me of a cross between fish guts and pumpkin pie spice. Humans call them musk and pay big bucks for them. You now wear natural garbage can smells. The same smell, marketed and priced out of the reach of an ordinary man, becomes valuable. You have to price what you and your smell are worth. I am a rich man with thousands of dollars in the bank, a cook at home to fix me anything I want to eat, and a maid to bring it here and serve it to me. However, I am into being the god of my world wherever I am. I will rule my world, here in this hospital, not be ruled by it. I am a god and a creator."

"That is a good thought. However, are the pretty nurses you speak of going to let you rule?" I replied asking. "They ignore my grandfather here like he is white trash. No one wants to associate with a garbage dump individual because of who we are."

"What would you like the nurses to do for you, or your grandfather?"

"Respect would be nice for a starter. What do you want from them, if you already have everything including a cook, maid, etc.?"

"You want respect. I want a piece of Banana Crème Pie. The pie is the respect I will demand from them. I am king of my world. Anyone that wants an audience with me and wants favors must pay my worth. If they want me to do what they ask, they will first present me with a piece of my favorite pie. If they want me to quit pushing the nurse's call light button, they will have to pay my price. As the ruler of my world, I am worthy of Banana Crème Pie. You must figure out your worth, one day at a time, and demand it from people. The nurses, your school classmates, and all people in general are little gods walking around you with items of respect you want. You won't get any of their offerings unless you walk right up to them, push their buttons, test them, get what you want, and then run away laughing with your pie. Life is what you take from it. If you want respect, demand it. If you want to be someone other than a dump kid, reinvent yourself."

"I hate my grandfather's trash truck business. He is ill and expects me to take over his garbage trucks when I graduate high school in the spring. I want more out of life."

"We have no control over the families we are born in to, or how we are raised up to a certain age. You are a garbage man's kid and I was a fish monger's son. However, there comes a time in every young man's life when he must test the gods and run. Your grandfather chose his life career, just as my father chose to run a fish market. However, I am not my father and you are not your grandfather. You and I must be what we are intended to be. One day, after cutting out the guts of my ninety eighth fish for the morning, a light bulb in my head went on and I realized what I would really be good at."

"What was that?" I asked all ears.

"I was a perfect candidate to become a surgeon! I was sure that the guts of humans couldn't be much different from those of the fish I had honed my skills on. That moment, in my father's fish market, I reinvented myself and quit telling people I was a fish gutter. I started telling people I was going to medical school and one day would be a surgeon, a doctor. Everyone started treating me differently and seeing me differently. They even ignored the fish smell on me."

"I am the bottom of the garbage barrel in my world. My classmates have never wanted anything to do with me. At graduation in the spring, we seniors are required to pair up to walk down to get our diplomas. You are guaranteed that I will walk alone at the end of the line. All the kids I have grown up with refuse to be my partner. It has been that way my whole life. When I take over a garbage truck for my father next summer, I will be doomed to a life of being socially unacceptable."

"You are looking at what you do not want, when you should be looking forward and choosing what you do want. Smart guys reinvent themselves." The old man stated giving his nurse's button another push. "Right now, I am reinventing myself to be a Troll god who wants Banana Crème Pie. Before coming in here, I was a doctor. A doctor doesn't mean anything sitting here in this bed. A troll is who I need to be to get what I want out of hospital life. Many nurses will be crossing my bridge today. Tomorrow, I will reinvent myself again. There is no stopping place. A smart man reinvents himself in every situation he encounters."

"There isn't much hope for me doing much reinventing. My low class family intends to suck the life out of me and chain me to their trash business. I won't be going off to Ivy League colleges like my classmates, although I would like to go. I will be driving a trash truck down a never ending, life road."

"It is not where you won't be going; it is where you will be going in spite of the fact you are temporarily a fish gutter or a garbage collector. There are lots of opportunities out there. You just have to walk up to the gods who control them, poke them in the ribs, demand Banana Crème Pie from them, and then run like hell forward toward your next opportunity. I was a fish gutter, but I am not one now." He replied and then asked. "What did you say your name was?"

"Chester Holly," I replied enjoying the old man's attention. No one had ever took an interest in me. I was drinking the old man's attention in.

"Well Chester Holly, if I were you, I would test the Gods and run every moment of every day till you find yourself my age, lying in a hospital bed like me, and with your clothes and running shoes hidden by the nurses. Even half naked, flat of my back, and tied to this bed; I can still test the gods and get what I want. Right now, I don't need clothes, shoes, or my medical degree. My stomach does want to eat Banana Crème Pie."

"Are you telling me to annoy people and opportunities till I get what I want?" I asked laughing.

"Annoying the nurses is not my game. I am testing them to see what I can get out of them." The old man replied grinning. "What we get from testing the gods could be our next step forward or our next meal. I happen to be craving Banana Crème Pie. At the present, here in the hospital, I am on a tea, gelatin, and bullion soup diet. I am supposed to have surgery tomorrow and they are cleaning me out, or so they say. If I die on that operating table, I want to go to meet my maker with pride knowing that my stomach is full of respect or Banana Crème Pie. I can lie here and accept a garbage collecting or fish gutting death bed meal of meaningless liquids, or I can test the gods and die tomorrow with my sweet tooth satisfied." He replied with a smile from ear to ear. "In the moment, I am a Banana Crème Pie man. Obtaining a piece of pie is just as important to me as the day I obtained my medical degree."

"Are you telling me not to be satisfied with what life is currently forcing down my throat?" I asked to clarify what he was saying to me.

"More than that son . . . I am telling you to walk right up to whatever it is in life you day dream about and annoy the devil out of the gods till you get what you want from them. Test the gods of life and get what you want in every moment of every day. Run afterwards. Once you have obtained a high school diploma, or some other award, focus on what is next. Never settle for yesterday's garbage, or step backwards experience. My parents would have loved for me to have taken over their fish market. They would have loved to tie me to fish guts forever."

"Just where would I start on this adventure of testing the gods?" I asked with my own light bulb trying to turn on.

"For starters, I would introduce myself as Chet Holly to the girls and tell them that your parents are collectors of antiquities. Antiquities describe anything and everything thrown out that is more than one day old. Yesterday is gone forever. It is an antique."

"I had never considered that. Thanks man!" Chester replied rolling over the words 'Collectors of Antiquities' in his thinking.

"Walk up to those snooty, smell good, teen goddesses at your school and make them see you in a new way. Then, after you snag their attention, run. It is the snagging where life is at. There is a big world of opportunities out there, Chet Holly. Bored to death, wealthy gods and goddesses are waiting out there for you to come along, snag them from their boredom, and play games with them. Walk right up to them, tell them what you can do for them (not what they can do for you), snag their attention, get what you want and then run like hell, laughing as you go."

"So, you are telling me to annoy the devil out of my fellow man and refuse to get out of their face till I get what I want from them. Then I am to seize the next moment, run, and annoy the next rich god on my path."

"You are getting my point, Chet Holly. Present yourself as somebody, not a garbage man's kid or some beggar that won't see the insides of their mansions. The gods and goddesses of this world want to hang with those individuals who are going somewhere. They don't want to lie in the gutter with those who refuse to get up out of it. Calling yourself Chet Holly is a beginning. Chester doesn't attract girl's attention. Chet does."

"I have always hated my name. My mother named me after a pack of Chesterfield cigarettes she was smoking when she was in labor with me. Anyway, that is what she has told me. Who names their kid after cigarettes?" I replied in a sarcastic questioning voice.

"Where a man's thoughts are, is where he lives from. Where you let yourself think from, is where you will live your life. A woman with gutter mentality sees and thinks herself as worthy of a cheap free ride, raising her kids on welfare. She names her kids from what she hears and sees in that gutter. A cigarette name is one she would choose. A woman, with going somewhere thoughts, will work, go to school, and do whatever it takes to move up society's ladder, not down it. Not only that, a smart woman will use birth control and plan a good life for the children she will choose to have. Dump life, Chet, is a form of welfare. To you, it is gutter living. Just as a smart woman does not ever think about living on welfare, you should not think about the gutter you are in. Concentrate your thoughts always on living higher and higher standards. What you think is how you will live. You are a smart kid, Chet. You won't find smart kids choosing to live welfare or dump lifestyles."

"So, you are saying that I am currently living the choices made by my parents, but once I am out of school, it is okay for me to walk away and reinvent myself or choose higher god experiences."

"Reinvent yourself, Chet. Face life, test the gods, and get the respect you deserve. It will never come from following someone else's dream or living in their gutter life choices. Until this moment in time, your family has forced you to live in a dump gutter life or welfare state. You have the smarts to reinvent yourself and climb out of the gutter life you have been born into."

"I will give what you have told me some serious thought." I replied as I suddenly had hope for a future. "Do you have any suggestion as to how I might snag a date for prom? My reputation as the white trash kid already has me branded."

"I would pick out the prettiest cheerleader in your school. I would write her a note telling her that you are sorry but you cannot take her to the prom, because you don't find her as attractive as her best friend, another cheerleader. Then write her best friend the same note. The two will get into a fighting war over you, because no girl wants to be second best. Then you ask the third prettiest cheerleader to the prom, who will see it as one upping the other two. At the same time, you let it be known that you have just won a new convertible in the state lottery. You rent it a week before prom and start driving it to school. It will be classier than the wheels of any of the football team's piles of junk. Then on the night of the prom, you dump all three cheerleaders and show up with a model on your arm that has bigger endowments and figure than any of the cheerleaders. In doing so, you have tested the gods and run."

"And just where do I find this gorgeous girl with huge endowments?"

"Rent what you need in life, Chet Holly. Today it might be a limousine; tomorrow it might be a beautiful woman or a house in Hollywood. Hire an actress to play the model on your arm at prom. Everything and everyone you need is out there. You don't have to own anything to reinvent yourself. Life is all about the image you project of yourself. You can present yourself as a low class kid who lives in the garbage dump across the tracks or take what funds you have and reinvent yourself. Sooner or later, some rich man is going to ask you to be a car salesman, seeing what fine autos you drive. Then, he will introduce you to the mayor, the state's senator, and other rich men who will take note of you. They will in turn introduce you to others further up the success ladder. Someday when you are in business for yourself and you need a doctor's degree to pull off a deal, you go out and hire you one. Expensive things and men with degrees can all be rented."

"You are one smart dude." I replied in awe of what he had told me. "You are not annoying the nurses just to get attention; you want free Banana Crème Pie or the accomplishment of adding to your wealth the price of the pie."

"I am testing the nurse gods today. I will make them all want to kill me before this day is over by pushing their call light buttons one time too many. They will promise me anything before their shift is over. Right now, my anything is pie. When they give me what I want, Banana Crème Pie, I will run. They all will remember me and pray I never end up on their floor again. The frightened, non-button pushing patients like your grandfather, will be forgotten. Your grandfather will be just one of thousands that float in and out of this place. I have no intentions of being forgotten. I will be remembered as the Banana Crème Pie patient."

About that time, a young nurse flew into the room and headed straight for the old man's bed.

"Now, Doctor Mayo, I was just in her ten minutes ago. Is there something you need that you forgot to ask me for?" She inquired forcing herself to smile. Before this appearance at his bedside, she had been in every ten minutes for the last two hours.

"I want a piece of Banana Crème Pie and the personal phone number for your head nurse. I have a new, single doctor in my practice that thinks she has the prettiest legs of all of the nurses on this floor? I agree with him." He stated winking at me. "None of you younger nurses have legs that can compete with her gems. If I was a beauty contest judge, instead of a doctor, she would get my vote." The old man replied grinning from ear to ear and glancing at me out of the corner of his eye. "Anyway, this young colleague doctor friend of mine was thinking of asking you out, till he spotted her legs."

Instantly, the young nurse looked down at her own legs, blushed, and then quickly looked him in the eye. She had always been told she was the most gorgeous nurse on the floor, by most of the patients. It was an ego moment for her and a testing of the goddess moment for him.

"The head nurse weighs at least ten pounds more than me!" The young nurse huffed.

"Ten pounds makes the difference. You are too skinny and a little short in the endowments department. My doctor friend wants a woman with endowments. Don't take me wrong. You are cute, but your head nurse has what a man really wants." He stated in an apologetic manner.

"You are pushing my buttons." She muttered in an annoyed voice. "Who is this doctor friend of yours that thinks my head nurse has more to offer in the way of endowments than me?"

"You sneak me a piece of Banana Crème Pie from the hospital cafeteria and I will tell you. Otherwise, I am going to just encourage my colleague to pursue your head nurse. You should see his big, new mansion out in the suburbs. Your head nurse will be living the good life with a maid and a sports car to drive, if she plays her cards right."

"No pie! You know you are having surgery tomorrow." She retorted. "Now tell me which of your young doctor colleagues is interested in me and has a new mansion in the suburbs?"

The young nurse had one dream, to meet and marry a rich doctor. She didn't care who he was, or how she got him. She wanted the status of being a doctor's wife. That was her button.

"You sneak me a piece of Banana Crème Pie and I will tell you." He replied folding his arms across his chest. "Play your cards right and you might be married to him by New Years. Of course, you will have to take him away from your head nurse. He is currently infatuated with her legs."

"One piece of pie coming up . . ." The young nurse whispered, completely ignoring me. Then she spun on her heels and left humming the tune to 'Here Comes the Bride'.

After the young nurse was out of the room and out of hearing range, I walked back over to the bedside of the old man. "You conned her."

"No . . . I just dared to test the goddess she is and demand something from her. All gods and goddesses have buttons to push. You just have to figure out what they are. Female gods are vain. They all want to be worshipped and seen as the most gorgeous woman alive. They are competitive. If the young nurse sees the head nurse bringing me a piece of pie, she will sneak me two pieces. They will both compete for what they think I have to offer, a chance to date and marry a doctor."

"So, if I snag the attention of my school's prettiest cheerleader, a type of your young nurse, and then tell her that one of the other girls is prettier than her, I have tested her as a female god and set her up to compete for me or what she thinks I have to offer?"

"That is how it works. You just have to figure out what your school's cheerleader's buttons are. You reinvent yourself into being the fulfillment of her secret dream. In return, she will bless you with Banana Crème Pie or whatever it is that you are in need or want of. A smart young man moving upward must reinvent himself every day of his life." The old man stated and then he pushed his nurse's button again and grinned from ear to ear.

Suddenly, a stern nurse in her late twenties, flew into the room, pulled the curtains around his bed, and then asked. "What will it take for you to quit pushing that nurse's call light button every ten minutes? You are driving my nurses crazy, Dr. Mayo. Furthermore, what are you doing sharing a room with a garbage collector. You have insurance policies out the yang and can afford a private suite as well as a private nurse. I know! I used to be your office nurse; in case you have forgotten."

"You would love to see me isolated in a prison like, one bed dungeon where one nurse would have control over me. It isn't happening. Here, I have the freedom to ask for what I want and there isn't a dam thing you can do about it. Plus, I have ears in the second bed as well as the visitor's chairs, should you try to dismantle my call button or ignore me. This bed by the window and my new friend, Chet, the other side of this curtain, insures I am treated as well as every other patient on this floor and that I am not chained down by some private, weight lifter nurse and left in a dark dungeon of a room to die."

"I hated you when I worked for you and I still do. You push all my buttons. Be sensible, Mayo, tell me what it will take for you to leave that call light button alone. There are other patients on this floor who need my nurses worse than you. You are going to have one small hemorrhoid removed in the morning. That is hardly a reason to be pushing the nurse's call light every ten minutes. Just lay it on the line. What do you want in exchange for not pushing the call light button? I know you want something. You always have an agenda. You continuously pushed all of your staff's buttons when I worked for you. Don't beat around the bush. Just tell me what you want."

I grinned and slapped my hand across my mouth to keep from snorting. He was the man. No one walked on him or told him he was smelly. Then, I heard him reply.

"A piece of Banana Crème Pie from the cafeteria and you spoon feeding it to me. I am in need of a little TLC."

"No pie." She half shouted.

"Have I told you that one of the three new surgeons on my staff has a crush on you? Bring me the pie and I will tell you which one."

"Me . . . one of your colleagues has a crush on me? Is he the cute Jewish one with the name I can't pronounce?"

"Banana Crème Pie . . ." He replied and then he added as she pulled the curtains from around his bed, "Spoon fed!"

CHAPTER TWO

Embracing Mayo's Theory

After the nurse left, I excused myself to go to the cafeteria for a sandwich and soda. I laughed and shook Dr. Mayo's aging hand before leaving, telling him that he was the man. He threw back his top sheet to reveal five empty pie plates beneath his cover. I laughed.

"If you are going to the cafeteria, will you get rid of these for me?"

"Not a problem!" I replied stacking the pie plates and then removing them from his bed. I wondered how many more pieces of pie he would con the nursing staff out of before the day was over.

"Did you eat all of these?" I asked snorting.

"No, but they will think I did if they find them. I shared them with the housekeeper, a visiting chaplain, and your grandfather. I flushed a couple down the toilet when I was in there earlier."

"I will remember that!" I replied grinning and then left the room totally amused. I had my first super hero and he was wearing an open backed hospital gown, not a cape and mask.

"By the way kid . . ." Dr. Mayo called after me as I was about to exit the room, "What do you dream of being someday?"

"I would like to move to California and become a private detective." I re-

plied juggling the stack of dirty pie plates. Then in a moment of shared cama-
raderie I added testing him, "I will bring you a piece of Banana Crème Pie if
you will pay my bus fare out to California after I graduate. That is my price."
Then I laughed knowing I had him.

"You are a fast learner, Chet Holly. Bring the pie on."

I left my grandfather sleeping and walked down to the cafeteria to eat. When
I returned upstairs, carrying a piece of Banana Crème Pie, the old doctor by
the window was gone and his bed was being cleaned for a new patient. I was
sorry my super hero was gone. Not many people had been nice to me in my
life. Dr. Mayo had taken the time to talk to me like I was someone.

"Where did the old fellow go?" I asked while placing the piece of pie on my
grandfather's over the bed table.

"He just climbed out of his bed and walked out of the hospital not looking
back." She replied. "You should have seen the number of dessert plates he
had hidden beneath his mattress. I never saw such a mess."

I bit my lip and snorted. Dr. Mayo had tested the gods and run. Then, I just
had to ask, "Did the head nurse spoon feed him a piece of Banana Crème Pie
before he left?"

"She sure did. I was cleaning around your grandfather's bed and watched
her. Do you think they might have something going on? She is way too young
for him." The housekeeper inquired as she worked.

"I don't think age means anything to him." I replied.

About that time, my grandfather's doctor came in and motioned for me to
join him in the hallway.

"I gather you are Mr. Holly's family?" The doctor inquired.

"My mother is his only child and I am his only grandchild." I replied.

"I assume you are aware that your grandfather is slowly dying. In my opinion, he probably has till about the end of January to live. I am sending him home today and suggest that you and your mother spend some quality time with him. I should be sending him on to a hospice nursing home. However, I feel he would give up and die there by Christmas. Do you understand what I am telling you?"

"You are giving me and my mother a chance to spend quality time with my grandfather before he gets worse." I replied tearing up. My grandfather was the only person in my family who gave a damn about me.

"It is now November. I feel your grandfather can probably move about and do a few things till about Christmas. After that, he will go downhill fast. Make this holiday season a good one for him. Make memories."

"I promise you that I will." I replied fighting back tears. I was a man. Men were not supposed to cry.

"Have you ever asked your grandfather what the one thing is that he has dreamed about doing, but has never done?"

"No . . . but I will." I replied.

Whatever my grandfather wanted to do with what time he had left, I decided that I would help him do it. We would test the gods, extract Banana Crème Pie payment, and run just like Dr. Mayo, my new super hero.

With that said, my grandfather's doctor left and I reentered the hospital room where my grandfather was waking up from a drug induced sleep. I moved my chair to the side of his bed, so I could chat with him face to face.

"Was I asleep long?" He asked in a gravelly voice while running his bony, aging fingers thru his white hair.

"You were sawing some pretty mean logs." I replied smiling at him. "Your snoring sounded like a cross between a chain saw and a freight train."

"It is a good thing your grandmother wasn't here. She would have insisted they put one of those nose strip things on my snout to hold my nostrils open. In my opinion, snoring is just your body's way of saying that you are sleeping good. Whatever they are giving me is making me snore and sleep really good. Have you been here long, Chester?"

"I have been here about an hour or so. Your room-mate and I chatted while I was waiting for you to wake up." I replied.

"What roommate?" My grandfather asked glancing over toward the window bed. "Did they cart someone in while I was asleep?"

"I guess you slept thru the Banana Crème Pie man." I stated pointing to the slice of pie I had placed on his over the bed table.

"Take that piece of pie home to your grandmother, Chester. Tell her I sent it to her. It isn't fair for me to be in here eating pie and her not have some. She has never been much of a pie baker."

I knew how committed my grandfather was to my grandmother. However, it wasn't a two way street. My grandmother had always treated my grandfather like he was less than her. The piece of pie would not be appreciated by her. She was my grandma, but I didn't particularly like her. She treated me like she did my grandfather.

"Grandpa, is there anything that you have ever dreamed of doing, but have been too chicken to do? I was talking to your roommate, Dr. Mayo, while you were sawing logs. He told me I should boldly do some of the things I have never had the balls to do."

"Like what?" My grandfather asked.

"He suggested I ask a cheerleader type to my high school prom next spring. That is serious balls." I replied.

"When I met your grandmother, I asked her out fifty-seven times before she said yes. I knew she was the one and it took some serious balls on my part to keep asking. She worked in a flower shop. I was a trash hauler and emptied the shop's garbage cans. She couldn't picture herself on the arm of a garbage man and told me so in rather stout language at times. Asking her out fifty-seven times was some serious balls." He replied laughing. "Once, she told me to take my stinking body and go find a female skunk to date."

I didn't laugh. That was how the girls at school treated me.

"The elderly doctor, that was in the next bed, said I should walk up to the unobtainable in life and push buttons till I get what I want. I have never pushed anyone's buttons in my life. Maybe it is time for me to test the gods of life to see what I can accomplish."

"Have you ever thought about running for Mayor of Gardenia, Chester? I am tired of our dump town's self-proclaimed mayor, Gordy Gardenia, telling us we can only park two trash trucks in our yards. My grandson, running and becoming Mayor, could change that. Gordy Gardenia may be the self-proclaimed Mayor of Gardenia, he is not the legal one. A legal one could tell him to go take a hike."

"You want to test the dump's god, Gordy Gardenia?" I asked in shock. No trash man messed with Gordy Gardenia. He owned the dump and could refuse to let you dump your trash loads.

"He has twenty five super haulers parked on his property. My driveway is big enough to hold three garbage trucks, and I should be allowed to park three. Just because Gordy sold me and Gardenia's other haulers our small tracks of land to live and park our trucks on, doesn't mean he should be able to dictate what we park in our driveways." My grandfather replied in an agitated voice.

"Taking away Gordy's self proclaimed position would probably not be a good thing, grandpa. You have grandma to think about. She and Gordy have been friends since they were kids. Her opinion of Gordy differs from yours."

"I will vote for you for mayor, if you promise to let me have the right to park three trucks in my driveway. The others living in Gardenia will too."

"Your vote for mayor could be bought with the promise of a three truck parking permit?"

"That is my price. I have been trying to talk your grandmother into running for Mayor for years. She keeps turning me down, due to her being friends with Gordy. I don't know what she sees in him. In my opinion, he is a short, fat, little pig who has no respect for women, including your grandma. She is blind as a bat and continues to think he walks on water."

"Maybe grandma doesn't want three garbage trucks parked in the driveway outside of her kitchen window." I shot back in defense of my grandmother who had installed all sorts of air filters in her trailer to keep out the smell from the dump.

"It isn't the smell, Chester. It is politics with her. I'm a Democrat. Your grandmother and Gordy are Republicans. Republicans always stick together and try to stick it to the hard-working, lower class labor man. I am just a Democratic garbage man to your Republican grandmother. Self-proclaimed Mayor Gordy is upper class Republican. I am an outhouse and he is an inside toilet in her book, if you get what I am saying."

"I get what you are saying, grandpa. However, I don't ever recall grandma voting. I doubt that her friendship with Gordy is based on politics."

My grandmother idolized Gordy Gardenia. I had never quite figured that fact of life out. Gordy was short, obese, smelled like the dump, and lived in a rusted out older mobile home by the dump's gate.

"You should run for Mayor, Chester. You could have legal say in our dump town and be King of our world one day, when you inherit my trash trucks. You would be set for life."

"What do you think the other six residents of Gardenia would want in return for their votes?" I asked to pacify him. He was old and dying. Whatever he wanted to talk about was okay with me. However, I had no intentions of running for mayor or taking over his trash hauling business when he was gone. After my high school graduation in the spring, I planned to kiss Gardenia goodbye and never return. I planned to pursue my dream of being a detective in California.

"You have to study people and what is important to them, Chester. Rosa, across the road from your grandma and me, is distraught because her husband's urn of ashes is missing. You promise to help her find them and her vote is in your bag. It is important to her to take his ashes back to Mexico and bury him in their family cemetery. Rosa cannot go home to Mexico with head held high without those ashes."

"Promising Rosa to help find her husband's ashes will buy her vote?" I asked finding my grandfather's idea quite humorous. I was just sixteen going on seventeen. "That would be a weird campaign promise, grandpa. Wouldn't it make more sense to promise to fix the pot holes in the dump road?"

"That is her price." My grandfather replied. "Pot holes mean nothing to her."

I thought for a moment about Dr. Mayo telling me that every god and goddess had a button to be pushed. Maybe Rosa's was a little odd, but it was a button. I fantasized for a moment about her being a goddess who watched over cemeteries and dead men's ashes. The Romans had goddesses of love and war. Why shouldn't Gardenia have a Goddess of Ashes? Besides, Rosa was the only good looking woman in my dump town. However, I didn't dare tell my grandmother that. She hated Rosa for some reason.

"What about Snuff?" I asked. "What is his price?"

Snuff was an old bachelor who lived on the outskirts of Gardenia and was a garbage hauler like my grandfather. His land had not been purchased from Gordy. It was, at one time, a small farm. The dump's toxins and run off had ended the farming of it.

"Snuff wants one thing. He wants to hook on to our Gardenia community well, not that our water is any good. It is a matter of principle with him. He wants public water. The cistern on his place doesn't hold enough water to wash his garbage trucks out regularly. Your parent's small acreage is also outside of Gardenia and not purchased from Gordy. Snuff and your parents share a common need. If both of their properties were annexed in to Gardenia, they would have automatic water rights. Gordy couldn't prevent them from hooking on. He would not be the legal mayor and have any say into the matter. He would have one vote like the rest of us."

"So Snuff and my parent's vote price would be annexation and water rights?" I asked a little in shock. Being young, I had never considered what the problems were of my fly speck town and surrounding area. My only thoughts had been how to escape it after I graduated high school.

"They couldn't vote for you in the first election for Mayor. Only those who live inside Gardenia could vote the first round. Once annexed, they could vote in future dump town mayor elections."

"What about old, sourpuss, Mable? Her garbage hauling husband is long gone. What would be the price of her vote? She has no interest in parking haulers in her driveway or concerned with dumping rights. She is just old, cranky, and mean. She has rocked me home more than once over the years, when I have walked too close to the front of her property. She has one mean, throwing arm, grandpa."

"It isn't you in particular that she is trying to scare off, Chester. She has a still hidden in the back of the broken down old hauler her husband used to drive. She is dealing in moonshine now, instead of garbage. She has to make a living for herself; God knows her boys aren't going to help her. I think an offer of picking up a couple hundred wine bottles or fruit jars from the dump for her to reuse for her shine would get her vote. Gordy refuses to let her pick about in his dump."

"So, Granny Mable's price is glass containers to put her moonshine in?" I asked once more amused.

"Yep . . . !" My grandfather replied. "Getting close enough to make her the offer is the problem. I agree with you, she does have one mean arm. The seven pit bulls tied around her front door and the broken down hauler are nothing you want to mess with either."

"How many legal voters are there in Gardenia?" I asked.

"Six." My grandfather replied and then added, "That number includes me, your grandmother, Granny Mabel, Gordy, Rosa, and Carlos the dump dozer man. Four votes could be annexed for future elections . . . Snuff, Wolf Dog the hermit, and your parents."

"What do you think the hermit's vote price would be?" I asked remembering Dr. Mayo telling me you had to know what people's buttons were in order to push them. The hermit was mentally challenged, and had the mind of an eight year old.

"Wolf Dog may be touched in his attic, but he is smart enough to make himself a living, riding and picking on the back of our trucks. He spends all of his spare money on dog movies, books about Alaska, and dog food for his Alaskan huskies. I bet if you offered to help him build a dog sled that he could mush all the way to Alaska, you would have his vote. He has slept with eleven dogs or more in his camper trailer for years. He fantasizes himself a Yukon man."

"Build one rolling dog sled for Wolf Dog the hermit," I muttered to myself amused.

"Gardenia has never had a town election for anything. How would a person call for one, legally?" I asked continuing to pass the time with idle conversation.

"You get up a petition calling for an election. You get half of Gardenia's six voting residents to sign and then have Mr. Parks the county commissioner do the legal part. Three signatures are all you will need on the petition. I have tried to tell your grandmother that for years. A third trash truck in my driveway could make your grandmother and me quite comfortable in our old age."

I cringed at his last statement. The doctor had plainly told me that he would probably be dead by the end of January.

"You are serious about this idea of yours, aren't you?" I asked to pacify him. "You have really wanted grandma to run for mayor."

"I have tried over and over to convince your grandmother to run for mayor. She has the smarts and could put an end to Gordy Gardenia's dictatorship of our tiny dump town. I wouldn't mind being known as the mayor's husband. Now, I am asking you, Chester. Why don't you run for mayor and end Gordy's tyrannical grip on all of us? I would sign the petition calling for a mayor election, and then vote for you."

"It is an interesting idea, grandpa, but I am underage and not old enough to vote yet. I am only sixteen. I won't be seventeen till next June."

"We have no town rules stating how old a man has to be to run for mayor. You could set the precedence. You are smart, Chester, like your mom and grandma. You could pull it off. I wouldn't mind being known as the grandfather of a mayor."

"What would I have to know about grandma, to get her vote?" I asked, knowing that my grandmother and Gordy had a friendship thing going that baffled all of us. She was more likely to vote for Gordy, than me. Also, I had never felt like my grandma gave a damn about me.

"Your grandmother is a wild card. She was a wild card when I chased her and asked her out fifty seven times. You will have to figure out what her buttons are on your own. She still keeps me guessing what they are. Your grandmother is the pumpkin pie spice in my life. She makes this old can of bland pumpkin edible."

"I wouldn't call her pumpkin pie spice, grandpa. I think a mixture of mint and chili peppers better describes her. She definitely has her cold and heated moments." I replied.

"It is her heated moments that I live for, Chester." My grandfather stated grinning and then coughing a couple of times.

"It is her friendship with Gordy that baffles me, grandpa. He brings her fake, dirty, dump flowers and she treats him like he is visiting royalty bringing her dozens of real red roses."

"I have always feared she would one day dump me for Gordy Gardenia. I am not much of a flower man." My grandfather replied taking time to cough a couple of times more and then take a sip of water. "Gordy knows how to push all of your grandmother's buttons. Her love of flowers is one of those buttons. I regret to say that I haven't been much of a flower man."

"What about my parents?" I asked. "What are their buttons? How would I get them to vote for me after annexation?"

"They are like Snuff. If they could vote now, it would be water rights. Your mother detests Gordy Gardenia. She would just automatically vote for you some day. Your stepfather's vote could be bought with the promised hookup with a cheaper drug seller, I imagine. You wouldn't have to know one to make the promise. Politicians never keep their promises. Drugs, alcohol, and the white sheets are all your stepfather thinks about."

"Why haven't you run for Mayor, Grandpa? You seem to have it all figured out." I replied making bedside small talk with him.

"Your grandmother would have left me, had I run for Mayor. There is also the fact that Gordy would have denied me dumping rights. I have never been in a position to rock my boat, Chester. I love your grandmother, and trash hauling and dumping is my business. It is all I know. You don't own any trash trucks, yet. Gordy can't deny you dumping rights. You can be mayor, commute into town to work in one of the factories, rub Gordy's nose out of shape, and him not be able to do a thing about it."

I regretted that my grandfather did not see me as capable of being more than a trash hauler or a factory worker. I realized that he didn't have a clue that I was a 4.0 student and had worked hard to try to get a scholarship to get me out of my unwanted dump world. I planned to move to California, enter a university there, and become what I wanted to be; an educated man and a detective. His only interest in my being mayor of Gardenia was so that he could get to Gordy. My grandfather had no real goals or dreams for me, nor did my mother or grandmother. I bit my lip to control my frustrations. My family saw me as a no-body.

After a moment of concealing my hurt, I continued. My grandfather was dying. I wasn't going to indulge in a self pity party. Now was not the time.

"Changing the subject, Grandpa, I have a question."

"What is it?" He replied.

"Have you ever dreamed of doing something out of the ordinary; something that perhaps grandma or my mother would not understand?"

"Like what, Chester?"

"Have you ever fantasized about flying to Hawaii, making mad love to a hula dancer, or perhaps sitting in a Colonel's Restaurant and eating all the fried chicken you wanted?" I asked wanting to get an idea of what I could do that was meaningful for my grandfather, while he was still able to enjoy it. "What is your out of the box fantasy, grandpa?"

"You know there is one thing I have always wanted to do. However, I have never had the balls to pull it off."

"What is that thing?" I further pumped him.

"Your grandmother and I are both only children. Both sets of our parents died before your mother was born. Mine were killed in a car wreck and your grandmother's died in a freak processing plant accident. We have never had extended family to invite in at the holidays. It has always been just us, your mother, and you for the holidays. Your grandma and I have never known what it is like to attend a big family dinner where all the relatives from seven states pile in. I have always wanted to crash one of those big family affairs in the city, pretend I was some distant relative, and blend in for the evening; just to see what the gatherings are like."

"You fantasize about being a party crasher?"

"Not just any party, Chester. I want to crash a huge Christmas Eve family get together and convince them I am one of them. For one night, I would like to be a part of a big stranger's family, and they not know the difference."

"Somehow, I have never pictured you as a party crasher, grandpa." I replied laughing. "How would you choose which family's door to knock on?"

"I would choose the one with the most cars in the driveway and on the street."

"How long would you stay at the party?" I asked suddenly seeing an adventurous side to my grandfather I had never seen before. Until meeting Dr. Mayo, I had always seen him just as a low class, uneducated, trash hauler. I wondered if he, like me, had spoken with Dr. Mayo and now dreamed of testing the gods.

"I would stay till the party was over, Chester. A guest leaves early or on time. Family stays till he party is over and helps do the final cleanup. I want to tie the hostess' apron on her and help her wash and dry the final dish."

"When Christmas Eve arrives, Grandpa, you and I are going to test our balls and do a little party crashing. We will test the gods and see if we can get by with it." I laughed, hoping his balls were big enough for both of us.

My grandfather grinned and reached his hand out to shake with me while asking, "Who gets to ring the doorbell?"

"It is your fantasy, you do." I replied. "I, personally, am going to look for mistletoe and some pretty girl to steal a kiss from. I intend to do my own thing testing the gods."

"Have you ever considered kissing Gracie Gardenia underneath the mistletoe on Christmas Eve? She is an only child and will inherit all of Gordy Gardenia's trash trucks and dump someday. Marry her and you will be set for life, Chester."

I bit my lip and didn't reply.

CHAPTER THREE

Gordy's Fake Flowers

It was the end of November. Thanksgiving was history. I moved out of my mother's trailer and into my grandparent's mobile home, because my grandmother needed me to help with my grandfather and the trash route which he could no longer run. That made me an official resident of Gardenia, population now eight. Gracie Gardenia, Gordy's daughter, and I were the only two residents not of legal age. Gracie and I were both sixteen going on seventeen, although I was a year ahead of her in school. I always assumed she was possibly slow and had flunked a year somewhere along the line. She had been a dirty dump kid like me, that I had always ignored.

I hadn't had an opportunity to test Dr. Mayo's 'Test the Gods' theory yet. However, I was thinking about it constantly. I just couldn't decide which god in my world to test. The cheerleaders at school really weren't of any interest to me. Most of them were airheads and I wanted a future with professional women in it, not pom-pom wavers who had no future once high school was over. During my school years, I had watched which types of students went on to become someone. Usually it was the nerds and book worms that carved out future, prosperous niches in society for them-selves. I had no intentions of taking an air head, pom-pom girl with me as a tag-along on my future journey upward. Dr. Mayo was single and had gorgeous young nurses spoon feeding him. He was in his eighties. I wanted what Dr. Mayo had achieved. Also, I was in my senior year now and about past caring whether my classmates saw me as worthy of their friendship. In just four or five months I would be leaving for California and not returning, or ever looking back. I wanted to test the gods like Dr. Mayo and become who I really wanted to be, a private detective. I had read practically every detective novel there was in the school library.

As I stated before, it was late November. Heavy snow was predicted to fall upon top of three inches of white stuff that was already on the ground. After my high school classes were finished for the day, I decided to run a late route picking up trash in case I couldn't make the next day's pickups. I unloaded in Gordy's dump just before he closed the gates for the day. Afterward I pulled into my grandparent's drive and proceeded to take a water hose and rinse out my hauler which was a daily ritual to keep the smell down. The running water and the snow on the ground were making a sloppy, but necessary mess. I was just finishing my last chore for the day when I glanced up and spotted Gordy Gardenia heading toward my grandparents' rusted out mobile home with an arm full of fake flowers he had picked out of the dump. The thought that he might be making a play for my grandmother, before my grandfather was in his grave, annoyed me.

Turning off the water, I dropped the water hose to the ground. I decided to confront Gordy and insist he stop bringing my grandmother dirty, fake blooms. Dr. Mayo wanted pie. I wanted Gordy out of my grandmother and grandfather's lives.

I headed for the stoop entrance to intercept Gordy before he knocked on my grandmother's door.

"What are you carrying?" I asked the round, short, red faced man wearing a ten gallon black hat with pins all over its band from casinos he had been to.

"I found these in today's dump loads and thought your grandmother might want them." He replied.

"Why would my grandmother want smelly, garbage covered fake flowers?" I asked blocking the door to the trailer.

"That is for me to know and you to find out." He retorted in a huff. "Go back to washing your truck and mind your own damn business. Ask your grandmother if you want to know."

"It is my business. Are you trying to put moves on my grandmother?"

"Are you appointing yourself as your grandfather's personal detective or something?" He shot back not smiling. "Your grandmother and I just share a love of fake flowers, if it is any business of yours. Now get out of my way, or you will wish you had."

About that time, my grandmother opened the door, smiled really big, and invited Gordy in while pushing me out of the way. Then she closed the door in my face, telling me to go get lost. I was more than annoyed, I was pissed.

To cool off and get lost as she put it, I walked out to the slushy, snow covered dump road and then turned toward the garbage dump and walked toward it. As I neared Granny Mabel's place, all of her dogs came unglued and started howling. I ran knowing she would fly out of her trailer to throw rocks at me. I wasn't in the mood to deal with her and her craziness. I continued to walk toward the dump. Then it occurred to me, why not push Gracie Gardenia's buttons and get the answers I wanted. I whistled as I turned in her yard. She and her father lived in the first rusted out mobile outside the dump's gate. Once on her ice covered small front porch, I took a deep breath and knocked.

"Chester . . . what do you want?" She asked after peeping out and slowly opening the door. Sixteen year old Gracie was wearing one pink platform hi heel with her jeans and carrying the other in her hand. She probably had been in the process of trying them on when I knocked.

"Er . . . uh . . ." I stammered as she put on the other pink heel. I could tell she had great legs in her tight jeans. I wondered why I had never noticed that before.

"Well, spit it out and quit wasting my time, Chester Holly. I am in the midst of packing. I am leaving for California in the next few minutes. I have got to finish my packing before my dad returns. How do you like my new traveling shoes? She asked turning around so I could see her feet in her pink spikes."

"You are going to need snow boots out here, not pink spikes." I replied forgetting why I was there. "Why hasn't anyone said anything about you leaving?"

"No one knows that I am leaving, if it is any of your business. I am catching a ride out of here with one of Rosa's drivers in about ten minutes. I am going to California." She stated twirling another time to show off her pink hi-heels.

I could see her back pack on the floor behind her and she had stuffed it with her personal possessions.

"You are going to California?" I asked with a twinge of jealousy. That was my dream.

"I am going to become a hair dresser there and wash the hair of the rich and famous in Hollywood. Now get off of my porch so I can finish up and get out of her before my dad returns."

"You should think about this, Gracie. You are just sixteen and don't have your diploma yet. You can't go to cosmetology school, if you don't have a GED or a high school diploma."

"I know when my time is up Chester Holly. I will be making money and living in California when you are carrying your diploma in the back pocket of your trash hauler's coveralls. You are a loser who will end up driving your grandfather's trash trucks when he is gone. If I want a diploma, I will buy me one or print me one. It is just a piece of paper. Knowing when to move on is far more valuable than that piece of parchment you will be handed in the spring. My life depends on me leaving in the next ten minutes. Now, get lost."

"Getting an education is important, Gracie. Your hitchhiking off to California could get you raped or killed. You need to think about it."

"You don't understand, Chester Holly. If I don't leave tonight, I may never leave here. I know things you don't know. I unlocked and looked thru a door today. That bit of snooping could get me killed by my father, when he discovers I have seen something I shouldn't. I saw your grandmother doing her thing."

"If you are trying to tell me that you have looked in either your or my trailer and have possibly seen my grandmother and your dad in bed together, I don't really want to hear about it."

"Think what you want to, Chester Holly." She replied. "I will be gone as soon as you leave. I have purposely flirted with one of Rosa's drivers to obtain a ride with him. If it means having sex with him to get out of this place, so be it. I have my life to think about. If you were smart, Chester, you would go with me, forget about your diploma, and not look back."

"I am smart, Gracie Gardenia. I will wait four months and then start a new life with a real diploma in my hand. You may beat me to California, but I won't be far behind you." I huffed.

"And just what do you plan to do in California? Are you going to sign on to be a picker on some low life's trash hauler there? That is all that this dump life has qualified you for."

"I am going to be a detective, for your information." I retorted in an angry voice. She was pushing all of my buttons. It was suppose to be me pushing hers.

"Prove it to me, Chester Holly. You use your private eye skills to track me down after you graduate next spring. I will be in California living the good life and using a brand new name. If you manage to find me, I will let you crash at my place free for a couple weeks till you get your act together. Personally, I think you are a Gardenia, garbage hauling, dim wit who will never make it out of here. That is my opinion of you."

"I will find you next summer, just to show you I can. Furthermore, I wouldn't crash at your place if you begged me. You are the Gardenia dim wit. For one thing, you don't go hitch hiking in pink hi-heels. Men will think you are a tramp." I retorted with a run-away mouth. She had insulted the secret me, the one that wanted to be somebody.

Then, Gracie slammed her rusted out trailer door in my face.

As I walked back toward my grandparents' mobile home, I heard Dr. Mayo speaking in my head, "Run up to the gods, push their buttons, get paid a price, and then run."

I had approached the goddess, Gracie Gardenia, pushed her buttons, got a door slammed in my face as payment, and forgot to run. I definitely had not got the answers I went there looking for. Flunking my first TEST THE GODS endeavor was a blow to my ego.

CHAPTER FOUR

Testing the Gods

I didn't give Gracie Gardenia any further thought on my walk back to my grandparents rusty mobile home. That was due to Granny Mabel's dogs barking, lunging at me, and stretching their chains as far as they would go. The crazy old trash hauler's wife flew out the door of her rusted out trailer, using profanity, and picking up anything she could get her hands on to throw at me. I instantly broke out in a run and made a mad dash past her place. One crazy old woman and seven lunging pit bulls is nothing to mess with.

Returning to my grandparents' dilapidated mobile home, I was relieved to see that Gordy was gone. I went inside, did my homework, and then dozed off on the couch. I dreamed of my super hero, Dr. Mayo. He had a dozen or so beautiful nurses lined up with pieces of Lemon Meringue Pie to feed him.

"You are eating the wrong kind of pie." I yelled at him in the dream.

"Banana Crème Pie was yesterday's choice. Today is a new adventure testing the gods, Chet Holly. Lemon Meringue is today's choice for payment."

"I will join you for pie tomorrow!" I shouted from behind the long line of women that were gathered carrying pieces of pie to feed him. "Save some of those nurses for me!" I shouted to him as the dream started to fade and become misty.

"Test a chocolate goddess!" Dr. Mayo shouted back, as the dream faded."You are a chocolate pie man."

~ ~ ~

The doze turned into an all night crash. Morning came and I gathered up my homework and made my way thru the new fallen snow to the end of dump road where it spilled out onto the main highway. That junction was where Gracie and I had boarded the county school bus for the last eleven plus years. It was a little shocking to not see her standing there with her nose stuck in a movie magazine, ignoring me. Boys in elementary school don't particularly want to be friends with a girl; much less a white trash, dump girl. By the time middle and high school rolled around, I had been used to ignoring her. Now, I wish I hadn't been such a jerk. She was gone, and I felt a little guilty.

November faded into December. My grandfather, although very ill, was still able to move about. He drove his trash route, but he hired someone to do the loading. When I got out of school in the afternoon, I took over any late day runs. Each afternoon, as I emptied wealthy people's trash cans, I could hear Gracie telling me that I would never escape who I was. Her words had really stuck a knife in me. I kept telling myself that I was just running my grandfather's trash route till the night I graduated. When I got that diploma in my hand, I was kissing the dump town of Gardenia goodbye forever, just like she had. It was annoying to know that a girl had beaten me at my own game.

December was a monotonous repeat of every other day of my life, except for the fact that my grandfather was readmitted to the hospital for ten days due to pneumonia, a complication of what was slowly sapping the life from him. He had lung cancer due to smoking and dump life. He got out of the hospital on Christmas Eve morning. Driving one of his trash haulers, I picked him up at the hospital door. My grandparents didn't own any ordinary vehicles.

During his hospital stay, I visited as before and often thought about Dr. Mayo and our conversation concerning testing the gods. I really hadn't tried out his theory, other than a failed attempt on Gracie. I felt a little guilty about not putting his words of wisdom into practice. He was a fish gutter who had made it out of his fish market gutter. I was a garbage man and still embracing the life in my dump gutter. There was restlessness in me! Down deep, each and every day, I wanted to just step out of the trash hauler, leave it on the shoulder of the highway somewhere, hitch a ride, never look back, and discard Chester Holly. I wanted to be the Chet Holly that Dr. Mayo had seen in me. The receiving of my diploma in the spring was the only thing that kept me pursuing my daily grind of school, studying, and trash hauling. I hated who I was. I hated who my family was, I hated having no friends. I hated the kids at school who avoided me like I was a smelly pig.

After dropping my grandfather off at home, I ran a last minute route emptying Christmas Eve trash cans for the wealthy who had called and didn't want trash sitting around for Christmas Day. Then, I headed for dump city. As I drove, I thought about my grandfather's dream of crashing a Christmas Eve party. I also considered my promise to do it with him. Gracie's face then popped into my head. I would always feel guilty about the ten years I ignored her, when I could have been doing things with her. I didn't want to feel guilty about not keeping my promise to my grandfather. I might not ever see Gracie again. I did have the time to indulge my grandfather with his fantasy. Dealing with the guilt of not being Gracie's friend gnawed at me. I didn't want anything to feel guilty about, after my grandfather passed on. Gracie had already passed on to her new life. She had left me forever, going to California. My grandfather was about to go to the great beyond and never return to me.

Just as I was about to turn on the dump road, my cell phone rang. I flipped open its cover and saw that it was my grandmother.

"What is up, Grandma?" I asked being a man of few words.

"Wherever you are at, turn around and go back to the hospital and pick up your grandfather at the Emergency Room door."

"I picked grandpa up early this morning and brought him home." I replied thinking my elderly grandmother might be losing it.

"I know you did. Midmorning he took a coughing spell with his asthma, and was having hard time breathing. I sent him back by ambulance. The old SOB was probably faking the asthma attack to get away from me. He wanted fried chicken for lunch, that greasy stuff from the fast food place. I told him no, that Gordy was coming to eat lunch with us and I was serving clam chowder. Anyway, he has had an asthma treatment in the emergency room and they are sending him home. Personally, I think he has worn out his stay with the nurses and doctors there. The nurses are tired of trying to wash the dump smell off of him and the doctors are just sending him home to die."

"He is dying grandma. You should have let him have the chicken. You are married to him, not Gordy." I spit out not thinking.

"If your grandfather gave a damn about me, he wouldn't have asked me to get out in the cold and snow to go buy the fast food chicken. He would have been happy just to be home and respected what I had on the stove cooking. Instead, he grabbed a beer, turned on his four televisions, and demanded I call a taxi and go get fried chicken. Your grandfather is a disrespectful old fart that I am going to be glad to be rid of when his time comes. He has been a noose around my neck, my whole life. Gordy is the only one in my world that gives a damn about me."

"He might feel the same about you, Grandma." I replied half mad. "You don't exactly respect him, always hanging out with Gordy Gardenia. You are married to my grandfather. You should show him a little respect. He is sick and won't be with us much longer."

"Longer can be an eternity, Chester." She shot back sarcastically. "Now turn your hauler around and go pick him up at the emergency room."

"I am now turning around and going back to the hospital to pick him up." I replied as I flipped my cell phone closed. I was sure this was not how normal folks spent Christmas Eve. My grandma was not the little apron wearing, white haired woman who baked cookies and hugged you at the door on Christmas Eve. My grandmother had always had a screw loose. The problem was, I never could figure out which screw! She was quirky, hateful, and sometimes sarcastic to go with it.

After reaching the hospital, checking my grandfather out of the emergency room, and helping him get in the passenger side of his trash hauler pickup, I headed for the dump and a non existing Christmas Eve celebration. My grandmother didn't seem to give a crap about Christmas. Her holiday eyes lit up only when Gordy came to call. There would be no Christmas Eve dinner or gifts for me or my ailing grandfather. It had always been that way. Glancing over at my pale, sick, bag of bones grandfather, I made a decision. It was time for me to become Chet Mayo. It was Christmas Eve and my grandfather deserved a pleasant holiday memory to die with. I was ready and willing to TEST THE GODS with him.

"Have you got your party crashing shoes on, Grandpa?" I asked as I drove away from the hospital with him in his pajamas and house shoes.

"I don't have much of a party left in me, Chester. I will be lucky to have enough energy to kiss your grandma tonight beneath the fake mistletoe, if she bothers to hang it."

"Well, grandpa, I don't want to leave this life without accomplishing my secret dream. You shouldn't either. I remember you telling me last fall about wanting to crash a family Christmas party. Tonight, we are going to put on our best clothes and do it."

"I couldn't leave your grandmother alone on Christmas Eve, Chester. Gordy Gardenia might take my place beneath the fake mistletoe. He has a thing for your grandmother."

"Well, grandpa, there is no fake mistletoe hanging. If you don't knock on the door of the gods tonight and test your dream, you fail your earth life mission. Face it, grandpa, if Gordy's one big mission in life is to kiss Grandma beneath her fake mistletoe, he will do it whether you are there or not."

"You are right, Chester. He has probably already stolen more kisses from her than I can count. This is my last chance to follow my dreams, isn't it?"

"We are on then," I stated, suddenly feeling alive like I was going to accomplish something other than emptying trash cans.

"What are we going to tell your grandma? She will want to know where we are going when we leave in our best clothes." My grandfather asked between a couple coughs. "It is Christmas Eve and I have never left her alone on a holiday before."

"I will tell grandma that you and I are going to get dressed up and go to the mall and have a family photo made of the two of us. The photo will provide us an excuse."

"You are a smart boy, Chester. Tonight I will see if I can pull my fantasy off. What is your dream, Chester? Is it bigger and more exciting than mine?"

"All I am going to say, grandfather, is that it has something to do with Gracie Gardenia. I am going to go find her next year, after I graduate. I have a pretty good idea of where she has run away to."

"Is there something you are not telling me Chester? Has Gracie run away because she in the family way? Are you the reason?"

I blushed. "You don't have to worry about Gracie and me. We are just friends, or are going to be. She dared me to visit her next year out on the west coast. I think a little vacation jaunt out to California might be nice." I replied not wanting to go into any details about Gracie's great legs, or the fact that I wanted to be a detective in California.

"You can't fool an old guy like me, Chester. You have the hots for Gracie. Is she out in California getting an abortion, Chester? Do you need money to pay for it?"

"Think what you want to grandpa." I replied rolling my eyes. Why did my family, classmates, teachers, neighbors, etc., think the worst when it came to me?

"Young women don't like to be pregnant. It takes away their bikini beauty. Is that what your Gracie is afraid of?"

"I can assure you Gracie is not carrying my child. Also, she wouldn't go out with me, even if I asked her. She is interested in movie stars and non-dump men."

"Have I told you that I asked your grandmother out fifty-seven times before she said yes. Maybe Gracie Gardenia is like your grandmother, a fifty-seven times girl. When Gracie comes wandering back here with her runaway tail between her legs sooner or later, make another play for her."

I rolled my eyes again and bit my lip. He didn't have a clue what I or Gracie wanted out of life. In some ways, he had a white trash mentality. I hated to admit that.

"If you manage to catch Gracie, after I am dead and in my grave, the two of you can move into your grandmother's trailer and takeover my trash trucks. Your grandmother has never liked Gardenia. It is okay with me if you put her in a nursing home, or send her to live with your mother."

"That is an awful thing to say, Grandpa. I would never put Grandma out of her home. Are you nuts?"

"Your grandmother is not a garbage dump lady. She is a religious nut and roses girl. She only lives in Gardenia because of me and Gordy. Sometimes, I think she lives here just because of him."

"Why would she stay with you in Gardenia for Gordy?" I asked stopping at a four way stop and then driving thru it.

"I took her away from Gordy Gardenia when we were young. He was not in the garbage dump business back then. His parents were florists in the city. Your grandmother was their teen assistant and had a thing for arranging their weeds. Gordy had a thing for toying with your grandmother. He would toy and then she would get roses. He was also toying with someone besides her. Gordy chose the other girl and I got your grandmother."

"Gordy doesn't bring her roses now." I huffed, suddenly realizing that Gordy and my grandma had been lovers in their younger days, before grandpa. My grandfather had possibly caught her on the rebound.

"Gordy still toys with her and picks her fake flowers from his dump?" My grandfather stated, pausing to have a little chain coughing episode.

"You should tell Gordy Gardenia to take a hike. Grandma is yours. You are married to her." I shot back in disgust while thinking about Gordy and my grandmother once being lovers. My grandfather marrying her on the rebound explained a lot of things.

"I have always known your grandmother loves Gordy Gardenia and not me. When we were young, your grandmother walked in on naked Gordy in a compromising position with the funeral home owner's daughter. It was my lucky day. Your grandmother got even with him by marrying me. His naked butt day was my lucky day. I asked her out the fifty-seventh time and we eloped that night."

"How lucky were you, grandpa? Grandma disrespects and ignores you! It is embarrassing to watch her light up like a Christmas tree when Gordy calls with his fake flowers."

"Your Grandma would run off with Gordy Gardenia, if he would ask her. She has forgotten about the naked butt of the funeral director's daughter who is dead now. She would like to forget about the hermit."

"Why would she want to forget about Wolf Dog the hermit?"

"It is a long story, Chester. Gordy has people in his life that he won't give up for her. He just toys with your grandmother to annoy me. He isn't interested in old wrinkled skin. He likes his lady friends young."

"You must really love her grandpa." I stated shaking my head in disbelief.

"I am a lucky man, Chester. Someday, when your grandmother catches Gordy again with a naked woman, I might just be lucky enough that she will consider having another baby with me."

"For God's sake, Grandpa . . . Grandma is over seventy. She is hardly young enough to give you a child."

"It is the trying that makes you a lucky man, Chester. She just might be mad enough at Gordy to elope with me again. That is how we got your mother." Then my grandfather smiled from ear to ear.

When I pulled into the driveway of my grandparents' rusted trailer, I helped my grandfather out and inside where he settled down in his worn out recliner that faced four televisions sets. They were his version of a big screen. After a couple of coughing bouts, my grandfather dozed off in his chair. My grandmother ignored him and me. I plopped down on the couch and joined my grandfather for a short Christmas Evening nap. We had an hour or so before we could knock on some family's door, hug a bunch of strangers, and then let them figure out who the heck we were.

CHAPTER FIVE

The Scented Pink Envelope

About six-thirty, I woke up from my Christmas Eve nap. Sitting up, I ran my fingers thru my hair and then checked the time on the kitchen clock. My mother had slipped in for a visit with my grandmother while I was asleep. They were sitting at the kitchen table, drinking coffee, and smoking. Rarely did my mother visit my grandmother, even though they lived the equivalent of a couple of city blocks from each other. On holidays, my alcoholic mother would come for short, strained visits. My grandmother didn't usually welcome her with open arms. It was my mother that tried to foster a relationship. My grandmother ignored my mother, like she did my grandfather.

I stood up and made my way over to where my grandfather was still dozing in his recliner. He was snoring obnoxiously loud and his four television sets were blaring. I shook him and then turned the antiquated sets, his idea of a big screen, off. It was time for us to get dressed for our adventure testing the gods.

"Why are you waking the old fart up?" My grandmother inquired, as she sat exhaling smoke at the kitchen table.

"I have made a late appointment out at the mall for Grandpa and me to have our photo taken." I replied as I shook my grandfather a second time. "He asked me what I wanted for Christmas back at Thanksgiving. This is what I want, a photo of the two of us together."

"Well, don't have an extra made for me." My Grandmother replied tapping her cigarette ashes into an empty beer can on her table. "This trailer is full to overflowing. I don't have any place to sit one."

I bit my lip. Most normal grandmothers, in my thinking, would be thrilled at the possibility of having a new photo of their grandchild.

"Make me a wallet, Chester." My mother replied as she tapped her cigarette pack on the table, finding that it was empty. "You'll have to pay for it. I am a little strapped for cash at the moment."

"My mother was always short on cash. She and my step dad spent every cent they had on cigarettes, drugs, alcohol, and lawyer fees keeping them out of jail for this, that, and the other."

"Sure mom." I replied in an effort to keep it a secret what my grandfather and I were really up to.

I had long ago given up on my mother paying for anything pertaining to me. She lived in a bottle and most of the time was totally oblivious to me and my needs. I had been loading trash or driving one of my grandfather's trash haulers, since I was eleven. I bought and paid for my own clothing and school supplies. My grandfather had always paid me at the end of each day, before he turned over his earnings to my grandmother. She thought I should work for them for free, to pay for the couch I had slept on most of my life. When my mother's addictions got out of control, I had always slipped out of my mother's mobile home and made my way to my grandparents. My grandfather was always glad to see me and made me a bed on the couch. My grandmother had always been a cold person and ignored me when I came. It was the security of my grandfather's arms that I had always made my way to. I have no memories of my grandmother ever hugging, kissing, or doting on me. To her, I was a little, unwanted bastard.

Accompanying my grandfather to his bedroom, I pulled clothing from his closet. Then, I helped him change from his pajamas to his dress clothes. I could tell that he was appreciative. Just as I was about to slip his Christmas blue sweater on him, I heard my grandmother yelling from the kitchen table.

"Get the lead out, Chester, and get the old fart back in here. He has a visitor."

I did as I was told and hurried my ill grandfather along. At the same time, I wondered what my grandfather's Christmas Eve visitor thought about my grandmother's less than appropriate language. A real grandmother would have walked back to the bedroom and said something sweet like, "Chester, it is Christmas Eve and your grandfather has a visitor." Then she would have placed a sweet little peck on my grandfather's cheek, smiled sweetly at me, and then left us to feel like we were the two most important men ever. That was not the case with my grandmother. My grandfather was an old fart to her and I was an unwanted fly speck on her wall paper of life.

After straightening my grandfather's clothing, I helped him back to the living room and into his recliner to sit, till it was time for us to go. Granny Mabel was standing waiting for him. My grandmother hadn't even asked her to sit down. I was embarrassed. It was Christmas Eve. The least my mother and grandmother could have done was ask the elderly woman to sit down with them at the table. I would have, even if she was the one who often rocked me and encouraged her pit bulls to lunge at me every time I walked in front of her place. In my book there was no excuse for blatant rudeness.

"Have a seat, Mable." My grandfather said to her once he was settled.

"I can't stay, Woody. I have just dropped by to bring you a little Christmas gift." The rock thrower stated handing him a pint jar of what looked like water. It had a red Christmas bow stuck in the center of its lid. The container had once been a mayonnaise jar.

"Thank you, Mable." My grandfather stated accepting it. He then pulled his wallet from his pocket and handed Mabel a twenty dollar bill. "Merry Christmas to you too!"

Then Mabel, the Moonshine Maker, stuffed the twenty in her pocket and left ignoring my grandmother and my mother who were equally ignoring her.

"Are you going to share that with me dad?" My mother asked after Mabel was gone.

"Did she bring it to you?" My grandfather retorted, pulling the bow off the lid. Then he unscrewed the cap from the pint jar, sniffed its contents, and took one tiny sip.

"What is it?" I asked a little naively. I was just sixteen going on seventeen.

My grandfather motioned for me to lean down. I accommodated him. I could tell he wanted to tell me something that he did not want my mother or grandmother to hear.

"It is shine, Chester. Go pour it down my bathroom sink. It is good stuff, but I don't want your mother to drink it while we are gone. Tomorrow is Christmas. I don't want to have to put up with Liz being a ranting, rambling, damn drunk tomorrow."

Liz was my mother's nickname. Her actual name was Elizabeth.

"Will do . . . ," I whispered back taking the shine from him. Then I headed back to his bathroom and did as I was told. I fully understood his request. My mother was an alcoholic who would drink anything from your baking vanilla to moon shine made by a dirty, old, dump woman who had probably not had a bath in weeks. My grandmother kept her vanilla, which had a high concentration of alcohol in it, hidden from my mother.

After I dumped the shine, I rinsed out the pint jar and lid in my grandfather's lavatory. Then I set it on a shelf above his sink for safe keeping. Granny Mabel would want the pint jar back. Drying my hands, I heard another knock and headed back down the narrow, long, mobile home hallway to the living room.

"Answer the door, Chester!" My grandmother demanded not making any effort to get up from her smoking position at the kitchen table, which was riddled with cigarette burns. My grandmother complained continuously about the smells from the dump, but thought nothing about destroying her lungs or her kitchen table with cigarettes.

I opened the front door to see who our next Christmas Eve visitor was. There were no cookies or other holiday goodies to offer whoever was knocking. My grandmother had recently joined the Jehovah door knockers. They didn't believe in celebrating holidays.

Opening the door, I saw that it was Rosa, the gorgeous, Hispanic, widowed, neighbor across the road.

"Feliz Navidad . . . Chester! Is your grandfather home from the hospital?" Rosa asked with a flirtatious voice that just reached out and grabbed you. I had fantasized a few times about her. She was the best looking female in Gardenia, even if she was fifty.

"Come on in, Rosa. He is sitting in front of his big screen" I replied standing back to let her enter.

Rosa walked over to greet my grandfather who did not stand. He was saving his strength for our party crashing adventure. My grandmother didn't get up from the table to greet her. My grandmother, with a mad icy stare, just remained seated and kept on smoking, as did my mother. My grandmother had pulled a fresh pack of cigarettes from her pocket, and was reluctantly sharing them with my mom.

"How are you feeling Woody?" (Woody was my grandfather's nick name. His actual name was Woodrow.) Rosa asked stooping down and hugging my grandfather. She placed her cheek next to his and whispered something inaudible in his ear. Then, she resumed a standing position all smiles.

"I am still alive and kicking, Rosa. The doctors keep sending me home. I assume that is a good thing. The day they keep me in the hospital, I will know my number is up."

"You look very festive. Are you going to a Christmas party?" Rosa asked handing my grandfather a saucer wrapped in clear food wrap. It contained homemade cookies. A green bow was attached to the top of the food gift, along with a tag with my grandfather's name on it.

Standing listening, I eyed the cookies and counted at least five. My mouth watered and I swallowed. I couldn't remember the last time my mother, or grandmother, had baked cookies for me.

"Thank you Rosa." My grandfather replied pulling out his billfold. He pulled out a twenty and handed it to her. "I haven't been well enough to shop this year, Rosa. You will have to buy your own present."

Rosa smiled and took it. "Thank you, Woody. You know what I will do with this twenty, and think of you when I am doing it." She stated not saying what that something was.

I was a little annoyed. Why would Rosa bring my grandfather cookies, and not my grandmother? Was it possible that Rosa and my grandfather might have some private thing going between them? I glanced over at my grandmother, seated at the kitchen table, to see what her reaction was. She was ignoring Rosa as though she didn't exist.

After a short conversation about trivial things, Rosa left.

"Take these over to the table, Chester, and let Liz and your grandmother eat them. You and I will have Christmas Eve treats later." He stated winking at me.

I grinned and did as he said. My mother immediately tore off the clear plastic wrap from the saucer and pulled a huge sugar cookie from the dish. She then started devouring it, like she hadn't eaten in awhile. My grandmother picked up one of the cookies and held it up to the light overhead. She then stared at it, like the cookie was a sealed envelope that she wanted to secretly look in.

"Why are you holding the cookie up to the light?" I asked out of curiosity. My grandmother had her quirks and odd reactions to life. You never knew what to expect from her.

"I am looking to see if Rosa put her husband's ashes in the cookies." My grandmother retorted as my mother instantly gagged and spit out the mouth of chewed up cookie that she was about to swallow.

(Rosa's husband had died a couple of years prior and was cremated. To Rosa's horror, his ashes had been stolen from a shelf in her mobile home, shortly after his death. No one in Gardenia knew who stole the ashes or why they chose to do so.)

"Rosa's husband's ashes would be dark like pepper." I retorted rolling my eyes. "Those cookies do not have any dark, pepper like specks in them. They are white sugar cookies."

"Get off mom's back," My mother huffed. "It was rude of Rosa to bring dad cookies and not her."

"Grandma was equally as rude." I replied in disgust, thinking about my family's lack of social graces. "She didn't ask Granny Mabel or Rosa to sit down at the table and have a cup of coffee with the two of you. It is Christmas Eve."

"I don't entertain women who have a thing for your grandfather." My grandmother retorted in a sharp voice. "Mabel has always had a thing for Woody, and so has Rosa. Until I divorce him, or kill him, he and all his obnoxiousness belong to me. Rosa had no business hugging him and Mabel had no business enticing him with her shine."

I broke out in a snort. "Granny Mabel is a good twenty years older than grandpa and Rosa has more men chasing her, than she can shake a stick at." I shot back. "Rosa is just Rosa. She is a beautiful woman and the two of you are just jealous of her."

"I will jealous you!" My mother stated. She then threw one of the sugar cookies at me.

I ducked, and then was saved from having a second cookie hurled at me, by another knock sounding.

"Get the door, Chester." My grandmother demanded with a definite hint of disgust for me in her voice.

I could tell that I had somehow hit a raw nerve in my grandmother. I didn't have time to consider what that raw nerve button was. Walking to the mobile home's front door, once more, I opened it to see who our next Christmas Eve visitor was.

"Hi Snuff." I warmly greeted my grandfather's trash hauling buddy. "Come on in!"

Snuff was an old bachelor, about Rosa's age, who lived on the road that ran on the backside of the dump. He owned a small acreage there.

"Merry Christmas, Chester. Is your grandfather home from the hospital?" Snuff asked.

"He got out of the hospital today." I replied standing back.

Snuff entered and slid past me.

"You are looking good tonight, Woody. Are you going to Christmas Eve mass and confession?"

"Chester and I are going to get out and make a round shortly. What are you up to?"

"I have just returned from church and the confessional. Once a year, I clean my plate of sins. The priest told me it would take a whole year, of my emptying the church's trash cans free, to get the absolution I need."

My grandfather snorted. "He pulled that one on me last year, Snuff."

"Look at the bright side Woody. Father John will stick it to Rosa next year." Snuff replied laughing and slapping my grandfather on the shoulder.

"To answer your earlier question, Chester and I are headed down to the mall to have our photo made. A shot of our mugs together is what he wants for Christmas."

"He is one smart boy . . . , your Chester. I wish I had a photo of me with my grandfather or old man. You never think about that sort of thing when you are young."

"Chester is a good boy." My grandfather replied. "Why are you wasting your

Christmas Eve on me, Snuff? Don't you have a pretty, female elf and some mistletoe waiting on you somewhere?"

"You know better than that, Woody. When you have been with the right woman, there is no need of settling for second best. I won't spoil the memory of Jennifer, by crawling in bed or standing under mistletoe with someone less than her."

Glancing towards my mother, I was shocked to see a faraway look wipe the smile from her face. Snuff's words must have struck a nerve with her. Then I glanced at my grandmother. She seemed equally as distracted. I wondered what Snuff had said that had pushed their buttons.

"I have a favor to ask of you, Woody?" Snuff asked as he sat down on the ottoman in front of my grandfather.

"What is it?" My grandfather asked in reply, oblivious to my grandmother and mother's suddenly antsy dispositions.

"That elderly aunt of mine, who lives up north in Canada, has passed on. I am her only relative and I need to go north for a few months to get her estate settled. I was wondering if I could leave the keys to my place with you, in case there is an emergency or something. I see no need to turn the utilities off. My pipes would freeze and break this winter. I need someone to check my mail and door every couple of weeks."

"What are friends for? I haven't forgotten your loaning me one of your haulers when mine was broken down. I owe you more than some simple mail checks." My grandfather replied simply.

"My route of customers is another thing I want to talk to you about. You can service them and double your income till I get back, if you want." Snuff stated handing my grandfather a handwritten list which consisted of several pages. "You could take the extra money and buy Chester his first used trash hauler as a graduation present. It would give him a good start in the business."

I cringed at the suggestion. The last thing I wanted for my high school graduation was a used trash hauler. I had plans to go to California, attend a university there, and become a respectable detective.

"That isn't a bad idea, Snuff." My grandfather replied.

"What I am inheriting from my aunt will cover my backside for some time. I may give up the trash business altogether when I get back. Just like you, Woody, I am not young anymore. The only reason I have stayed in the business has been to make money to pay private eyes to look for Jennifer."

"Your hired detectives still haven't come up with any clues as to what happened to Jennifer and your baby?" My grandfather asked.

"Not a single clue has surfaced, Woody. It is as though she dropped off the face of the planet."

"Maybe you should just let it go, Woody. Perhaps, it is time for you to think about moving to some seniors golfing community, meet a nice little widow, and enjoy what time you have left on this planet. You know, as well as I do, that Jennifer is not coming back after this many years."

"I know, Woody, but I just can't let her go. You have hung on to your Erma in spite of everything." Snuff retorted.

"I get what you are trying to say, Woody. Let us not discuss that in front of Chester. He is too young to hear the details of my younger day's love life." My grandfather stated turning his head to look at me. He then winked at me. I wondered what that was all about.

"I was talking to the sheriff down at the church. He was in the confession line with me. He told me that over the last six months, a couple of older door knockers and a young, door to door, cosmetics woman have disappeared. I hope I am wrong, Woody, but I think our county has a killer working it, and he has been working it for maybe twenty years or so. I think Jennifer might have been one of his early victims, although I don't have anything but my theory to go on."

"You have to have bodies to say you have a killer, Woody." My grandfather replied.

"Jennifer would not have just walked off and left me sixteen, going on seventeen, years ago. We were in love, happy, and she was about to pop, being nine months pregnant with my baby."

"She might have had reason to walk, Snuff. As I recall you were not at home the day she walked. You were indisposed as we say."

"That dump girl made that story up, Woody. I was out on my hauler and not indisposed as we say. I was thirty-three years old. That fifteen year old dump girl was hardly my type. She had the hots for me and chased me, but there was nothing between us." He whispered, so my mother and grandmother couldn't hear.

"You know my opinion on your woman's disappearance." My grandfather replied. "I know the dump girl, and also that you did not put a ring on Jennifer's finger. In my opinion, it is disrespect not to marry a woman who is carrying your child."

"You are right on the disrespect part. I was a young Jackass who was a little slow in the commitment department. That doesn't diminish the fact that I was, and still am, madly in love with Jennifer. She was the other half of me, my soul mate as the young folks call it today. I was faithful to her back then, and I have been faithful to her in death."

"I have to give you credit for your obsessive faithfulness to her, since her disappearance. I wish my Erma was that obsessive in her feelings toward me." My grandfather replied.

"You want to insist that Erma keep this trailer's doors locked when you aren't here. I am going to have a talk with Rosa and Mabel about it. The two missing door knockers worked this area for their Jehovah Hall. The young cosmetics saleswoman also sold her products in this area. The killer, I fear, could live in our vicinity."

"I think my seventy year old, wrinkled skin Erma is probably safe. Killers usually pick on young pretty women. Just between you and me, Snuff, my woman hasn't aged well."

"You are probably right, Woody. Erma doesn't fit the female profile that most sociopath's go after." Snuff replied lowly.

"Are you listening, Liz?" My grandfather suddenly yelled across the room to my thirty thirty-two year old mother. "Make sure your trailer doors are locked. Three women are missing."

I glanced at my mother and she had a look of horror on her face. However, she didn't reply to my grandfather's demand.

"The killer isn't just picking on women, Woody." Snuff stated. "Make sure that you instill in Chester the danger of picking up hitch hikers in your trash hauler. He is the right age for a killer to pick on. Don't forget that young minister that disappeared on the road behind the dump a few years back. He was just twenty-three, and straight out of Bible College."

"Have you forgotten that it was rumored that he ran off with the pianist?" My grandfather retorted eyeing Snuff. Then he turned to me. "Did you hear that, Chester? No hitch hikers in my haulers . . . !"

"I hear, Grandpa." I stated rolling my eyes.

"Don't you be picking up any hitchhikers; especially any Bible thumping or piano playing ones." He then added in an amused voice.

"You don't have to worry about that, Grandpa. I doubt very seriously that I am going to find a broken down piano on the side of the highway, with a pianist sitting on a bench thumbing a ride and a Bible thumper laying in wait, to beat me to death with his good book." I replied to get him and Snuff off of my case.

Snuff snorted and my grandfather grinned at me.

"Will you watch my place and check my mail for me while I am gone?" Snuff asked returning to what he had come for.

"Of course I will." My grandfather replied, ignoring the fact that his health was on a steady decline. "I will send Chester over to get the mail and check the doors once a week. How long do you think you will be gone?"

"The old girl has left me everything, Woody. It may take me a few months to sell off her real estate and personal possessions. I may be gone till the first of summer."

"Give your keys to Chester. He will hang them on the hooks by the door, and they will be hanging there when you get back."

At that point, Snuff handed me a ring of keys. I hung them by the front door on a board of hooks where we kept all of our personal keys.

Snuff further visited with my grandfather for a few minutes, and then left.

"I don't recall Snuff ever saying much about his missing girlfriend." I stated making idle conversation with my grandfather, after Snuff was gone.

"He doesn't like to talk about her, Chester." My grandfather replied. "He is obsessed with finding her, although he is also trying to forget her. I personally think she found out about the dump girl and walked. Snuff wasn't much in the commitment department back then. Having two women on the line wasn't a smart move on his part."

"Do you want to tell me who his fifteen year old lady friend was?" I asked, continuing to make idle conversation to pass the time till we could leave.

"It is a long story, Chester. Snuff didn't know what he had, till she wasn't there anymore. He wants to believe his Jennifer has been a victim of foul play, somehow. In my thinking, his pride just won't let him admit that he did her wrong, and that she had the guts to leave him being nine months pregnant and about to pop."

"Was the fifteen year old dump girl pretty?" I asked thinking that girl had to be about the age of my mother now.

"I think so." My grandfather replied in a whisper. "However, a father always thinks their kid is pretty."

"Are you inferring that Snuff was seeing my mother?" I asked forgetting that my mother was sitting at the table.

"That is enough, dad." My mother demanded in a loud voice from her position at the table. "I was fourteen, not fifteen, and had a crush on Snuff. I did stupid things when I was young, and I have lived to regret them. Now, drop the subject of Snuff and I. I am not the reason Jennifer left him."

"Yes Mum . . . !" My grandfather replied.

My mother got up and stomped off to the bathroom.

"Was Jennifer a pretty woman?" I asked running my hand thru my red hair. "Was she as pretty as Rosa?"

"No one is as pretty as Rosa, Chester. When God made her, he broke the mold." My grandfather stated suddenly grinning from ear to ear.

"So, Snuff just can't admit to himself that his girlfriend walked on him?"

"Yea, that is my opinion." My grandfather replied. Then he had a short round of hacking and coughing. He was dying from lung cancer.

"So, in your opinion, Jennifer is just a single mom who split and decided to raise her baby on her own?"

"There are lots of single mothers out there raising kids on their own, Chester. In my opinion, Jennifer is one of them. Snuff should have put a ring on Jennifer's finger and left your mother and her flirting alone. Your mother was a wild card when she was young."

At that point, my mother returned from the mobile home's bathroom. We dropped the subject of Jennifer and Snuff.

"What about Gracie Gardenia, Grandpa? Who is her mother?" I asked continuing to make idle conversation with him. "I don't ever remember seeing her mother at any school functions, or here in Gardenia?"

"Gracie is the child of a young wife Gordy married and kept in the city. You best leave that subject alone. It pushes all of your grandmother's buttons."

"I heard that, Woody." My grandmother stated in a loud agitated voice, from her seated position in the kitchen.

"Why would Gordy, having a young wife and Gracie, push grandma's buttons?" I asked in a low voice glancing over at my grandmother and then at my mother who had two cigarettes lit at once. I could tell that something was pushing my mother's buttons big time. Her hand was trembling as she flicked ashes from the end of her cigarette into a beer can.

"Gordy and your grandmother have been friends since they were young. Your grandmother worked for Gordy's parents in their flower shop back when she was about sixteen. He was in his mid twenties at the time. From what I hear, Gordy's young wife in the city was quite beautiful; anyway that is what Gordy has said. Gordy and your grandmother had words when he first married the pretty young thing. Mad at what your grandmother was saying, he told your grandmother that she was a wrinkled old witch who was jealous of his young bride. Anyway, Gordy dumped his friendship with your grandmother over her." My grandfather replied in a low voice, muffled by his four televisions.

"Was his young wife prettier than Jennifer and Rosa?" I asked, not really being interested. I was just trying to keep my grandfather company and spend some quality time with him. It didn't matter to me what we talked about.

"I never saw her, Chester. However, I think Gordy was actually in love with her, and Gracie is his love child by her. Liz is my love child by your grandmother."

"What happened to Gracie's mom and why did he bring Gracie here to the dump to rear?"

"Gracie didn't come to live in Gardenia, till she was about a year old. Her mother died in a car crash, according to Gordy. Granny Mabel became Gordy's friend and baby sat Gracie till she started kindergarten."

I glanced over at my mother who looked like all the blood was drained from her face. She was biting her lip between puffs on her cigarette. She was listening to our conversation. My grandmother had us tuned out for the moment. She had picked up a page of Jehovah literature and was reading it. I knew whatever was bothering my mother would cause her to crawl into a bottle before Christmas Eve ended. I recognized the signs. She drank when she couldn't handle whatever her nightmares were.

"So, Gordy told Grandma to take a hike over Gracie?" I asked surprised. My grandmother lived and breathed Gordy Gardenia like he was a god.

"He did just that. Your grandmother was furious when she found out he had Gracie and his secret young wife stowed away in a really nice apartment in the city."

"Tell me about Gracie." I replied in a low voice.

"You and Gracie are just about the same age. She was born a week or so after you were. It must have been something in the water that year. Snuff's Jennifer was about to pop, your grandmother was pregnant, Gordy's secret woman was pregnant with Gracie, and your mother . . ."

"Don't go there . . .," My mom sputtered loud and angrily.

"Don't you think Chester should know that he has a sibling that you lost before becoming pregnant with him?"

"I guess he knows now." My mother replied in a mad voice and lit another cigarette. "I had a miscarriage dad. Those don't count as siblings and women don't talk about such things in public. Now, cool that subject."

It didn't really matter to me one way or the other about my mother having a miscarriage before me. There were times when I wish she had aborted me. I had a miserable childhood and my teen years were worse. I was the dump kid no one wanted anything to do with. In my opinion, the miscarried kid was the lucky one.

"You were telling me about Gracie's mother . . ." I whispered to my grandfather. Gracie, I wanted to hear about. I could still see her great legs in the pink hi-heels she was wearing the day I knocked on her trailer door. If Gracie's mother had legs like that, no wonder Gordy had fallen madly in love with her.

"None of us, here in the dump, ever met Gracie's mom. She was high class and Gordy kept her in style and in the city. Mabel told me she died in a car crash when Gracie was an infant. Gordy brought Gracie to the dump to live because he needed Mabel for a baby sitter while he ran his business."

"He didn't ask Grandma to baby sit for him?"

"Hell . . . no! He told Snuff there was no way he was going to trust Gracie to your grandmother, that she had a screw loose. I had to agree with Gordy. Your grandma didn't do a very good job raising your mother. She ran wild in the dump, especially when she turned about fourteen. I personally think Rosa's husband Ricardo killed himself over Liz. I think he might have been toying with your mother. I found out after she run away that she was pregnant. Maybe Ricardo couldn't live without your mother, although he was married to the sexiest, best looking, woman in Gardenia. Rosa is a goddess. When you are married to a goddess, you don't mess around with lowlife."

"I heard that dad." My mother once again interrupted. "I was not pregnant by Ricardo. He killed himself because Rosa had one too many men in her bed, in my opinion. I was fifteen, has it ever occurred to you that I might have been in love with another fifteen year old. I did ride the school bus and there were boys on that bus."

I just didn't understand why my mother kept the father of her miscarried baby such a secret, as well as mine. She had always refused to tell me who my real father was. I had a stepfather, but she had met him when she returned after running away. She already had me. It was possible my father was a John, or some jerk she met on the streets somewhere in the south.

I returned to my conversation with my grandfather.

"So, you are telling me that Gordy chose his young wife and his infant daughter Gracie over grandma's friendship."

"Gracie has always come first with Gordy, from the day he brought her here to the dump. Your grandma told Gordy that he should adopt the baby out, get rid of her. Gordy told your grandmother, in no uncertain terms, to shove her opinions up her . . . and take a hike. Your grandmother was furious. He then hired Mabel to help him with Gracie. That act stuck in your grandma's craw. She was Gordy's friend, but he placed Gracie in Pit Bull Mabel's care. Mabel is the nearest thing to a mother that Gracie has known."

"That is how it should be, Grandpa. Your kids should come first when you have them." I replied and then bit my lip knowing that I had insulted my mother. I had lived with my grandparents for two thirds of my life.

"It was a bad time for all of us, Chester, and each of us in a different way. The police questioned Snuff and the rest of us Gardenia men relentlessly about Jennifer's disappearance. Your grandmother went to her room, when she learned about Gordy's secret wife and infant. She didn't come out for weeks. Your mother ran away from home being pregnant by someone. She has always refused to tell me who by."

"Why would grandma get that upset about Gordy's secret wife and child?"

"Get a life and grow up Chester." My mother spit out. "Dad knows, I know, everybody knows. Your grandma lives and breathes Gordy Gardenia. He can do no wrong in her book." Then she nervously chuckled. "I think it is funny that Gordy rubbed a young wife and child in her face. She doesn't love dad, she doesn't love you, she doesn't love me, and she wasn't there when I needed her when I was fifteen. She only lives and breathes Gordy Gardenia."

"That is enough!" My grandmother spouted angrily at my mother as she slammed down the newspaper she was reading. "You stabbed me in the back when you were fifteen. I have no reason to love you."

My mom spit back. "I didn't stab anyone in the back. Your precious Gordy was already married to his young wife and she was about to pop the day I ran away. Gordy is not the god you make him out to be. My dad is, and you don't see it."

"There are some things in life that you can't fix, Chester." My grandfather half whispered. "I have always known that your Grandma loves Gordy Gardenia. I have also always known that Gordy does not love your Grandmother. It is something that I have dealt with, in my way."

"What . . . ?"

"I tricked your grandma into marrying me. We were both Catholic. Once those vows were said and I slept with your drunken grandma, there was no turning back. Your grandma got pregnant with Liz on our wedding night. The church refused her an annulment. Gordy is also Catholic."

"You tricked grandma into marrying you? How . . . ?"

"Your grandmother was sixteen and in love with Gordy. She did not know that Gordy played the field and had half a dozen girls on the string. Anyway, she walked in on him in his parent's apartment above the flower shop. He was butt naked on the sofa, and on top of the funeral home man's daughter. Your grandma bought a fifth and was drinking it in the shop when I walked in and asked her out for the 57th time. She was half drunk and said yes. She eloped with me in a drunken state to get even with him. I was in love with your grandmother and just counted my lucky stars. I was even luckier when she woke up the next morning pregnant. That meant I got to keep her in the eyes of the church."

"That would be considered rape, now-a-days, grandpa."

"Times were different back then, Chester. Gordy didn't want your grandmother. He really didn't want her after he found out she was pregnant. Your grandma got as big as a cow."

"Why in the hell would you move grandma here to the dump and why would she be willing to live with you all of these years here in the dump? She hates this place and you." I asked in a low voice.

"I was a trash man when I met your mother. I emptied the floral shop's dumpster. As long as I live in this dump town, your grandmother will never leave me because this mobile home is about as close to Gordy Gardenia as she will ever be able to get. I pacify her obsession with him. In return she is mine till I die. After that, she still won't have Gordy. He likes his women young. Old pregnant broads don't interest him."

"If you want to be sleeping in this mobile home tonight, Woody, you had better cool the subject of me and Gordy." My grandmother spouted angrily, having tuned into our conversation.

"Oh, that is not all, Chester. Your grandmother sleeps with Gordy when he is in between young things. She is an easy, cheap lay. Your grandmother got pregnant by Gordy. He laughed at your grandmother and told her the baby had to be mine." My grandfather retorted to her outburst. "He burst her bubble in the morning of the same day your mother run away from home. She took her frustrations with Gordy out on Liz and nearly beat her to death. Your mother had good reason for running away that day. Maybe she was pregnant by some fifteen year old school kid; she didn't deserve her mother's rage."

"Mom... You were pregnant by Gordy the night I ran away?" My mother asked with a really shocked look on her face.

"Just go and tell all of our family secrets!" My sixty plus grandmother yelled from across the room."While you are at it, tell Chester how you took up with a pretty, dark skinned, young thing. I wasn't the only one having an affair."

I looked at my grandfather in shock. He had always been nuts about my grandmother. The affair accusation shocked me. It was the first I had ever heard of infidelity on his part. My grandfather's washed out, white, sick face turned red.

"Leave her out of it. I needed her." My grandfather shot back. "You were pregnant with Gordy's baby and my only child had run away from home. I didn't have anyone to turn to."

"Neither did I!" I heard my mother mutter.

"You little good for nothing spread your legs tramp . . .," My grandmother exploded turning to glare at my mother. "That fight with you caused me to lose Gordy's baby. I wanted that baby!" Then my elderly grandmother got up and stomped off down the hallway to her bedroom and slammed the door.

"Are you okay, mom?" I asked seeing something in her eyes that said she was reliving some sort of nightmare.

"I . . . I . . . just need a drink . . ." My mother replied. Have you got anything Chester?"

"I think there are a couple of beers out in the cab of Grandpa's trash hauler. Do you want me to get you one?"

"I will get them after I finish smoking this cigarette." My mother replied in a really nervous voice. I could see her hands trembling.

I then returned to my conversation with my grandfather. I had not expected family secrets to be the Christmas Eve presents bestowed on me.

"Let us get back to Snuff, grandpa." I whispered. "You are unintentionally pushing all of grandma's buttons. That might not be a good thing. You and I could be sleeping in the cabs of your trash haulers tonight. I am not sure Santa will be able to find us there."

My grandfather grinned. "Could I ask Rosa to join me and Santa in mine?" He whispered back as my mother got up to go outside and retrieve the two beers.

I cringed. I now knew why my grandmother hated Rosa. It must have been Rosa that my grandfather had his affair with, the one with darker skin. Rosa was Hispanic.

"Rosa is too old for me; and too young for you and Santa." I retorted.

"If I could go back Chester, I would choose my dark skinned girl, and let Gordy have your grandmother." He stated loudly as my grandmother returned from her bedroom carrying a carton of cigarettes. There was already a blue, second hand, cloud of smoke floating around in the kitchen of the mobile home.

My grandmother yelled back at him, "You are lucky the white sheets haven't cut your manhood off. At least I stick to my own race, a superior race."

"You are not superior to her in bed or in looks." My grandfather yelled back at her. "If I had chosen her, at least I would have a beautiful warm body to sleep next to while I am dying. You would be sleeping alone! Gordy doesn't like old wrinkled hags."

My grandmother stomped out of the kitchen and down the hall again to her bedroom and slammed the door. Christmas Eve in my grandparent's mobile home was turning out to be a words war.

"Since you and grandma are airing all of our family's secrets tonight, who is my father? Mom has refused to tell me." I asked not realizing my mother had stepped back inside. She had entered by the rear door of the trailer.

"Don't answer that, dad!" My mother's voice suddenly exploded, while stepping from the hallway.

My grandfather didn't answer my question, but changed the subject to asking what time it was. He then proceeded to discuss our plans to have our photo taken. I knew he was letting the temperature in the trailer cool down. He winked at me. About fifteen minutes later, my grandmother returned to the kitchen table and threw a small bottle of vodka and a pack of little cigars on the table. She then bit the end off of one of the cigars and lit it. She smoked little cigars when she was highly agitated. She drank Vodka only after funerals. Apparently, she was having one of those moments. My mother stuck to the cigarettes and beer. However, I could see her eyeing the bottle of booze. My grandmother bringing the vodka to the table seemed as though she wanted my mother to get drunk, so she would shut up.

"How long have you had a thing going on with Gracie Gardenia?" My grandmother asked in a harsh voice, puffing away in an agitated mood.

"Who are you asking Grandma, Grandpa or me?" I asked confused.

"Cut the crap, Chester. Are you the reason Gracie run away?" My Grandmother asked, but didn't give me a chance to answer. "Just so you know, Gracie is not welcome in this trailer and neither are letters from her."

"What are you talking about?" I asked wondering how we had gotten to the subject of Gracie.

"Did you give him the letter?" My grandmother asked my mother harshly while pushing the small bottle of Vodka towards her.

"I almost forgot!" My mother replied. She then turned to me after pulling a folded pink envelope from her jeans back pocket. "I pulled this letter from mom's mailbox earlier before coming in. It is a letter for you from a girl. Mom thinks it is from Gracie. The perfume on it is too expensive smelling. I think it is from one of your class mates at school."

My mother then waved a pink envelope in front of me.

"It is probably just some advertisement, Mom." I replied reaching for it.

My mother immediately started playing keep away with me, to annoy me. Then, she smiled from ear to ear and held the hot pink envelope up to the light, like she was trying to read its content thru the envelope.

"Just give the damn thing to him, Liz. He is probably right; it is just an advertisement. Gordy wouldn't let our bastard within ten feet of his perfect little Gracie."

"Do you have a high school, girl friend . . . possibly on vacation in California?" My mother asked in a prying voice. "The postmark reads California."

"Did you say California?" I asked trying again to grab the hot pink envelope that she was waving about. I had no friends at school and had never had any outside of school. I was the smelly garbage dump kid that no one wanted anything to do with, much less play with. The pink letter was a first for me and I knew it had to be from pink, hi-heeled Gracie. I was excited. Good things didn't happen to me too often. Her great looking legs flashed across my thoughts causing me further excitement. I couldn't believe that I possibly had a letter from her.

"Chester has a girl friend . . . Chester has a girl friend." My mother taunted blowing me an air kiss.

I immediately blushed. Then, I grabbed the pink envelope from my mom's grip and quickly exited the trailer to open the letter and read it in privacy. It was cold outside and snowflakes were swirling in the air. I climbed into the cab of one of my grandfather's trash haulers to read my first correspondence from a girl.

I smelled the letter a couple of times and then laughed. Gracie had purposely sprayed the letter with perfume and was trying to push buttons she saw in me. That pleased me. At least she saw me as a god who needed his buttons pushed. She was one up on me in the 'TESTING THE GODS 'department and she definitely had my attention.

Tearing the pink envelope open, I was surprised to find that there was no letter inside. Instead, there was a folded newspaper clipping. I was really disappointed and bit my lip. Then, after a moment of descending from cloud nine, I unfolded and quickly scanned the newspaper clipping. It was an article about a young guy my age. He had opened a detective agency named 'Zeke's Feet' out in California. I was very much interested in what the clipping had to say. It was the success story that I wanted written about me, someday. My dream was to go to California and become a detective. Dr. Mayor was my first superhero. Now, I had a second. Whoever Zeke was, I wanted to be like him.

Gracie knew me and my buttons better than my family did. That surprised me. I wondered how many times she had studied me as we stood, not talking at our county school bus stop. I was sorry that I had not taken the time to study who she was. She was a better goddess that I was a god. She had taken the time to reach back to me in the gutter dump life of Gardenia and offer me a hand up. The clipping was her way of doing so. She was willing to invest the price of a stamp in me. That was an act of charity on her part, because there was no return address on the pink envelope. She was giving, not wanting anything from me. The perfumed, hot pink envelope was just to get my attention; push my buttons. Someday, I would find her and do a little button pushing of my own, I told myself.

CHAPTER SIX

First Detective Lesson

Have I failed to tell you that my grandmother, about six months prior, embraced the door knocker's religion? This really baffled me and my grandfather. My grandmother always had an agenda, and was not a charitable person. We knew she was milking her new religion for something. We just could not figure out what. My grandmother was a devout Catholic and continued to go to mass and confession, even though she had joined the witnesses. That told my grandfather and me that something was up. We just didn't know what.

It was seven in the evening on Christmas Eve. Snuff was my grandfather's last visitor. Gordy Gardenia had dropped by with an armful of dirty fake flowers from the dump for my grandmother. She quickly asked him to sit with her at the kitchen table, and offered him coffee. She was in the process of pouring him a cup as I turned off my grandfather's big screen. My grandmother's face was beaming. She was a different person, when Gordy visited. As my grandma offered him cream and sugar for his coffee, my mother Liz got up immediately and left. She always did that when Gordy came around. I disliked Gordy, but my mother seemed to dislike him more.

It was about time for my grandfather and me to take off on our night's adventure. I stepped into the trailer's hall where a full length mirror hung, and checked out the green college logo sweatshirt I had on, to make sure I looked presentable. Grandpa had found the discarded university sweatshirt in one of his trash loads the previous summer. Most of our clothes came from his dump loads. I was pleased with how I looked. Also, I was sure that guys my age didn't go in for dressing up for family Christmas Eve parties. I wanted to dress down, not stand out. Jeans and a college sweatshirt, in my thinking, was a good choice. I also planned to wear a green sports ball cap that I had retrieved from my grandfather's closet, when I was helping him dress earlier. Wearing the green cap and green sweatshirt, I was sure that I would look Christmas Eve festive. At the same time, I would not stick out like a sore thumb.

Christmas was foreign territory to me. My grandfather talked about the Christmas traditions of his youth. My grandmother ignored the holiday altogether. I don't ever remember being told there was a Santa Claus or being taken down town to sit on his knee. My mother had been a lifelong drug addict and alcoholic. If there was money during the holidays, she spent it on booze or drugs. My mother went on a yearly drinking binge during the holidays, and Santa Claus never visited me. Since joining the Je . . . ovas, my grandmother insisted that she no longer celebrated Christmas at all. However, I had watched her get in a taxi at daybreak and make her way to the church for her Christmas Eve confession. She had always wanted to be first in line on Christmas Eve. Why? I don't know.

"Chester . . . what do you have on?" My grandmother inquired loudly, looking up from her visit with Gordy. "That better not be a Christmas sweatshirt you have on. You know the rules in this house. We do not celebrate Christmas, especially now that I know better. Je . . . ova has shown me that celebrating Christmas is a sin."

"You don't celebrate Christmas!" I returned a little bit annoyed. "I seem to recall you going to confession early this morning. I personally think St. Nicholas is pretty cool! I might embrace him as my patron saint."

"Christmas is a pagan holiday." She shot back. "Only a 144,000 will live and reign with God and rule his New Heaven and New Earth. I will be number two of that number."

"Well, grandfather and I have not embraced your Je . . . ovas. We will take our chances with Saint Nicholas." I shot back while helping my grandfather up out of his recliner.

My grandfather looked sharp in his navy blue, button up, jacket sweater that had knitted snowflakes falling down one arm. Beneath it, he had on a white dress shirt and a navy blue necktie with Rudolph and Santa screen printed on it. He looked like a fun loving old man ready for Christmas.

"Woody . . . where did you get that pagan necktie and sweater?" My Grandmother demanded in a loud voice. "You know I don't allow Christmas garments to be worn in this house. You are going to bring the curse of God down on us. I am already knocking on double doors to keep Gordy from destroying you and the other heathen who come and go beneath my roof. Pagans will die by the sword in that day."

"It is just a sweater and a necktie, grandma. Get off his case. I bought him the sweater and tie to wear for our photo." I shot back lying to cover for my ill grandfather. I was sure he had pulled the sweater and tie out of some trash load over the previous year. People on his routes had a tendency to throw out holiday clothing and decorations after their parties.

"One day you and Woody will regret not listening to me. I am going to live and reign in the new Heaven with the chosen door knockers. Gordy will be God."

I ignored what I thought were mixed up words on her part. My grandmother had probably taken a few nips earlier of vanilla or something when she was cooking dinner. It was possible she was a tiny bit high. My grandma didn't drink often. When she did, it was always sparingly. She always claimed she didn't like the taste of alcohol.

Glancing over at my grandmother, I was annoyed to see Gordy put his hand roughly on top of hers. He had an eyebrow raised, and he wasn't smiling at her. My grandmother immediately bit her lip and shut up. I wondered what the act of aggression on Gordy's part was all about. My grandmother had screws loose at times. My grandfather called it quirks. Gordy was probably just trying to keep her from starting in on a ranting craze about her Je . . . ova religion.

In my opinion, my grandmother had a dark side, an insane side. She functioned in her day to day life, paid bills, and kept house. She didn't kill cats or beat children. However, I felt she walked a fine line between sanity and insanity. I could see it, but my mother and grandfather seemed oblivious to it.

There was cold silence in the trailer. Gordy had not removed his hand from on top of my grandmother's. I ignored them and helped my grandfather up, and then out the door to his trash hauler which would be our transportation. Gordy could have grandma for the evening. Let him deal with her loose screws.

~   ~   ~

In about fifteen minutes, my grandfather and I had made our way into the city and had started driving the streets of one of the wealthier neighborhoods. My grandfather had chosen what neighborhood he wanted to Christmas Eve crash in. Snow was falling and the ground looked like it had been dusted with powdered sugar. I drove slowly eyeing all the elaborately, decorated houses with their twinkling lights and festive displays. What I was marveling at, was what I wanted someday. I wanted a respectable life and skin that hadn't absorbed the odors of the dump. I wanted to be, what I thought at sixteen, was normal.

"What about that one?" I asked pointing to a huge Victorian house that was all lit up with candles burning in every window. It had two cads and a couple of four doors parked in the driveway.

"Not enough cars, Chester. They are probably having a quiet little sit down dinner for six or eight at the most. We need a party where there are so many people, there is standing room only and the men are spilling out on to the front stoop to smoke." My grandfather stated continuing to look out his passenger window.

I was proud of myself. I was helping my grandfather do the one thing he had always wanted to do. It was a 'Test the Gods' moment for him; a chance to successfully crash one Christmas Eve party and stay till the end of it, pretending he was one of them. I was giving him a gift that no one else could ever give him. Thanks to Dr. Mayo, I knew how valuable that gift was. A price tag could not be put on his chance to 'Test the Gods'. This would be his chance to crawl up out of his garbage dump existence and be someone else. Afterward, he would return to the dump gutter, and die there.

"There is one!" I stated pointing to a ranch style home with three men standing and smoking on the front step. It had three cars in the drive and a couple of beat up pickup trucks on the street. The only nice car apparently was owned by the owner of the residence. A gold Cadillac was parked in the garage. The door was up for some reason, making the luxury car visible to the street.

"That is a family get together where they will exchange their gifts, eat a cookie or two, and then everyone will go their way to other parties." My grandfather answered waving me on.

"How can you tell?" I asked.

"One of the pickups has a diaper bag on the dash. A mother would take a diaper bag in, if she were going to be there for more than an hour. Two of the cars haven't been washed and have fast food containers thrown up on their dashes. The occupants of those two cars ate before they entered. That means that no meal is being served inside. The three bored guys on the front stoop are just putting in their hour, till their wives say it is okay to move on to their next stop for the evening. If they were higher class and somebody, they wouldn't be flipping their cigarette butts onto the front sidewalk. They are low class jerks who are married to the daughters of some couple who probably made their money after the kids were gone. The garage door left up is so that all of the company will enter there, instead of thru the front door. The home-owner is trying to protect his carpets from the jerks who probably have never wiped their feet in their life. The home owner is probably someone from the other side of the tracks who made, inherited, or won a lot of money. They have made it out of the gutter of life, but their family still has low class mentality and ways."

"You have a keen eye, grandpa. You could have been a detective." I replied shocked at his insight into people.

We drove on down a couple of blocks and then turned onto a tree lined street of magnificent older, wealthy homes. My grandfather had motioned for me to turn on that particular street.

"That looks like a winner!" I stated pointing to a Tudor style home with a huge twinkling Christmas tree in its window and its driveway full of foreign import cars. A black airport limo and a taxi were parked along the curb. A neon sign, in the front yard, was flashing season's greeting in a foreign language.

"That one definitely won't do, Chester." My grandfather replied.

"Why not . . . ? It has at least nine cars and there is a Christmas tree."

"They don't speak English, Chester. See their flashing Christmas greeting? They are French, Hungarian, German, or something. If I can't read their flashing Christmas greeting, I definitely cannot hold my own inside in conversation. If they are terrorists or something, you and I might get shot for being Christmas Eve spies. Do you want me to die before my time?"

"I get your point. However, this is the middle of the United States, Grandpa. I doubt very seriously that there is any spy activity going on around here. If we lived in New York, New Jersey, or on the coast, you might be right." I replied.

In our shared moment of looking for a god to test, I was seeing my grandfather in a new light, one of respect. He was teaching me to read people by what was in their driveway and yards. It was a lesson in being a detective that I did not expect to learn from a garbage man.

"Where and when did you hone your detective skills?" I spit out asking.

"Well, Chester, it is like this. A girl who has worked in a man's clothing store for years can tell what size pants a man wears, just by looking at him. I service the same trash routes year in and year out and have done so my whole life. I know which families purchase big screens, stereos, and shop at exclusive dress shops. I also know the ones that do rip off shopping. The boxes and things in their trash cans tell on them. The rip-off shoppers want to appear wealthy. The live in their big houses, but can barely make the payments on them, much less shop for big screens or high end clothing. The wealthy are frivolous and don't worry about tomorrow. They throw their last season's high end purchases in the trash at the end of the fashion season. The pretend wealthy have garage sales. I have learned to read my customers by what they throw away or don't throw away. For instance, the rip-offs discard a lot of generic macaroni and cheese boxes in their trash. The wealthy throw out half a roasted duck, a huge tray of cold cuts, and a half gallon of peppermint ice cream with one scoop out of it after a party. The rip-offs will feed their last cold cut or stale cookie to their kids for the next two weeks. I read their cars and their lawns the same way."

"My hat is tipped to you grandpa. I want to be a detective someday. However, in this moment, you are the man."

"I am just good at what I do, Chester. I know which of my customers will pay and which will not. I eventually weed out the rip-offs. Your grandmother and I have lived quite well on what the rich have thrown away. We may live in Gardenia, but we are the upper crust of Gardenia. Gordy gets the leftovers from my route. I sell all the good stuff in my loads, before dumping. I have a route of antique and flea market dealers in the city. I call on them, when I have something good on my truck. The good stuff never goes home to the dump, unless it is something I think your grandma might want. I keep a storage locker downtown for anything that might take a week or so for me to dispose of."

"The smell, grandfather . . . people treat us differently because our skin absorbs the smell of the garbage dump. Doesn't that bother you? How often do you and grandma get invited to social gatherings beyond the dump? I don't. The kids at school have made my whole life miserable telling me I stink."

"I am what I am, Chester, and I make a good living at it. I make a lot of money and your grandma and mother spends it. Those in the dump are used to the smells and do not smell each other. It is your grandmother that I want to be with, not the fancy pants that live in these houses. I have a social life. Snuff, Rosa, and the other haulers are my friends. Rosa never forgets me at Christmas and Snuff trusts me enough to leave his keys in my care."

"It is a small world you live in, Grandpa. I want a social life filled with more than six to eight people. Don't you ever dream of more?"

"The only thing that has been missing in my life is a large extended family. When I was young like you, I wanted a trailer house full of children. Your grandma did not. Tonight, I get to have the one thing that is missing in my life, a large family to be with on Christmas Eve. I won't be seeing another Christmas Eve, Chester. Thank you for this once in a life time gift. After tonight, I can truthfully say that I have accomplished all my dreams. I will be able to truly rest in peace."

"Why do you put up with Gordy, grandpa?"

"Putting up with him is my key to keeping your grandma. She and Gordy, you might say, come as a package deal. Some men marry a woman who has been married before and has two or three children. What she has in tow doesn't keep her and a man from having a lifetime of loving each other. Gordy is your grandma's baggage from a former life, just like some women have children. That doesn't keep me from loving her."

"I will never fall in love with any woman that has a bunch of kids or an ex-lover in tow." I shot back shaking my head. "You should tell Gordy Gardenia to take a hike."

"Do you see that lit up, two-story house on the left?" My grandfather asked pointing and ignoring my comment.

"Are you pointing at the one with the younger couple necking on the side porch?"

"That is the one. How many cars do you see, Chester?"

"It's a double driveway. I see six in the double drive and seven along the curb." I replied after quickly counting.

"Are there any beat up wrecks amongst them?"

"No, they are all cads, sports cars, jeeps, black limos, four door family cars, and a catering van."

"Circle the block and turn down the alley. I want to get a look at what is parked behind."

I did as my grandfather said. Driving to the end of the block, I made a right and then turned right again heading down the alleyway that ran behind all the huge houses. I slowed the hauler down to a creep as we neared the house he wanted to check out. I put my foot on the brake and brought the trash hauler to a running stop behind the house. My grandfather eyed an array of dented up heaps and older sports cars parked in the alley drive.

"What do you see, Chester?"

"I see an array of dented, older, expensive vehicles with high school and college stickers on them. Also, there are a couple of thirty year old looking, cheap four door wrecks that look like they don't belong. Why do you ask?"

"These rich folks have made their kids park behind the house for the evening. Their college and high school students are driving mom and dad's old sport cars. This party will have young folks your age to blend in with. If anyone asks you who you are, just point to some guy across the room and say you are with them. College kids are notorious for bringing someone home for the holidays."

"That is brilliant, Grandpa."

"What can you read from the two older four door wrecks parked back here, Chester?"

"Well, I see some type of white waitress' cap hanging on the rear view mirror of one and a change of men's clothes hanging in the other. The cars are beat up, rusted, four door salvage yard heaps. People in this neighborhood definitely would not want cars like that seen in their driveways, in my opinion. The one with the waitress cap has two car seats in the back seat. I assume it belongs to some young mother. The car with the jeans and shirt hanging in the back has to belong to a guy. He eats cheap fast food. He has a burger sack up on his dash."

"Those two cars belong to back door people, or servants. You must learn to study the little things about people if you want to be a detective, Chester. You did good spotting the car seats and the man's clothing. The young mother is probably broke, or she would be home with her children on Christmas Eve. She probably needs the cash from working tonight, to run out to an all night discount store afterward and buy her kids something for Christmas. The guy with a change of clothing in the back of his vehicle is probably working for the caterer parked around front. He, like the young mother, needs cash. He probably needs it for gas money to get home for Christmas in some other city. He will leave as soon as he gets paid around midnight. Then, he will drive all night to make it home for the holidays. Cars parked behind mansions on holidays are usually not guests."

"Where are we parking?" I asked.

"Back here. We don't want the police called on us. We could get a ticket for parking a commercial vehicle around front. We will park back here with the servants and then walk around front and ring the front bell like front door guests. As a garbage man, I would never ring the front bell of a house like this, if I wanted to keep them as a customer. The rich are all about appearances. A catering truck in a driveway is status. A garbage hauling truck is not."

"Won't the hired help be suspicious of our truck being parked back here by them?" I asked.

"The hired help will think we are here to clean up after the party." My grandfather replied pointing to a parking spot by the trash cans.

Grinning, I parked where he pointed. I had read detective magazines for years. However, it was my grandfather who was giving me a crash course in reading people, their houses, cars, lawns, and rear entrances. I was in awe. His trash route had just been something I ran to keep the family afloat when he was ill. Running his trash route was like reading a detective book to him.

A light bulb went on in my head. I needed to read the people in my world as though they were houses and decide if they were rip-offs or real McCoy in their presentation. At school, after Christmas, I would pay more attention to kid's lunch trays and what they were raking off or folding in napkins and sticking in their purses and pockets. I also would pay more attention as to how I was presenting myself to the world around me. Maybe Doctor Mayo was right. Maybe I was presenting myself as a garbage man, when I should be presenting myself as the grandson of a detective, or a collector of antiquities.

As I helped my grandfather from the passenger side of his trash hauler,

I wondered what Zeke, the detective in California, was like. He hired only women, from what the newspaper article said. I wondered why. In that moment, I decided that Zeke was a god, and I intended to test his buttons one day. I would walk in his agency's front door, demand to fill out an employment application, and then push his buttons till he hired me as his first male detective. I would apply sixty times if I had to. Dr. Mayo pushed his nurse's call light button over and over till he got what he wanted. Dr. Mayo had gorgeous nurses spoon-feeding him Banana Crème Pie. I could see myself working with a whole group of gorgeous female Private Eyes and them catering to me.

CHAPTER SEVEN

Blending In

After a little slow walking in a blowing snow that was accumulating fast on the ground, my grandfather and I made it around the huge, two-story, Victorian home and approached the steps leading up to the front porch and door. A teen guy wearing black pants, a white shirt, and a black string tie was standing on the front sidewalk talking to some girl on his cell phone. He ignored us.

"He is hired help . . . probably a server." My grandfather whispered to me as we neared the door, after climbing onto the sprawling porch. "He will get fired, if the homeowner catches him out front. Servants are always required to use rear entrances and walks."

I looked the young black guy over. He appeared to be about my age. My grandfather was probably right. No one my age wore a white shirt to a Christmas party. He had to be the guy who had the change of clothes stashed in the dented wreck out back.

"Are you ready?" I asked as I raised my hand to knock on the door. We had purposely left our coats in the truck. If we had to make a quick exit for any reason, we didn't want to have to take time to search for coats. There was also the chance we might get thrown out without the chance to look for them. I quickly sniffed myself trying to decide whether I smelled like the dump. I was sure I did.

"Don't be sniffing yourself, Chester. If anyone asks, tell them it is a new musk scent you are trying out. You can always say the scent doesn't seem to agree with your skin's natural oils."

"That is your line?" I asked refraining from anymore sniffing.

"That is my line and I am sticking to it!" My grandfather replied running his hand thru his white hair to make sure it wasn't falling forward anywhere. "How do I look, Chester. Read me like I read the houses of the rip-offs and wealthy?"

"Well . . . You are a casually dressed older man, probably single or a widower because you do not have a woman on your arm. You love snow because of your choice of a blue sweater with snowflakes on it. Your color is blue. You probably have some health problems, since you have me driving you to the party. Your white hair won't threaten anyone. If anything, someone will grab you by the arm and help you find a chair and maybe even carry you a drink. Some money grubbing, old lady is probably going to put the moves on you because you look like you are single and might just be about to kick the bucket. She will probably think you have money and can see herself inheriting everything you have. She will be a rip off woman. All the young folks will just see you as some old dude who is a friend of someone in the family who had nowhere to go on Christmas Eve. How is that?"

"I will tell you if you are correct after the party. If you see the money grubber heading my way, run interference. Your grandmother will kill me if I end up under the mistletoe and kiss some rich old broad who wants me for my money."

I laughed. "I am going to knock. Are you ready?"

"Lay it on the door, Chester. It is time for us to blend in and do our thing."

I gave the door three sturdy knocks. After a moment, a black girl wearing a starched, gray maid's uniform opened the door.

"May I help you?" She asked.

"We are here for the party." My grandfather stated. "This is my grandson,

Chester. Can you show him where to find his college friend? He forgot his contact lens and he can't see two feet in front of himself without them. A girl looks like a guy to him without them. I wouldn't want to see him end up under the mistletoe with the wrong sex."

The maid snickered. "Come on," she said taking me by the arm. The party, as you call it, is that way." She stated pointing my grandfather toward a set of double doors. "You will find Miss May Belle in there. I will see that your blind escort makes it to the back where the younger crowd is gathered."

"Double doors it is." My grandfather replied winking at me and smiling.

"Just wait till Miss May Belle's kids see that sweater you have on." The maid added and snickered again.

"Am I overdressed?" My grandfather asked winking at the maid.

"I would say you will be the only life in this party." She returned and snickered again. "Are you the old dude, Miss May Belle's lover, that the kids in the back are joking about?"

"The one and only . . . ," My grandfather replied.

At that point, the maid ushered me down a hall and to the rear of the house where she stopped pointing me to the door of a huge kitchen.

"Go on in! You will find your college buddies in there, somewhere. The snoots up front, where your older dude is headed, are snacking on escargot and goose liver pâté. The younger crowd back here is pigging out on pizza and beer."

"Thank you!" I stated and looked into the kitchen a little nervous. Then I muttered, "So much for blending in."

My grandfather had picked an all black Christmas party for us to crash. My lily white skin and red hair made me stick out like a sore thumb. It was too late for me to retreat. I stepped into the kitchen nervously, removed my ball cap, grinned, and asked, "Is this where the good party food is?"

"Yeah man, come on in. That wake food up front is just for show for Auntie's rich friends and her old white dude lover that hasn't arrived yet. Goose liver pate and Escargot on little crackers is all you are going to find up there. Are you by any chance, her lover?" A six foot black teen in a college logo sweatshirt asked laughing. "Rumor has it that she has been seeing some lily white older man. Was the older part wrong?"

"It is not me, but I did drive an older white man here. He has joined the goose liver eaters up front."

The tall, skinny, black teen laughed and slapped me on my back in a good natured fashion. Then he asked, "What is your name?"

"Chess . . . Chet!" I replied remembering Dr. Mayo had told me I needed to up my game and change my image. "Chet Holly is my name."

"Hey guys, look who is here. This is Chet Holly, Aunt May Belle's white lover's driver. Dish this dude up a plate of pizza and toss him a coke from the fridge. I think he might be a bit too young for one of the beers." Then he slapped me on the back again. A well dressed black girl walked over from the breakfast bar, took me by the arm, and ushered me back to the bar to sit with her. Then the party was on. One of the guys turned up a kitchen stereo system and the others pushed back the kitchen table. The kitchen's marble tiles became a dance floor. In the back of my mind, I told myself that I was going to have to learn to dance, if I wanted to fit into future scenarios like this.

"What is that cologne you are wearing, Chet Holly?" The black girl seated next to me asked.

"It is called Gardenia Musk. I am going to throw it away when I get home. The old dude I drive for gave it to me for a Christmas present, just before coming here. The scent seems to be having a reaction to the oils in my skin. Musk and I just don't agree."

"Yeah . . . I agree with you. Definitely throw that gift in the trash. Here!" She said pulling a tiny metal flask of women's perfume from a big sloppy purse she had thrown on the kitchen bar. "This will cover up anything, even Gardenia Musk."

With that said, she sprayed the heck out of me. I didn't refuse. I was on her turf and I was sure my grandfather didn't intend to leave anytime soon. To my surprise, I liked the smell of what she sprayed me with. I sniffed my sweatshirt.

"I like the smell of your perfume. What is it?" I asked.

"Emile Five. It should be good. I paid seven hundred dollars for this little flask of it. A girl or guy is only as good as they smell."

I sniffed myself again. She had just sprayed me with at least fifty dollars worth of expensive perfume.

"I owe you one, a spray of perfume." I replied.

"I will collect later under the mistletoe." She replied grinning.

"The mistletoe it is." I replied not knowing how to answer. Then I gave her the most flirtatious wink I could muster up. Winks worked for my grandfather.

Then her cell phone rang and she ignored me. At the same time, the black maid stuck her head in the kitchen door and then walked over and took me by the arm. "Excuse him leaving your party so early. The old dude he brought here is calling for him. Your Aunt May Belle has reduced the old fellow to tears."

I immediately got up, thinking my grandfather and I were about to be thrown out. I smiled and waved at all the high school and college kids in the kitchen. "I will catch you later. Save me a plate of that pizza and ribs." I stated waving at everybody.

"Will do, Chet . . ." The guys echoed each other.

The girl on the phone waved at me and threw me a kiss as I left. She had the most luscious, milk chocolate, brown skin. In my thinking, she had to be the most gorgeous girl alive, next to Gracie. What made her that way, was the fact that she had not turned her nose up at me. She had befriended me. I had no friends. I had never had any friends. I was the smelly kid from the dump. She could have stuffed me in her big sloppy handbag and took me anywhere. I would have tripped all over myself going willingly.

Once out in the hallway, the rent a maid said to me. "You should have grabbed you a plate of those ribs. Those fools in the kitchen aren't going to save you a plate. This party is about over. Those free-loading yahoos are going to eat their last free meal, grab what they can get, and then run when Miss May Belle's party bites the dust. Her limo is outside now, waiting for her. When she goes, the party is over. Those rich kid's parents are saying their good-byes up in the front room now. Your grandfather is taking her leaving really hard."

"He is?" I asked sounding a little confused. If he was taking it hard, it had to be because the party was a dud and ending too quickly. Maybe he had sent for me, so we could exit quickly and look for another party to crash.

As the maid and I were walking down the hallway toward the front, I spotted mistletoe hanging from a hallway light fixture. It was my first chance to test a goddess.

"Hold it!" I stated reaching out and taking hold of her arm lightly as we reached the mistletoe.

"Is something wrong?" She asked turning towards me.

I pointed to the mistletoe hanging above us, "Mistletoe . . . one kiss is due me."

"Why would you want to steal a kiss beneath the mistletoe from me? I am hired help." She replied in shock and then continued, "Not to mention that you are as lily white as a bed sheet and I am dark brown rye bread. Why would you want to waste a kiss on me?"

"For starters, you have the greatest legs of any woman at this party. Second, I like a girl with a sun tan. Third, I can't argue with mistletoe on who it wants me to kiss."

"Okay . . . kiss me before my boss sees you do it. I might as well have one Christmas Eve moment to remember. That will be the only thing I will be getting this year."

She did not know how excited I was on the inside. I had walked up to my first goddess, tested her, and was about to claim payment. I took her in my arms and kissed her like I had seen them do in the movies. It was my first time kissing a girl. When I let her go, she looked at me big eyed.

"Until this moment, I have always been a woman who preferred a rye bread man. However, I think I have just developed a taste for white bread. That was one toe nail curling, turn my heart upside down, passionate kiss." She replied fanning herself with one hand. "Where did you learn to kiss like that?"

"What is your name?" I asked ignoring her question. "I want to remember you and this mistletoe moment forever."

"Believe me, the feeling is mutual." She stated fanning herself with one hand. "My name is Keesha."

"My name is Chet Holly!" I replied and then gave her a little wink.

"Meet me under this mistletoe later when all the guests are gone, Chet Holly." She replied laughing and giving me a wink. She then pointed me toward the double doors of the front room.

I was proud of myself. I had just successfully tested the gods, claimed a kiss and a girl's wink in payment, and was about to run. I returned my attention to thoughts of my grandfather. I figured he was in over his head and we would be thrown out on our butts in the next two minutes. Peeping in the entrance to the massive living or great room, I looked sheepishly around for my grandfather. A group was gathered at the far end of the room. That is when I spotted an open casket placed in front of a Christmas tree. There was a huge, black woman's body in it. I gulped. This was Christmas Eve, not Halloween. Was I in some sort of time warp? I turned to the rent-a-maid with big eyes. "Is that . . . ?"

"That is Miss May Belle. She died yesterday morning. Her last request was for her wake to be held on Christmas Eve and that she lay in state in front of her Christmas tree till her white lover had a chance to make it here and claim his last kiss."

I grabbed the door frame. My grandfather and I had crashed a black woman's wake. Not only that, it was possible that some other old white guy might show up at anytime and beat the crap out of my grandfather for kissing his Miss May Belle in death. I now knew why my grandfather was taking it bad. However, he was putting on a good act of crying and holding her cold, limp, dead hand.

"Excuse me, Keesha! I have got to go and pay my last respects." I whispered and then headed for the casket.

Then, I heard Keesha whisper loudly behind me. "Don't kiss her goodbye like you kissed me under the mistletoe. She just might rise from the dead."

I turned around, winked at her again and said, "I will never kiss anyone like I kissed you. I promise!"

She grinned.

Afterward, I walked to the end of the room, pushed my grandfather aside and took Miss May Belle's hand and pulled it up to my lips and kissed it. Then I leaned down and put my cheek against hers and whispered, "This has been one of the best nights of my life. Thank you, especially for the mistletoe you hung in the hallway. I will never forget your Christmas Eve Party."

Then I felt a hand on my shoulder. I let go of Miss May Belle's hand, stood up straight, and turned to see who was trying to get my attention. It was one of the older boys from the kitchen.

"Aunt May Belle is one big woman. Would you give us an extra hand carrying her and her casket out to the hearse?"

"You've got it." I replied.

~   ~   ~

After the casket was in the limo, I returned to the house for my grandfather. The old white dude lover had not shown up. My grandfather shook everyone's hands and carried out the part as good as any actor would have. The family gave him a huge portrait of Miss May Belle to take home with him. I wasn't sure what grandma was going to think about that. She was a wild card, as grandpa put it.

Outside, we paused a moment to take a breath of the cold, December night air. Then we walked around the mansion and returned to the rear parking. I helped my grandfather in the passenger side of his trash hauler that was parked by the trash can. He was quiet. I figured the party had pretty well zapped what strength he had for the moment. He was just weeks away from joining Miss May Belle in death. I walked around and got in the driver's seat. That is when my eyes wandered to Keesha's wreck of a car. I lived in a dump. However, I did not want for money. I reaped a weekly wage off of my grandfather's business. It was possible she was living in the city's ghetto, a dump all its own.

"How much money have you got on you?" I asked my grandfather. "I forgot my wallet."

"I have twenty or thirty dollars . . . why?"

"Hand it over. I need to pay the rent-a-maid for a favor."

My grandfather grinned and handed me the cash he had in his billfold. "I hope you are not paying for something that I am going to have to take you to the doctor for next week."

I ignored his innuendo and grabbed an envelope from the dash. We kept statements and envelopes on the dash to bill customers. I stuck the money in the envelope, and then quickly wrote Keesha a note on it. Then, I jumped out of the trash hauler and secured it beneath her window wiper on the driver's side.

The note read:

Merry Christmas! The memory of your kiss will be a gift I will treasure for a lifetime. You are a Rye Bread Goddess.

Chet Holly Mayo - Your Mistletoe Man

In that moment, I decided I was changing my last name to Mayo when I got to California.

CHAPTER EIGHT

Unanswered Questions

T he end of January rolled around and my Grandfather took a turn for the worse. After a short hospital stay, he was placed in a hospice nursing home, because he was past the stage of caring for himself.

Before I went to school in the mornings, I ran a quarter of his trash route. After school, I ran another quarter. My step-father picked up the remaining half on the end of his trash hauling route. It seemed the forced taking over of my grandfather's trash business was sucking the life out of me. I was headed for the end of my senior year and there was no hope of my partaking in the senior hoopla that went along with that moment in time. When I wasn't hauling trash, I was studying or making a late night visit to my grandfather in the nursing home. He was the only member of my family that gave a damn about me. I felt obligated to visit him every night. My grandmother didn't visit him at all. She had stuck him in the nursing home and left him there to rot. My mother visited my grandfather when she wasn't stoned.

It was on a Friday night time trek to the nursing home that my grandfather and I got around to talking about Grandma and Gordy. I was giving my grandfather every chance possible to say anything he wanted to say before he passed on. There were two family mysteries in particular that bothered me. One was what my grandmother did with the hundreds of fake flowers that Gordy brought her on a regular basis from the dump. The other was who my father was. Maybe it was time to see if my grandfather, in the face of his impending death, would answer my two questions.

"What is on your mind, Chester?" My grandfather asked as I fluffed his bed pillow and tried to make him more comfortable.

"I was thinking about Grandma and all the fake flowers Gordy brings her from the dump. What does she do with all of them? One morning there will be a black trash bag full stashed in the laundry room. When I come home at the end of the day, they are gone."

"You are the one who wants to be a detective, Chester. I don't know what she does with the fake posies. When I leave out on my trash route in the morning, there is usually a bag in front of the washer and dryer just like you say. When I return for lunch, they are usually gone, just like you say. I think she might be graciously accepting them from Gordy and then tossing them back in one of my garbage haulers later. Then again, she might be taking them to a cemetery somewhere and putting them on some ancestor's grave. She is a cheapskate in some ways. Who knows! Your grandmother has always been a wild card, Chester."

"Do you think Gordy, as old as he is, has a thing for grandma?" I asked cringing.

"It is more than a thing for your grandma, Chester. They have a history together. I think they will be buried next to each other after I am gone."

"Well, he won't be buried by Grandma if I have anything to say about it." I huffed.

"Did you know that your grandmother plans to cremate me? She has bought a little wooden gnome man that is hollow on the inside. She plans on putting my ashes in him. I don't want to be cremated, Chester. I want to be buried in a casket wearing the snowflake sweater I had on when I crashed the Christmas Eve wake of Miss May Belle. I also want Miss May Belle's picture taken from its frame, rolled up, and buried with me. Miss May Belle gave me one of the best nights of my whole life."

"That was some night . . . , grandpa. We went to crash a party, but attended a wake."

"I should have known by the black hearse out front. I am sorry about that, Chester. Even I don't always get every detail right. Did I tell you that I sampled the escargot and the goose liver pâté? For one night, Chester, I was someone. I was Miss May Belle's man." My grandfather replied and then he started coughing. After a moment or so, his coughing subsided.

"We did screw up not reading the hearse. However, everything turned out okay. I had a great time." I replied, while thinking about Keesha and our mistletoe kiss. I just couldn't get her out of my thoughts.

"Promise me you won't let your grandmother cremate me, Chester. Promise me! I want to lie beneath the ground in a casket in peace. Being cremated extra crisp, like a strip of bacon, just isn't my style."

"I will do my best to see that you are buried properly, Grandfather. I promise."

He had another hacking spell. I gave him a drink from one of those hospital water containers with the flexible straw.

When he calmed down, he looked me in the eye and said, "Put your grandmother in a nursing home and throw away the key when I am gone. She is a wild card, Chester. I think she killed the two missing Je . . . ova ladies. I can't prove it, so I have kept my mouth shut. She went door knocking with both of those missing ladies. She returned home to the dump in a taxi. Your grandmother may have killed Gracie too."

It was at that point that I felt my grandfather was slipping into a state of dementia or deathbed craziness. My sixty plus, skinny as a rail grandmother was hardly able to kill two women that were in their thirties. Also, I knew that Gracie was safe in California. She had sent me the pink envelope with the article about Zeke's Feet Detective Agency. My grandfather's mind was slipping, in my opinion, and he was becoming a little delusional. I decided to tell my mother what he had said, but not my grandmother.

"Gracie is fine, grandpa. I got a letter from her at Christmas. She just ran away."

"Gracie did not run away without reason, Chester. Have you asked yourself why she left a doting father, and has not kept in touch with him? I think Gracie may have discovered something concerning your grandmother and her father that she could not handle."

"Are you trying to insinuate that Gordy and Grandma have something shady going on?"

"Gordy is a wild card, like your grandmother. He has a screw loose and it has to do with young women. I have my theories, but I cannot prove them. You are young and have the time to do so. I am asking you to keep an eye on Gordy and read him the way we did the houses on Christmas Eve. Your grandmother was sixteen when he toyed with her. Gracie's mother was very young when he married her. Gordy's first wife, the funeral home girl, was fifteen. How would you read a man who prefers very young women? Gracie was barely sixteen when she ran away last fall. Does that suggest anything to you?"

"I get what you are trying to say, Grandpa. I will keep an eye on Gordy. However, I doubt very seriously that he and grandma are killing Je . . . ova women! As you have pointed out, he likes young women below the age of twenty. The missing Je . . . ova women were in their late thirties."

"Maybe they looked young," My grandfather replied still holding on to his theory.

I rolled my eyes.

"I have another question for you, Grandpa. I know that mom is never going to tell me, but I think I have the right to know. Who is my real father?"

"I honestly don't know, Chester. Your mother was fifteen and pregnant when she ran away from home. She lost that baby. A month afterward, she got pregnant with you while she was down south somewhere. She met your stepfather when she secretly moved back here into an apartment across town. I honestly don't know, Chester."

"Why did grandma go berserk and beat mom the day she ran away? Mom miscarried because of that beating."

"I didn't hear your mom's story that day. I walked in, after my trash route, just in time to stop Erma. Your mom made a run for the door and I didn't see or hear from her for years. When she did come back with you in tow, she was of legal age, and immediately married your step father. I think she came back so you could get to know me. Your mother and I had a good relationship till the day Erma beat her. Your mother hasn't trusted anyone since that day, not even me. You were conceived down south somewhere."

"I guess I truly am a bastard child with no father." I replied feeling like a knife had been stuck in my gut.

My grandfather entered another round of coughing. I offered him another sip of water. Sitting the water container back down I asked, "What about the fake flowers, grandpa. What do you think the real secret behind them is?"

"You know, Chester, I would like to know the secret of the fake flowers myself. I will make you a deal."

"What kind of a deal?" I replied asking.

"If you do a little detective work, discover what happens to the fake flowers, and then tell me, I will tell you who I think Gracie's mother is." My grandfather stated suddenly smiling from ear to ear. "You might just be surprised. It is a theory on my part, but I am sure that I am right about it. She was one of our dump girls. That is what has pushed your grandma out of shape. Gordy took a dump girl to the city, treated her like she was a queen, and had Gracie by her."

"Gracie's mother, the young one that died in a car crash, was a dump girl?" I asked in shock.

"Yep . . . !" My grandfather replied. "You figure out the mystery of the missing flowers. I will tell you the name of the dump girl that Gordy was in love with."

"You are on, grandpa." I stated seeing a chance to hone my detective skills.

"Hurry with your detective work concerning the fake flowers, Chester. I don't feel like I have much time left. Did I tell you that Miss May Belle stood at the foot of my bed last night and told me she was waiting to cross over with me?"

I bit my lip. My grandfather was definitely losing it. Our conversation ended when a hospice nurse informed me it was past visiting hours. I left the nursing home with my detective curiosity roused. My grandfather had pushed my buttons. In return, he was getting what he wanted from me, someone to listen and pursue his theories.

CHAPTER NINE

The Fake Flower's Secret

Early the next morning, which was Saturday, my grandmother informed me that I had to take time out from my morning trash route to take her to do her weekly grocery shopping. I was slowly assuming a lot of responsibilities that my grandfather was no longer able to do. I kept telling myself that my mother would take over some of the chores and cares for my grandmother, once my grandfather was gone. I was lying to myself and I knew it. My grandmother was depending on me, more and more. As much as I loved her, I felt like I was being sucked down the tube of her chosen dump life. I had dreams of going to California after graduation, not taking over my grandfather's trash business and the care of her.

Taking time out from my busy Saturday morning trash pickups, I picked my grandmother up and drove her to the market in the city and parked as far away from the front doors as I could get. I had almost a full load of garbage on. I was sure the market manager would run me off, if I parked any closer. I had my school books in the front seat. I decided to spend the time studying for my high school finals. Books were my best friends. They took me places that were far away from Gardenia and the dump life I hated.

"Do you need me to go in with you?" I asked my grandmother who was opening her door and about to climb out and down.

"I can handle the shopping. The grocery boy can push my cart out here when I am done. However, when I come back out here, I will need you to help me lift the groceries up and in. Today is bleach and drinking water day. I will have at least twelve gallons of drinking water and six gallons of bleach to load plus groceries." She replied. "The grocery boy will run when he smells the hauler."

"The water I understand, grandma. Why do you buy so much bleach?"

"You want clean coffee and a clean rosy place for me to be buried, don't you?"

"Clean coffee and a clean place to be buried . . . what do you mean?" I asked in a confused tone. Her screw had to be loose for the morning.

"I don't have time to go into it right now." She replied as a cold wind blew thru the door of the garbage truck. She hurriedly got out and scurried across the parking lot toward the market. A fierce winter wind was blowing. Her coat tail and head scarf were whipping about. She was hunkered down to fight off the cold and the force of the wind.

I was glad she didn't ask me to go inside with her. Several of my high school classmates had part time jobs as register clerks and sackers inside the store. I was dirty and smelled like the morning's garbage. I didn't want to subject myself to any more turned up noses and ridicule from them than was necessary. I just had a couple of months or so to go and my school days were over. I just wanted to slide thru it, grab my diploma, thumb my nose at all the kids who had belittled me, and fly off to California never looking back. I had six thousand dollars saved. I planned to fly to California, rent myself an apartment, and buy myself a street bike for transportation. I had every detail of my future life planned, including attending the university there and getting hired by Zeke's Feet Detective Agency.

My dreams were all I had to cling to, I had no friends. My family didn't know or give a crap about me. I had always signed my own report cards. I was two hands on the wheel of one of their trash trucks. That was all I was to them. I had lived my whole life in a rusted out, falling down, mobile home just a few hundred feet from the Gardenia dump. There were no expectations for me, other than taking over the family's trash business.

My step-father took me aside when I was sixteen and told me that I could quit school if I wanted. It didn't take a diploma to be a trash hauler or own several trash trucks. He said, in his opinion, that I was wasting my time in school. My being an honor roll student meant nothing to him.

After meeting Dr. Mayo, when my grandfather was in the hospital the previous fall, I had begun to see myself as someone, not a fish gutter or a garbage can emptier. I saw possibilities for myself and nurses with call buttons in my future. Just like Dr. Mayo, I intended to reinvent myself and be who I wanted to be for a change. My grandmother, grandfather, and mother had their chances at life. It was my turn. My future choices, if I had any say concerning them, would not be gutter or the wrong side of the tracks ones.

I picked up my biology book and studied till I heard my grandmother return and bang on the truck door. I immediately closed my book and got down to help her. I shivered as I walked around the front of the truck. A blizzard was eminent. Before the day was over, the weather would become hazardous. I made my way to the passenger side and helped her back up in. Then, I placed all the water and bleach jugs around her feet. She put her feet on top of them. Then I worked all the sacks of groceries in. I didn't know why she always had a compulsion to buy all of a month's groceries at one time. She even had sacks on her lap when I was finished. I closed the passenger side door carefully, so I didn't crush anything or her. Then I returned to the driver's side, climbed in, started up the engine, and headed home to Gardenia.

"Do you think you could make me a thermos of coffee to take back out with me, Grandma? I am sure it is going to ice and snow before I return later. I know I am going to be late getting home. It might be after dark."

"I am not your slave, Chester. Make your own pot of coffee. I have all these groceries to put away. Then, I have to tend to a bag of flowers that Gordy brought me this morning."

"Sorry I asked . . . ," I muttered.

"You just don't appreciate all I do for you and your grandfather. You want what you want and when you want it. Well, your grandfather is no longer my boss and I do not want to make you coffee. I have had it with you and him and your constant wants. I am thinking about asking Gordy to let me move in with him."

"What has got your underwear in a wad?" I asked. "Whatever it is, don't take it out on me. I took time out from my schedule to run you to the store. I am the only kid in this town that is working on Saturday to make his grandmother a living."

"I am not the only one in a piss-poor mood. What is your problem, Chester?" She demanded sharply. "Do you want more money to pay for the services of the black whore you met? I know about that black girl you kissed on Christmas Eve and that your grandfather gave you money to pay her for her services. I also know all about Miss May Belle and your father kissing her goodbye."

I bit my lip wondering how she had found out about the Christmas Eve adventure my grandfather and I had made. I hadn't told anyone and I was sure that he hadn't.

"The black girl was not a whore. She was a maid. Furthermore, who I kiss is my business. I know you are mad at me about something. Just lay it all out, grandma."

"I will never forgive you, Chester, for taking your grandfather one last time on Christmas Eve to see his dark skinned lover."

"What?" I asked.

"You heard me. May Belle and your grandfather were lovers. How do you think she made her money and bought that big house? She was an expensive call girl and your grandpa paid for his share of her."

"Rosa was not his lover?" I asked in shock.

"Rosa toys with your grandpa. Your grandfather met Miss May Belle on his trash route. Your grandpa got to know her, and fell in love with her. He has only hung on to me, to keep me from Gordy."

"Have you ever considered that grandpa might have turned to Miss May Belle because you have had a lifelong insane attraction to Gordy Gardenia and have refused to let Grandpa sleep in your bed?" I asked mad at her and angry with my grandfather. He had lied to me about the house he chose. He was the old, white dude lover that was supposed to show up at the wake. He had played me.

My grandmother pressed her lips together mad and didn't say anymore. Arriving back at the mobile home, I pulled into the driveway and helped her out. Then I carried the groceries in for her, in spite of the fact that we had just entered a serious cold war with each other. I walked over to the kitchen cabinet to make myself a thermos of coffee. I never made coffee. This would be a first for me.

"Where do you keep the coffee filters, Grandma?" I asked opening up a canister where she usually retrieved one from. Inside the plastic container were little circles of white cloth that had a tiny hole in the center of each. The outer edges of the circles had in and out cuts like the leaves of a flower.

My grandmother didn't answer me, so I improvised. I stuck a paper napkin in the basket of the coffee maker, added coffee grounds, and made myself a thermos of coffee. I was proud of myself. I stuck the lid back on the container of little round cloths and pushed them back on the cabinet. They had to be something my grandmother was saving to use in a craft project.

After putting her groceries away, my grandma walked down the mobile home's long hallway, entered her bedroom, and slammed the door. I knew she wouldn't throw me out. She needed me to run the trash route and do all the little chores my grandfather could no longer do. I was wanted but not wanted. That was an unpleasant place to be. At the same time, I felt a little sorry for my grandmother. If she were telling me the truth about Miss May Belle, she had a right to have a screw loose. Never once had I dreamed that my grandfather had played around on my grandmother. He had always spoken of how crazy he was about her. Maybe he had a screw loose too. Maybe my whole family was crazy. They definitely didn't have any morals, in my opinion.

~   ~   ~

The weather turned bad after I returned to running what was left of the Saturday route. I drove slow and took my time. I wasn't exactly looking forward to returning to the trailer and the cold war with my grandmother. I was sure she would not be cooking me any dinner. I would need to pick up some fast food on the way home. I would pick something up for her too.

As I drove, with snowflakes swirling outside of the cab and the windshield wipers on high, I thought about Gracie and my deal with my grandfather. I wanted to know more about Gracie, and that included who her mother was. My grandfather wanted to know what was happening to all the fake flowers. I needed something to think about besides the words I had with my grandmother. Gracie and the fake flowers seemed to be what was available to think about.

Tomorrow was Sunday and the Gardenia dump would be closed. I didn't run my grandfather's route on Sunday for that reason. I decided I was going to sleep in, stick around my grandmother's trailer, and perhaps discover what she was doing with the fake blooms. I knew there was a fresh black trash bag full of them in the laundry room. I had carried the bleach in there for my grandmother earlier. Gordy apparently had been there sometime earlier in the day.

Turning off the main highway into Gardenia, I got in line with the other trash haulers on dump road. I was last in line. When it came my turn, I entered the dump and discarded my load of garbage. Afterward, I drove back to the entrance gates to pay Gordy my dump fee. He was standing waiting with a padlock and chain in his hand. I rolled down my window to make my transaction with him.

"Hurry up Chester and get your truck out of my gate. I have a date."

"You have a date?" I asked in a shocked voice. Gordy Gardenia was an old man, at least seventy five possibly. "Who with . . . ?"

"Gracie's mother, if it is any of your damn business. Now, get the lead out."

"Gracie's mother is coming here?" I asked. "Is there any chance of me dropping by and meeting her? I have never met your daughter's mother."

"Gracie's mother is already here and no you cannot meet her. Now, get the lead out. Today is a special day for me and her."

"What kind of a special day?" I asked trying to pump him.

"It is an anniversary of sorts." He replied taking my dump fee and giving me a receipt. "Tell your grandmother I will be over in a few minutes. I found her some good flowers in today's dumped loads."

"Why are you wasting your time with my grandmother, if you have a date?" I shot back.

"A man needs more than one woman in his life. Your grandmother and I go back a long way. She keeps my head straight. Gracie's mother keeps something else straight."

"That is kind of crude, Gordy." I replied to his insinuation. "My grandmother deserves more than fake flowers and keeping your head on straight."

"Your grandmother knows where she stands with me. I don't love her, I have never loved her. It is Gracie's mom that does it for me. Now get the lead out."

I bit my lip. When my grandfather was gone, I was telling Gordy Gardenia where to stick it. Afterward, I would place my grandmother in a nursing home with instructions he was not to visit her.

After pulling the hauler in my grandmother's drive, I parked and then headed for the trailer to spend another boring night watching one of my grandfather's four televisions. I had no friends and my weekends sucked miserably. Even if I went back into the city, there was no one to hang out with. I was the smelly garbage dump teen that everyone backed off from. I gave myself a pep talk as I approached the door of my grandmother's mobile home to enter.

"Two months and you are out of here, Chet Holly Mayo."

Heavy snow was falling. About three inches had now accumulated on the ground and the sky was almost at the point of being a white out. When I opened the door of the mobile home and stepped inside, I was relieved to be out of the icy wind and blowing snow. I shivered and decided to make a fresh pot of coffee to go with the fast food I had brought home. I had learned to make coffee earlier in the day.

"I'm home!" I yelled down the hallway. "I have brought you a burger and fries."

"I will be there in a minute Chester. I am starting a bleach load." She yelled back, apparently being in the laundry room.

I got down the monster can of coffee and opened the cabinet doors trying to find filters. The paper napkin had left a funky taste in the thermos of coffee I had made earlier. I couldn't spot a filter anywhere. As I was closing the cabinet doors, my grandmother entered the kitchen and took her spot at the kitchen table and started going thru the fast food.

Glancing up at me, my grandmother asked, "What are you looking for Chester?"

"I can't find a coffee filter anywhere, grandma. Where do you keep them?"

"They are in that round canister next to the coffee maker where they always are." She replied as she started to pick at her French fries. "Did you bring any ketchup home for these fries?"

I reached for the round canister with the intent of opening it and showing her that she had craft supplies of some sort in it; not coffee filters. I opened the can, removed the lid, and held the canister so she could see into it.

"This can doesn't contain coffee filters, grandma. Where are the filters?"

"Those are the filters. What is the problem?" She asked while she opened a tiny pack of fast food ketchup.

"These are not filters, Grandma. They are little pieces of white fabric with a hole in the center. See!" I stated pulling one from the can and holding it out for her to see.

"Don't you know anything about recycling, Chester. I made those filters."

I turned the crinkled little piece of white cloth over in my hand and looked at it. Then I looked in the can at the others. That was when I saw that they were all sizes and some looked like they were once flowers of some sort. I grabbed the edge of the cabinet and steadied myself with one hand. Surely, I wasn't seeing what I thought I was seeing.

"Grandma . . . what did you make these floral shaped coffee filters from?" I demanded, knowing what the answer was going to be. I was just about to gag and throw up.

"I make them from the blooms Gordy brings me. I keep half and give him half." She answered looking up from swirling one of her fries in ketchup.

My stomach was suddenly churning, thinking about all the thermos bottles of coffee she had made me and my grandfather over the years. "You make coffee filters out of those nasty flowers Gordy picks from garbage loads?" I asked and then put my hand over my mouth.

"Haven't you ever heard of recycling, Chester. I do my part. I separate the glass and plastic from the paper. I wear second hand clothes and recycle fake flower blooms into coffee filters. You should be proud of me. Gordy does his part too. He has his own recycling project going. I save half the bleached blooms, the leaves, and stems for him."

"What do you do, just keep the white fake flower blooms?" I asked not wanting to really know. I was already about to throw up thinking of how much coffee I had drank that had been filtered thru garbage covered fake flowers. I didn't think my grandfather was going to be overly thrilled at what I had discovered.

"It doesn't matter what color the blooms are. I use them."

I thought of all the smelly, garbage stained flowers that Gordy had brought my grandmother over the years and then I thought of my stomach. My grandmother could have killed me or my grandfather with her germ laden filters. My stomach was rolling and I was about to puke. I tried to control my gag reflex.

"Coffee filters are cheap, grandma. Why would you make your own filters? You could have killed any one of us with a virus or germs from the dump. I immediately walked over and dumped her tin of blooms into the kitchen trash can. "I will buy you filters out of my money. If I find any more bags of fake dirty flowers in this trailer, I am going to personally recycle them by stuffing them down Gordy's throat. Do you understand me, Grandma?"

"Don't get your boxers in a wad, Chester. The filters are clean. I bleach them along with our laundry. I put them in a little mesh bag and throw them in with our white sheets, towels, and underwear. They come out white, sanitized, and ready for use."

"Is that the reason you purchase so much bleach?" I asked in shock, while recalling the four gallons I had loaded into the truck after her morning shopping trip to the supermarket.

"Gordy pays for the bleach. I help him and he helps me. I keep what filters I need and give him the rest. Everyone needs to do a little something for the environment. I make washable coffee filters for me and him." She replied oblivious to the fact that I was about to barf.

My grandmother had just said she washed the filters along with our underwear.

"What does Gordy do with the stems?" I managed to ask while hanging my head over the kitchen sink. My stomach was rolling. She had said that she had washed the filters with my grandfather's dirty underwear, as well as mine and hers.

"He stirs his coffee and ice tea with them." She replied not offering anything further.

At that point, I threw up in the kitchen sink.

"Are you coming down with the flu or something?" My grandmother asked.

CHAPTER TEN

Key to my Heart

On Sunday afternoon, the snow quit and I climbed in my grandfather's monster garbage hauler and headed for the hospital to visit him. The new fallen snow was no match for the weight and huge wheels of the truck. As I was about a quarter of a mile outside of Gardenia on the main highway, I spotted a snow covered old wreck of a car with its hood up. A girl with no coat on, and her face wrapped with a muffler was waving for me to stop. I brought my trash hauler to a halt on the shoulder, about fifty feet in front of her vehicle. I reached over and swung open the passenger side door.

In a moment or so, a girl climbed upon the running board of the passenger side of the truck, and pulled the muffler down from her face.

"Could you give me and my two boys a lift into town? My wreck of a car has blown its engine. I don't have the money to have it towed anywhere, much less repair it. I am just going to have to leave it and move on." She stated. "Could you give me and my kids a ride to the Bell Ringers' shelter for the homeless?"

I was instantly embarrassed! I pulled my own muffler upon my face as high as I could get it and my stocking hat down as low as I could get it. It was my mistletoe girl, Keesha. She, apparently, did not recognize me in my dirty, trash hauler coveralls and stocking hat. I wanted to turn her down and speed off into oblivion. Kissing her on Christmas Eve and being somebody for once in my life was one of the few good memories I had to cling to.

Sucking it up, I bit my lip and smiled saying. "Sure, go get your boys and your car seats. I will throw your seats in the back till I get you where you want to go. You will have to hold your boys on your lap in the passenger seat."

"Thank You . . . ," She replied shivering. Then she trudged back toward her car with its hood up.

I got out and walked to the back of the trash hauler. After a few minutes, she returned with two seats. I secured them in the back, so they wouldn't fall out or get garbage on them. By the time I had that accomplished, she returned with the two little boys. They had no coats on. I quickly scooped up the bigger of the two and then helped her walk thru the snow to the passenger door. Once there, I helped the three of them up and in. I tried to keep my muffler covered face turned from her. I was in a panic, but she didn't know it.

I returned to the driver's side of the truck, climbed in, closed my door, put on my seat belt, shifted gears, and started to creep forward. I had left the engine running. The heater was on full tilt. I glanced over and eyed her, as she held her and her little boys' hands to the heater vent to warm them.

"Thank you for stopping. The heat feels so good!" She replied, letting go of her little boys' hands, and suddenly rubbing her arms with her tuxedo black hands.

"I will have you at the shelter in about fifteen minutes." I replied simply, praying I could get her to the shelter and out of my truck before she recognized me. I pulled my stocking hat down and my muffler up till it was under my nose.

"Where do I know you from?" She asked, after she started to warm up and she had her two boys settled.

"I don't know you!" I stated shifting gears and peeping out the driver's side window to try to keep my face turned from her as much as possible.

For a few minutes, she ignored me as she pointed out the window for her two little boys to watch a deer standing in the distance in a snow covered valley. Then suddenly, she returned her attention to me.

"I know you! You are my mistletoe man." She stated big eyed. "You left me thirty dollars in a trash hauler's payment envelope."

"You have me confused with someone." I replied in a panic thru my muffler.

"No . . . You are my mistletoe man. I bought my boys milk and their only Christmas gift with that money. Miss May Belle's family stiffed me that evening. They accused me of taking a couple of sterling silver serving pieces from the escargot and goose liver pate' platters, while she was being loaded into the hearse."

"You have me confused with someone." I lied.

I didn't want my Christmas Eve memory of her, or her memory of me, spoiled. She had kissed a nice looking guy in a college logo sweatshirt, not a trash hauler.

"It is you, Chet Mayo. I am not blind."

"My name is Holly." I replied simply.

"Chet Holly Mayo, don't you mean?" She retorted. "Don't play mind games with me. I don't wear glasses and I know who I am looking at. Now cut the crap."

"They say everyone has a twin. I don't know you." I repeated with my stomach in knots. I didn't want her to know me as Chester Holly the garbage hauler.

"Oh . . . I get it . . . you are probably married and that is the reason you are trying to deny kissing me beneath the mistletoe. Am I right?"

"I have a twin brother. Maybe it is him you kissed." I replied out of desperation with my muffler slipping down. "And no, I am not married."

"You are biting your lip, Chet Holly Mayo. That is a sign that a man is lying.

You don't have any twin brother. Are you ashamed of kissing me, an ebony black girl? Is that your reason for denying knowing me here and now?"

"I have a cold sore on my lip." I replied. "It is bugging me."

"Well, I don't see any cold sore on your lip and you need to get over whatever your problem is. If you regret kissing me, it is okay. It is not like I am going to tell anyone. We don't exactly run in the same circles. Just so you know, I don't regret kissing you. It was the only gift I got for Christmas."

Then I really felt bad. At the same time, I just didn't want to admit to being the smelly dump kid to her. I wanted to keep the 'me' that had kissed her on Christmas Eve alive.

"I am not who you think I am," I replied once more trying not to look at her.

"I don't know what you are ashamed of Chet Holly Mayo. I am the one who has things to hide. My boys and I have been living for the last month in the Army's homeless shelter. If I don't get my act together, I am afraid I am going to lose my two boys. I have no home and now no car. The boys' father, whom I am divorced from, is in prison for life. He killed a man robbing a store. What do you have to be so ashamed of?"

"I am not who you think I am," I replied once more.

"Are you ashamed of being a trash hauler? Is that your problem?" She asked eyeing me. "I would gladly drive a trash truck to feed, house, and clothe my boys. I just don't have that skill. Waitressing and hiring my-self out as a temporary maid is all I know, and it hasn't been paying very well lately."

I bit my lip as I pulled into the parking lot of the homeless shelter to let her out. I just could not let my good memory of kissing her bite the dirt. I had so little to hang on to. I got out of the truck and walked around to the passenger side and helped her and her two little boys down. Then I retrieved her two car seats and carried them to the door of the shelter for her. She met me at the door with her two little ebony black skinned sons in tow. The three of them were shivering.

"Why don't you and the boys have coats?" I spurted.

"Someone took them, one night last week, while we slept here. I guess some low life mother thought her kids needed them worse than mine. I was headed south when my car broke down. I figured we wouldn't need any coats when we reached Florida. My plan was just to keep my boys in my car with the heater running till then. I am doing what I have to do to survive."

I once again bit my lip and my eyes filled with tears. I removed my muffler and put it around the four year old boy's neck. Then I pulled off my stocking hat and put in on the two year old. They were two little boys starting out life in the gutter, just like I had always lived in the garbage dump gutter. The thought sickened me.

"I've got to go." I replied and hurriedly walked around the nose of the trash hauler, opened the driver's door, got up in, and left without looking back. About a quarter of a mile from the shelter, I pulled alongside the curb and buried my face in my arms on the wheel. I knew I was going to have to go back for her. As bad as I hated to admit it, I had fallen in love with her when I kissed her beneath the mistletoe. Was my pride more important than possibly her falling in love with me? Those two little boys needed me. How could I walk away?

Returning to the shelter, I parked and got out. I headed toward the door and was about to open it, when it opened and Key was standing there staring at me, holding her two sons' hands. She was just about to exit.

"Why are you leaving?" I asked looking a little confused.

"There is no room for us." She replied. "They are full up. I was about to walk across the street and hang out in that laundry till I figure out what to do next."

"Keesha . . . I am ashamed of being a garbage man. That is why I didn't want to admit knowing you. I am sorry. I was pretending to be someone else at the party that night. I don't like who I am in my every day existence."

"Come here," she said motioning for me to stoop a little. When I did she put her face next to mine and her arms around me. "I was hoping you would come back for us. I need you Chet Holly Mayo, or whatever your name is. My boys desperately need you. You are a god to me, not a garbage hauler."

I put my arms around her and nuzzled my face next to hers and whispered. "It is me that needs you. Do you believe in love at first kiss?"

She pulled away and looked at me grinning. "You felt it too?"

"We will discuss that later. For now, let us get back in the truck till the four of us figure out where home is."

I picked up the four year old and Keesha picked up the two year old. We hurriedly made our way back across the un-cleaned snowy parking lot and got back in the trash hauler where I had the heat on high tilt. I suddenly felt alive.

Putting my seat belt back on, I prepared to shift gears and take off. Pausing for a moment, I looked over at Keesha and said, "I love you, Keesha. I fell in love with you when I kissed you that night. I am sorry I was such a jerk earlier."

I then felt her hand reach over and rest on my leg. "It is okay Chet. We all wear false faces at times, when we are trying to survive. It doesn't matter to me what occupation you follow in life. As long as you treat me and these boys right, I will stand beside you and always have your backside."

I took my right hand off the wheel and placed it on top of hers. "I have no doubt that you are that special one that comes along only once in a lifetime."

"I feel it to! Something inside tells me that you are the other half of me. Destiny has let us find our way to each other. I have thought about you every waking moment since Christmas Eve."

"How do you feel about going to California three or four months from now? After I get my high school diploma in May, I plan to move there, enter the university, and be a Private Detective."

"Wow . . . you are going to be someone special. I am just a waitress, Chester

Holly. I was a foster child who got raped by her foster dad, got pregnant, and then run away and became a street kid at fifteen. The tenth grade in school is as far as I have made it. I married the first guy that half way showed interest in me, needing a father for my baby. I don't have a clue as to who my real parents are. I was dumped in foster care when I was eighteen months old. Ebony Black kids don't always find people willing to adopt them. Now, I am divorced and Social Service has been hot on my tail for the last month. I was leaving the state to free myself of them. I am no one special, Chet Holly Mayo! I am just confessing it up front to you."

"You are someone, Keesha. You are the other half of me. Whatever I become, you are."

"I like the idea of being a detective's woman. That is wow!"

"My wow moment was meeting you." I replied grinning and suddenly giving her the Chet Mayo wink.

"If you treat me and these boys of mine right, I will waitress in California and pull in my share of the expenses while you go to the college. My boys need a role model. If I stay here, they are going to turn into ghetto dope dealers or pimps. They are jet black skinned like me. For some reason, white and black people are scared of really black skin. I am just a human being, a gift to Earth like everyone else. I just happen to be wrapped in really black paper. I am a black tuxedo, girl. Those around me just don't see it. I want to be a wow someone!"

"I am a white tuxedo man, but people around here don't see that either. They don't want anything to do with me because my skin has absorbed the smells of the garbage dump and I am always dirty. The dirt on me is honest dirt. I work and I get paid for it. I am just the smelly, dirty kid from the dump that they see as never going to amount to anything. I can't live that image down here. California is going to be my chance to crawl out of the garbage dump gutter and wear my white tuxedo skin with pride."

"It takes individuals like you and me, who have been on the bottom of the trash heap of life, to appreciate the good things coming our way. Your Christmas Eve kiss was the only decent thing that has happened to me in years. You are not smelly to me, Chet Mayo. You are a god in my book."

I looked at her and wondered, for just a brief moment, if she was pushing my buttons to get what she wanted from me. Would she extract payment from me and then run away with my heart? I had quit trusting kids my age a long time ago. Then I discarded the thought. Dr. Mayo had his nurse spoon feeding him. Keesha was my nurse and I wanted her.

"Would you believe me, if I promise to be absolutely faithful to you and one day buy you and your boys one of the biggest damn houses in California you have ever dreamed of?"

"I don't want a big house, Chester Holly Mayo. I want a man who loves me and will be there for me and my boys. I want arms to hold me at night, arms that haven't disrespected me and held some other woman during the day. You treat me right and you will never have to worry about having someone love you. My arms will always be open for you to hide in."

"That is what I want, Keesha! I want someone to give a damn about me for once in my life. You are guaranteed I will treat you right. I want to be hugged, told to take a bath, and fed on time. I guess I want to be mother loved and hen pecked by a woman who loves me. I have never had that. I want a woman who cares enough about me to tell me what is what and hold me in the middle of the night when my nightmare memories of dump life come to call. I have spent my whole life living in survival mode. When I get my high school diploma, my survival days in the dump city of Gardenia are over."

"You are not the only needy one in survival mode, Chet Mayo. Both my boys need something I can't give them. I cannot give them a home, a family, a father. Living with them in a car or a shelter is not the life I want for them. I want out of the gutter's survival mode too."

"You will never live in the gutter once I get my high school diploma and we are out of here. That is a promise, Keesha." I replied glancing over at her.

Keesha looked a little funny.

"What's wrong?" I asked in a panic.

"You . . . you are still in high school. I . . . I am older than you. You aren't legally of age."

"So . . . ?" I replied.

"I thought you were a college guy." She sputtered.

"Is it a problem that I am a little younger than you thought?" I asked fearfully thinking she was going to dump me before our relationship got off the ground.

Then Keesha went to laughing and her eyes filled with tears. "I could get arrested for sleeping with you."

"The difference in our ages isn't a problem with me, if you don't have a problem with it." I retorted and then asked her, "How old are you?"

"I am twenty-one, almost twenty-two and you have to be maybe seventeen. Most kids graduate high school when they are seventeen."

Then I blushed. I had completed my high school education in three and one half years. I had gone to summer school two summers in order to do so. I was sixteen and would be seventeen a few days after my high school graduation. She was suddenly seeing me as a kid.

"Well . . . spit it out. I told you my age." She demanded. "How old are you?"

"I have purposely kept my nose in my books. I am graduating high school in three and one half years, instead of four. I . . . I am sixteen and will be seventeen a few days after my high school graduation." I sputtered, sure that she was going to tell me to pull the truck over so she could get out.

"Some men go for older women," she laughed. "Apparently, you do. Then, there are some women who go for younger men. Apparently, I do. We just won't tell anyone our ages, okay?"

I looked at her and grinned sheepishly. Not only was I younger than her, she was the only girl I had ever kissed. I knew I was going to have to tell her that I had never slept with a girl either. That was going to be a little bit embarrassing.

Keesha pulled her hand out from under mine and reached up and touched my cheek lovingly.

"I now have three little boys. However, you are going to be mama's special big boy. I am going to treat you really well, Chet Holly Mayo. You won't regret loving this mama."

"Mama . . . huh?" I replied grinning. She was going to make a man out of me; I could see it in her eyes. I pulled her hand from my cheek with my free hand and kissed it. "Is this big boy welcome to sleep in your bed tonight, mama?"

"You won't be doing much sleeping, Chet Holly Mayo. Your kiss on my hand was electric. I know, when I crawl in bed with you, I am not going to be able to get enough of you."

I smiled from ear to ear and then returned my attention to the wheel. That was my special moment in time. For the first time in my life, someone wanted me. My mother hadn't wanted me, my classmates didn't want my friendship, and my grandmother didn't want me. I had hit the mother lode, and Keesha was my gold. She was my payment for daring to 'test the gods' and kiss her on Christmas Eve. I was one happy man.

Stopping at a four way stop, I glanced over at the four year old.

"What is your name?" I asked and grinned at him.

"My name is Thaddeus and my brother's name is Thornton. Are you my father?"

"Yes I am." I replied.

"Well, I am glad you have finally come home. Where have you been?"

"Er . . . uh . . . I have been away in the army." I replied searching for a legitimate excuse that a four year old could accept. "Daddies who are in the military are gone for a long time, sometimes. I have just come home."

The four year old, ebony black skinned, little boy smiled from ear to ear. "Did you bring me anything?"

I removed a military camouflage cap from the dash. I had found it earlier in one of the trash cans I had emptied. Some dude had thrown away all of his military clothing. The rest was behind my seat.

"This is my army hat. I am home now and won't need to wear it." I stated handing it to the little boy.

"Me . . . me . . . ," The two year old chimed in.

"I haven't forgotten you," I stated pulling my billfold from my coveralls pocket. I removed my driver's license and other important items from it. Then, I handed it to him. "I carried this billfold while I was in the army. It is yours now." I replied handing the empty wallet to him while sticking my license and other items in the breast pocket of my coveralls. "If I ever have to go back to the army, the two of you will have to loan the items back to me, so I won't be in trouble with my sergeant. Okay . . . ?"

They both squealed with delight. I handed Keesha the forty or so dollars I had taken from the billfold saying, "This is just a start, Keesha. I promise you that one day, after I graduate college out in California, I will buy you the biggest damn house you have ever seen, bigger that Miss May Belle's."

"I believe you Chet Mayo." She replied with tears in her eyes and returned her hand to rest on my leg.

I was in Heaven.

"Where is home for us tonight?" She asked.

"A friend of mine has gone north for the winter to settle an estate. I have the keys to his mobile home. We will stay there till my graduation. I am watching his place for him. Don't expect much. He is an old bachelor and he probably hasn't cleaned the place in who knows when."

"Anywhere with you and my boys in my arms will be a mansion. Chet Holly Mayo. I know how to clean a place. Do you want me to look for work?"

"We won't owe any rent and I will make enough off this trash route to feed and clothe the four of us till I am out of high school. Just give me a chance to get past my high school graduation in two months. Afterward, I promise you that you will be carrying around more than forty dollars of my money. No, you don't need to look for work. Being a mother is full time work. It is okay with me if you want to be a housewife and rule the home roost. Later, if you want to work, it is okay with me. If you don't want to work, that is fine with me to. You will always be my woman and I will want what you want."

The light hadn't changed yet. I leaned over to the boys who were now playing with the hat and billfold.

"There is one thing I want you boys to always remember. Men who are loved by their women, families, and friends go by their nicknames. People give nicknames to those they love. Fathers nickname their sons. You tell your friends from now on that you are Tank and Tag."

"I am Tank," the four year old piped up with delight.

"You will always be my Army tank. You can go thru anything and laugh at anyone who tries to stop you."

"I Tag . . ." The two year old piped up smiling from ear to ear.

"What does his name mean, daddy?" Tank asked.

The word daddy melted my heart.

"A soldier wears Army Tags around his neck. They tell who he is. Tag is a good nickname for an army man's son. Everyone will always know who he belongs to.."

"My brother follows me everywhere," Tank replied, "Even to the bathroom. I think tag is a great name for him."

"Army tags do go with you everywhere." I replied laughing.

"I Tag . . . I Tag . . . I Tag . . .," Stated the two year old repeating himself.

I glanced at Keesha who was grinning from ear to ear. I could tell she was pleased.

"You need a nick name too, Chet Holly Mayo."

"Just call me Chet." I replied winking at her.

"Oh no . . . when we are in private, I am calling you Mistletoe. I now have three special men in my life; Mistletoe, Tank, and Tag."

"I am nicknaming you Key." I replied looking her over. She was beautiful, but very poorly dressed. As soon as the snow storm was over, I was taking her and my two new sons shopping. My family was going to dress upper-class. We were going to test the gods and be someone as a family.

"You are nicknaming me Key?" She asked with a confused look on her face. "Why?"

"You will always be the only key to my heart." I replied taking an imaginary key and twisting it in my chest and then handing it to her.

She took the imaginary key from me and stuck it in the pocket of her jeans. "You already own the key to my heart, Chet Holly Mayo."

I removed my right hand from the wheel and placed it on top of hers, which was resting on my leg. "I am a one woman man, Key. I promise you that I will give life one hundred percent and make sure you and our two sons have an uptown life, not a dump one."

"I believe you, Chet Mayo. Would you like to kiss me at the next light to seal our commitment?" She asked all smiles.

"I would very much like to do that! However, I have two sons now that I need to consider what is appropriate for them to see. My hands all over you, their mother, in public is probably not appropriate. Also, the touch of your hand on my leg is shooting electricity thru me. I don't think I can control my hands should I touch you at this moment. I don't wish Tank and Tag to see me as a pervert. May I have a rain check for that kiss after they are asleep tonight?"

"I think that can be arranged." She replied smiling. "However, I think it is me that is going to have my hands all over you. I would hate for my two Army sons to see their mother ripping their father's clothes off in public and raping him. Right now, Mistletoe Man, I see you naked and in my arms."

I blushed.

"Just so you know, Key, I have kissed only one girl in my life. Her name was Keesha and I kissed her on Christmas Eve beneath Miss May Belle's mistletoe. You may need to give me some pointers in the kissing and other departments. I have never slept with a girl." I replied and then I knew my face had to be forty shades of red.

~   ~   ~

Returning to the dump town of Gardenia, I turned the trash hauler into my grandmother's drive, parked, and left the truck running to keep Keesha and the boys warm. I then went inside to retrieve the key to Snuff's trailer. Key and the boys waited for me in the truck. I did not tell my grandmother about them. I just told her I was going to check on Snuff's place. I did not introduce Key or the boys to her. They were part of my new life. I didn't want my grandmother and her loose screws spoiling things for me. My being lily white and Key being Ebony Black alone would set her mouth in to overdrive. If at all possible, I was never going to let Key and the boys meet my dysfunctional family. Before picking up Snuff's key, I told Keesha my grandmother's trailer was where my boss lived. That way, I had an excuse to just run in and grab Snuff's keys and then back out again. I had no intentions of mixing my old life with my new one.

CHAPTER ELEVEN

Keeping my Tuxedo Girl a Secret

After getting my new family settled in at Snuff's place, I headed back into town to visit my grandfather and tell him I had solved the fake flower mystery. I wanted to spend as much time as possible with him. I knew he was dying and could be gone any day. He was living on borrowed time. The doctor had predicted he would have passed on two or three weeks before. My grandfather was fighting death.

The Christmas Eve party crashing had bonded my grandfather and me, even though he had played me. The sharing of that moment in time had made us friends. On the drive in to town to the hospital, I debated whether to tell my grandfather about Key. On the inside, I was whistling. Finding someone to love me had turned me on like flipping the switch in my grandparent's mobile home to turn the lights on. I was a different person. I wanted to tell my grandfather about my new, sudden family. I just didn't know whether I should.

My thoughts wandered to my grandfather's lover. He had kept Miss May Belle a well hidden secret. He had to of had a reason. In the back of my mind, I wondered if he had stayed with my grandmother because he wasn't man enough to buck the racial prejudices of his day and be with Miss May Belle. I did know that he was hanging on to my grandmother to keep her away from Gordy. He told me that on one of my hospital visits. He said that my grandmother was delusional thinking that Gordy wanted her. If he gave her a divorce, she would end up in a gutter somewhere, because Gordy had no intention of ever marrying or providing for her. It was her that wanted him. My grandfather said he stayed with my grandmother because he loved her enough to not want to see Gordy destroy her. People on their death beds tell you hidden secrets. My grandfather was slowly telling me his, just as his body was slowly dying.

My step-father and mother were racially prejudiced, as was my grandmother. My step-father was a profane, red neck who didn't think twice about using the 'N' word. My mother was the same. As bad as I hated to admit it, my grandfather was probably also prejudiced. He had kept his affair with Miss May Belle a well hidden, long term secret. I was ashamed of my family and my life as a dump kid. I didn't want Key and the boys tarnished by them. She saw me as someone; the first person who had ever saw me as someone.

There are tough decisions you make in life. Driving to the hospital, I made a tough one. I was never introducing Key and the boys to my prejudiced family. I planned to leave for California in a couple of months after graduation. There was no reason to introduce Key and the boys to people they would never see again. I never planned on returning to the dump town of Gardenia, or extend invitations for my family to visit me. I wanted to be free of them. My grandfather was the only one of them that I loved, and he would be dead when I left. There would be no one to return to.

The people in my life were misfits or social outcasts, and that was by their choice. My grandmother was an insane wild card, as grandfather called her, with more than one screw loose. My mother and stepfather were addicts and lush alcoholics. My grandfather had no goals for me beyond driving his garbage trucks and taking over his trash route after he died. Those living in Gardenia referred to me as the illegitimate son of my mother, like I was less than them. At school, I had always been treated as white trash. My world had not been a pretty one to live in. However, my time was close at hand to 'test the gods' and run.

Arriving at the hospital, I parked my grandfather's trash hauling truck in the rear of the hospital where commercial vehicles parked. Then, I entered the hospital and made my way to the third floor to my grandfather's room. He was awake and the nurses had his bed rolled up. He was propped up with pillows in a seated position. I grabbed a straight visitor's chair and placed it next to my grandfather's bed railing so we could talk quietly without disturbing the patient who was asleep in the second bed.

"I was beginning to think you weren't coming today." My grandfather stated in a weak, frail voice. "You wouldn't have a cigarette on you, would you?"

"You are on oxygen, Grandpa. Do you want to blow this place up smoking? No, I don't have a cigarette on me. Besides, you know that I don't smoke." I retorted.

"Oh . . . I forgot you don't smoke. You should take it up, Chester. A cigarette has a way of calming you and getting you thru some long, cold days on winter trash hauls." My grandfather stated and then he coughed violently a couple of times.

"Look what smoking has done to you, Grandpa. You are dying of lung cancer. I want to die a very old man, in my own bed, with good lungs to go out with."

"You will die just like me, Chester. If smoking doesn't get you, the air born toxins from the dump will. We trash haulers all die younger than we should from something or another."

"Whenever I die someday, when I am very old, it won't be from smoking cigarettes."

"When I was young like you, I dreamed of dying old and in your grandmother's arms. It looks like I am going to die instead in the aluminum arms of this hospital bed. Its arms are as cold as your grandmother's have always been. Did you know I haven't slept with your grandmother since the month we were married? She has always refused me."

"I don't think I want to discuss your love life with Grandma. Maybe we should change the subject." I replied a little embarrassed. "Let us talk about our deal instead."

"What deal Chester?" My grandfather asked as he hacked and coughed.

"Don't you remember? You agreed to tell me who Gracie's mother is, if I did a little snooping. I now know the secret of the fake flowers."

"Oh . . . I forgot, Chester. It must be all the pain killers they are giving me. My mind is a little fuzzy. Tell me about the fake flowers."

I proceeded to tell him about discovering that grandma was making coffee filters out of the fake blooms from the dump and washing them with our underwear. My stomach churned as I told him. I wasn't past puking a second time over my discovery. For a moment, my ailing grandfather looked like he was going to throw up.

"No wonder I am dying!" Grandfather stated holding his hand over his mouth and gagging. "You better hand me that puke dish the nurses call an emesis basin."

I handed my grandfather a little teal green plastic dish that was shaped like a kidney.

"Your grandmother has been purposely polluting my morning coffee all these years. She is after my insurance, Chester. She has been trying to kill me off for my insurance. I have been dying a slow death, the coffee filter death."

"Don't get excited, Grandpa. You are not dead yet, and I don't think Grandma has intentionally been trying to kill you. Some people recycle cans and bottles. Grandma, apparently, has a different recycling choice. A little bleach from fake flower filters has probably kept you from catching a lot of things over the years. We don't always have the cleanest of hands when we eat our lunch out on the route. If anything, Grandma's bleached, flower filtered coffee has kept your insides sanitized. I will have to admit that the coffee filters being washed with our underwear, has grossed me out."

"Well, if she hasn't killed me with her coffee filters, then she has probably made flower filters for our window air conditioners and that is where I got this lung cancer from. She is a wild card, Chester." He replied hacking a few times in a row. "Don't forget I told you I think she killed the two Je . . . ova women."

"Your lung problems are from your lifetime, three pack a day, cigarette habit." I replied rolling my eyes. "Now, tell me about Gracie's mom."

"Not till you tell me what your Grandma and Gordy Gardenia are up to with the flowers, Chester. There have been more flowers come and go in our trailer than we have ever had need of, for coffee filters. I think your grandmother has made a secret love mattress and stuffed it with all of Gordy's bleached posy blooms."

"That theory is a little out there, Grandpa." I replied thinking his medication had him a little loopy.

"I think that secret mattress is in that metal building attached to the back of Gordy's mobile home. I want you to find a way to get in there and take a peek. I want to know if Gordy is toying with your grandmother again. If so, when I get out of here, I will burn their mattress. You must peek inside Gordy's building and see if it is a love nest. After you come back and tell me what is inside of his building, I will then tell you, who I think Gracie's mom is."

"Grandpa . . . Grandma isn't about to sleep in a cold metal building with Gordy. He has a bed in a warm trailer and so does she."

"That 'Bed of Posey Roses' song is your grandma's favorite. Women don't like songs unless it means something to them. I bet she has made a secret bed stuffed with Gordy's fake roses."

"Come on, Grandpa . . . Grandma is sixty plus, and Gordy is a balding, stuffed, short, little pig who weighs at least three hundred and fifty pounds. He is at least seventy, and hardly a male sex idol. Grandma would have to roll him in and out of bed like a rubber ball."

"Some women like big boys." My grandfather replied. "If you want to know who Gracie's mom is, you must sneak in his building and find out if there is a love mattress there."

"All right, I will find a way to peek just to make you happy. On my next visit here, you have to promise to tell me who Gracie's mom is?" I stated adamantly.

I was a little disappointed that he hadn't accepted my explanation and told me which dump girl was Gracie's mother. I owed Gracie one. She had sent me the Zeke's Feet Detective Agency article. I didn't know who my father was. Perhaps Gracie didn't know who her mother was. I felt I owed her to find out all I could about her mother. One day I would share that information with her, if she didn't already know.

Thanks to Gracie, I had sent off a letter to Zeke's Feet asking him for an employment application, stating that I was moving to California in June and that I was going to study criminal law at the university there.

After pausing for a few minutes to control his labored breathing, my grandfather resumed conversation with me.

"I regret not waiting when I was young and marrying a woman that loved me. Your grandmother has never loved me. She has always played around with Gordy Gardenia."

"What about you and Miss May Belle? You haven't exactly been faithful to grandma?"

"Your grandmother had my heart. Miss May Belle had another part of me. I regret loving your Grandma, and I regret not loving Miss May Belle enough to leave your grandmother. I would have been happy with Miss May Belle. We understood each other. There is a difference, Chester, between loving someone and being in love with someone. I loved Miss May Belle, but I was in love with your grandmother."

"I will never love two women, Grandpa. I am a one woman man and I will be absolutely faithful to my one woman." I replied.

"I want you to promise me something, Chester!"

"What is it?" I replied, thinking he was going to swear me to secrecy before telling me more of his secrets.

"I want you to promise me that you won't let your grandmother cremate me."

I was a little taken off guard.

"I am sure that grandma is going to bury you with the rest of your ancestors and relatives in Mt. Pleasant Cemetery when the time comes." I replied.

"Your grandma cremated the baby she lost on the day she fought with your mother. It was a boy and she roasted him to a crisp like he was a little chicken. There was nothing but ashes left. I don't know what she did with his ashes. She won't tell me. She will cremate me if she gets a chance and then my ashes will disappear, Chester. Please promise me you will not let her cremate me. I think her baby is in Gordy's dump. I think she just threw him away, like he was nothing. She didn't even name him."

"That is a disgusting story, grandpa." I replied. "What kind of pills did the nurses give you today, anyway?"

"The nurse, who gave me a pill earlier, told me it was a happy pill. I don't feel very happy, Chester."

"You may not be happy, but you are definitely talkative today." I replied thinking that my grandfather was a little high and delusional on whatever the happy pill was.

"Just don't let her cremate me, Chester, is all I ask."

"I will not let her cremate you!" I replied trying to assure him and get him off of the subject.

"What would you think about me and Miss May Belle getting together after I cross over to the other side? Do you think it is possible for me to go to the Baptist's heaven? That is where Miss May Belle is. I would like to spend eternity in her arms. Your mother and Gordy will be in the Catholic one."

I bit my lip. I hated the fact that my grandfather disrespected my grandmother, and she in turn did the same to him. Sometimes, I felt guilty about not standing up for my grandmother. However, most of what my grandfather said was true about her.

"Grandma told me about you and Miss May Belle. Her version of life events is a little different than yours." I stated half way coming to my grandmother's defense.

"Someday you will find out about your grandmother's insane side, Chester. I didn't know she had screws loose till after I married her. I am Catholic. She is Catholic. I have stuck with her."

"A woman is to love, grandpa, not someone you stick with. You should be considering spending eternity with grandma, not Miss May Belle." I replied still thinking he was high on his meds.

"Your grandma has always wanted Gordy, Chester. She would leave me for him now, if he would have her. He toyed with your grandmother when she was young. He does not want to toy with her now. She is old and wrinkled like an ugly, old bull dog."

"Until I see grandma in a compromising position with Gordy, I think it is best that we drop this subject. You are high on your meds, grandpa. Gordy probably did have a thing for young women in his day. However, in my opinion, Gordy is too old and fat to be toying with anyone. He is over seventy years old. Girls want young guys like me. The girl I kissed beneath the mistletoe wouldn't give Gordy a second look."

"Are you telling me that you have a girl friend, Chester?" He asked perking up.

"No, grandpa, I don't." I replied lying. "Someday, I will."

I intended to keep Keesha and my new life a secret. She was part of my going to California, Chet Mayo new life. My family and their craziness was my old Chester Holly life, the one I planned to totally abandon in two months.

About that time, a nurse walked in with more pills for my grandfather.

CHAPTER TWELVE

Taking His Secrets with Him

After visiting my grandfather in the hospital, and before making my way to Keesha for the first night of our forever, I decided I needed to check on my grandmother and let her know that I wouldn't be spending the night with her. I was sure my grandmother would be glad to have me out of her hair. We did have a cold war going on over the coffee filters.

Arriving at my grandmother's mobile home, I got out of the trash hauler and went inside, after kicking the snow off of my boots outside. It was not a particularly nice evening. It was now sleeting and snowing. The roads had become treacherous. The trash hauler's side windows were covered with ice.

"Where have you been?" My grandma asked as I kicked off my boots and then my coveralls.

"I have been over at the hospital visiting Grandpa." I replied while picking up my coveralls and hanging them on a hook by the door. Beneath my work-alls, I always wore jeans and a flannel shirt in the winter.

"Don't give me that crap, Chester. You have been gone too long."

"The roads were bad and Grandpa wanted me to stay longer than usual." I replied grabbing my back pack from the end of the couch and stuffing my school books in it, while trying to think what I was going to need for my first night of forever.

"Why are you loading up your school books?" She asked coldly. "You won't be able to study at your mom's place. Your stepfather and mother are in the bottle again."

I ignored her question and comment. She was assuming that I was headed for my parent's place to spend the night. That was fine with me.

"Grandpa doesn't look good, grandma. Do you want me to get out the heavier truck and take you over to sit with him for the evening? He was talking out of his head just before the nurse gave him something to calm him."

"There is no need for that, Chester. When he dies, he dies. I quit caring about him years ago. I have only stayed with your grandfather due to my religious convictions."

"Do you feel the same about me, Grandma? Do you stick by me just because of your religious convictions? I know you have never given a damn about me." I questioned while zipping up my backpack.

"Your mother didn't care about taking something important away from me. Why should I give a damn about her or you?" She huffed.

"I just don't get what the lifelong feud between you and my mother is all about." I stated walking over to the cabinet and making myself a pot of coffee, using a paper towel for a filter. I hadn't made it to the supermarket yet to buy her some filters. "She is your daughter, Grandma. Whatever she did when she was fifteen, you should forgive her and move on. She was just a kid back then. I am just sixteen. Whatever you have against me, you should just can it and move on too. You are missing out on me, my mother, and my grandfather loving you."

"Your mother and your grandfather have each other. I don't want either of them, or feel any need to forgive them. You . . . I tolerate because I know that you are gay. You will have a hard time in life, being different. I have always been different, just in other ways. I have had a hard time in life."

"You think I am what?" I asked in shock as I sloppily poured myself a cup of coffee, with coffee sloshing out on to the counter.

"You have never had a girlfriend, Chester. You are almost out of high school. What am I suppose to think; that you plan to become a priest or something?"

I pulled open the drawer where cleaning rags were kept, with the intention to grab one quickly and wipe up the mess I had made.

"I am not gay grandma." I huffed. "The only thing different about me is the fact that I am a smelly dump kid. Girls don't like the smell on me."

"Gay or not, I let you stay with me. That is more than I will ever do for your mother. Also, hauling around black girls in your grandfather's hauler, behind my back, goes against everything your step father and I stand for. You know they are an inferior race. You need to repent of your perversion, Chester. Homosexuality is a sin, and hauling around black girls is a sin. Your stepfather is not happy with you."

I was in total shock as I fingered the rags in the drawer. How did she know about my picking up Keesha and the boys? My stepfather must have been out in his hauler or pickup and spotted me. That had to be the answer. He called my grandmother and told her. I needed to derail her thinking.

"I assume what you are referring to, is the black hitch hiker I picked up and took into town to the Bell Ringer's shelter. I couldn't leave her on the road to freeze. She didn't have a coat on, grandma. Her car was broke down. Grandpa would have done the same." I sputtered.

"Well, in the future, don't be picking up anymore of them. Your stepfather has his reputation to think about."

"What reputation, grandma? He is a damn drunk." I replied in disgust.

I longed for my grandmother to see me for the straight 'A' student and person that I was. Never once in my life had she told me she was proud of me and my accomplishments. Now, she was raking me over the coals for being an embarrassment to her and my drunken stepfather. I felt like I had a knife stuck in my gut. I wanted her to be proud of me. At the same time, I knew she was never going to. My grandmother lived in a self-centered world that my mother, grandfather, and I did not exist in it.

"That damn drunk could get you tarred and feathered." My grandmother replied. "Hanging out with black girls is beneath you and your stepfather's station in life."

"Since when have you seen my stepfather as someone? He is a drunk and an addict just like my mother. He hauls just enough trash to pay their utilities and most of the time, not enough to support their habits. He is a loser. I honestly don't know what my mother sees in him, other than he is big and likes to throw his weight around in bar fights."

"Your mother needs him to protect her from me." My grandma shot back. "I would cut her throat in a heartbeat, if it weren't for your stepfather. He would slit mine."

"You don't mean that, Grandma. My mother is your only child. You are going to need her the older you get."

"What is she going to do for me? She can't take care of herself. I would put my trust in your stepfather before I would her. He has the backup of his night riders. If you were smart, you would pay him a little respect and stay away from black girls and not let anyone know you are gay." She replied.

"I am not gay!" I once again replied.

"A duck is a duck." She retorted. "A gay duck is a gay duck."

I bit my lip and looked down into the rag drawer. That was when a very large, silver serving fork and spoon caught my attention. I had never noticed them in the drawer before. They looked to be real silver. I picked the fork up and turned it over. It read: Revere Sterling Silver.

"Where did this come from?" I asked holding up the valuable serving piece.

"Never mind where that came from. It was a Christmas present, although I don't celebrate Christmas and you know that."

"When did you get it?" I asked suddenly in a panic, wondering if it and the spoon were the serving pieces that had came up missing at Miss May Belle's wake. I wondered if my grandfather had taken them, and if he had told my grandmother about Keesha?

"On Christmas Eve, if it is any of your business." She replied.

"Where did you get it? You were home on Christmas Eve." I further asked.

"Haven't you ever heard of a woman getting herself a gift, Chester? I thought I deserved them and I took them."

"Took them?" I asked.

"You are damn right I took them. I followed you and Woody to Miss May Belle's house. Your step father drove me. We peeped in the windows, and I saw your grandfather kissing Miss May Belle's hand and crying over her casket by the Christmas tree. He spent Christmas Eve with her. I have never meant anything to him. He should have been home with me on Christmas Eve."

"What else did you see?" I asked nervously, wondering if she had seen Keesha and me kissing beneath the mistletoe.

"I saw a chance to slip inside and see where Woody has been hanging out all of our married life. Miss May Belle was a two bit, black whore that he spent most of his trash hauling wages on." My grandmother sputtered. "I deserved to see what she had purchased with my money. Your stepfather agreed to follow the two of you. I called him when you were getting your grandfather dressed for his hook up with his black whore. What your stepfather saw you do was an embarrassment to him."

"Did you take these two serving pieces from the escargot and goose liver trays?" I asked mad. Keesha had been accused of stealing them, and had not been paid because of it.

"Of course I took them. I slipped in while you, Woody, and the others were helping load May Belle's casket into the hearse. I slipped in the side porch door, took a quick look around, and left the same way. Your stepfather was waiting for me in the alley with his car running. For helping me dog the two of you, I gave your stepfather twenty dollars and an unopened bottle of wine that I found by the two trays."

"The serving fork and spoon are going back, Grandma."

"Touch them, Chester, and I will see that your grandfather goes to meet his maker quicker than expected." She replied.

Knowing that my grandmother was capable of doing most anything, due to her loose screws, I slammed the rag door shut. I wasn't taking any chances of her messing with my grandfather's fragile condition. I would return them in a day or so when she wasn't aware of it. I returned to the subject of her thinking I was gay.

"You are wrong about me being gay, grandma. I have a date with a girl tonight. That is the reason I am sleeping elsewhere."

"Who is she?" My grandma asked with her face suddenly lighting up.

My grandmother definitely had a Jeckel and Hyde personality. She could change from cold to warm in a heartbeat. "Is she one of your classmates?"

"She is a gorgeous waitress, if it is any of your business. I met her earlier today."

"Isn't a waitress a little beneath you, Chester? You can do better than a waitress. Everyone knows they sleep with every man that slips into their café booths. Waitresses are whores!"

"Well, this one isn't. She is my age and I like her. She likes me."

"What does she look like, Chester? Will I be embarrassed to introduce her to my witness friends? Does she have a nose ring or a tattoo? If she does, I want you to keep her away from here. It is hard enough to explain to my witness brethren why I live in this garbage dump. None of them will come here to eat a meal with me. I don't want to be further judged by some heathen waitress sporting a nose ring or a tattoo."

"She is gorgeous and has black hair. That is all I am going to tell you, grandma. You are also guaranteed I will not bring her here to Gardenia or this trailer to drink coffee made by you, using dirty, dump flower filters. She is a city girl, respectable, and she does not have a nose ring or a tattoo."

"You and your grandfather just don't appreciate who I am. I stand for recycling, cleanliness, and Godly living. The two of you could use a good dose of all three." She shot back and then continued, "You say she has black hair?"

"Yes grandma, she has hair that is raven black." I replied downing the cup of coffee I had made. It tasted a little funky from using a paper towel for a filter.

"Black hair is a good thing, Chester. If you and her have kids, the ones that have black hair won't be as likely to get head lice, like you always did in grade school. Blondish red hair like yours is always tempting to head lice. I read somewhere that the little devils prefer light hair. If there were any head lice at school, they jumped on your head. Your hair was like a bird's nest to them. I spent a fortune on head lice shampoo when you were little. Whoever gave them to you should have had to pay for the costly treatments. When you drag your little heathen in for me to care for someday, I hope they all have dark hair. I don't relish the thought of dealing with lice infested, bird nests like yours once was, again. You were always bringing home an infestation from school."

"Did you ever consider that it was dump life here, and all the old clothes from my grandfather's trash loads, that I got the lice from? I don't ever remember having a new stocking hat?"

"Why buy new things, Chester, when the rich throw out perfectly good things in their trash. I think your grandfather and I have done quite right by you, considering your good for nothing mother takes all of her money and buys drugs and alcohol with it. She has always dumped you and your head lice on me. You are lucky you have got what you have from me."

"I am indeed lucky to have you." I muttered rolling my eyes.

My grandmother ignored my comment and turned to pick something up that she had stored behind the kitchen table.

"I have something I want to show you, Chester. I know Woody is going to be gone before much longer. Back at Christmas time, I ordered him an urn for his ashes. It came in the mail a day or so ago. I just haven't had the opportunity to show it to you."

"You purchased an urn, and grandfather isn't even dead yet?" I asked in a shocked voice.

"I am not getting any younger and neither is your grandfather. I ordered me one too. He will just get to use his first." She stated setting two tall, bowling pin shaped figures on the kitchen table.

In shock, I touched the one that looked like a Hungarian peasant woman. Then I touched the male figure that looked like a bearded Santa or a garden gnome. They didn't look like urns to me. They looked like wooden dolls. Marble vases were what I considered to be urns. I was a little pissed. My grandfather had just begged me to prevent her from cremating him.

"What are they?" I asked thinking she might just have one of her screws loose in the moment. She couldn't put ashes in painted bowling pins. I picked the Santa one up and turned it over looking at it from different angles. It was about twenty inches tall.

"They are Russian nesting dolls, Chester. Watch . . . !" She stated pulling the top half of the hand carved bowling pin, wooden, lady peasant doll from its bottom. A smaller similar doll rested inside. She then pulled the second wooden figure's top half off and another doll appeared a little smaller than the second. Then she continued till she had eight of the lady dolls sitting in a row ranging in size from twenty inches down to two inches.

"What did you call them?" I asked pulling the top half of the Santa gnome off and looking at the smaller gnome inside. I was intrigued for the moment

"Russian nesting dolls . . . ," She replied speaking slowly to make sure I got it.

"I don't get what these have to do with burial urns. Aren't urns usually little square wooden boxes or marble vases with lids on them?" I replied lining up a row of Santa gnomes as I removed top half after top half revealing a total of eight Santa like gnomes ranging in size from twenty inches down to two inches.

"The two big dolls will hold Gracie's and my ashes. The lady is for mine and the gnome is for hers. Gracie collected Santa figures before she ran away. I think the Santa Claus urn fits her. The next two will hold your mother's ashes and your step father's. The third set will hold your ashes and those of the baby I lost seventeen years ago. I have the baby's ashes stored in my button can in the top of my closet."

I interrupted and asked in a shocked voice. "Your miscarried baby's ashes are in your button can in the closet?" My grandfather had never known what she did with her baby's ashes.

"I left the buttons in the can." She replied grinning. "I thought the baby might like to play with them till I decided where I would rest in peace one day. I have never planned to be put next to Woody. The baby and I will rest in Heaven with Gordy."

"Go on . . . tell me who the other peasant urns are for?" I asked, wondering if she were going to reveal any other family secrets in her apparently delusional state. A cremated baby in a button can was unfathomable.

"The fourth set of peasant urns will hold your dead children." She stated.

"What do you mean when you say dead children, Grandma?" I asked, feeling a little repulsed and edgy. My grandmother had screws that came loose on occasions. It was possible this was another of those times.

"Children sometimes die young, Chester. I want those of my family to look good in my Heaven. These urns will be very presentable when I personally accompany each to Heaven and sit them on the shelf behind God's throne. Children without urns must sit at the foot of the throne. All my family's little ones will look rich like the wise men. They will sit on a shelf behind God's throne like they are someone. I have given a lot of thought how to make all of you presentable enough, to get you into Heaven."

"What about Grandpa? You said you purchased an urn for him?" I asked, knowing she had already named who went in the first four of the lady and gnome dolls.

"I should put him in my button can, after I remove my baby's ashes. He doesn't deserve to go to my Heaven. However, I purchased a nesting doll to put him in to. Every Heaven needs a fallen angel to cast out."

At that point, my grandmother turned and retrieved from a cardboard box, behind the kitchen table, another set of Russian nesting dolls. They had the same bowling pin shape, except they were red Devil nesting dolls. I gasped.

"Your grandfather's ashes should fit nicely in him, don't you think? He will get to go to my Heaven, but god Gordy will then cast him out into the dump."

It was at that point that I became alarmed. My grandmother was entering a state of some sort of mental dementia or a step off into the realm of the insane. I didn't have a clue how to handle the off the wall comments she was making.

"I have just one question, Grandma. Why did you buy a nesting doll for Gracie and not Gordy? Gordy is your friend. Gracie barely knows you. She was raised by Mabel."

"Gordy doesn't need one, Chester. He is God. He will sit on his throne and we will all be members of his 144,000 chosen ones. We will all die, but Gordy won't. He is divine."

I didn't ask any more questions. It was very apparent that my grandmother had lost it. She was mixing up the two religions she embraced, and was somehow traumatized by my grandfather's future death. Gracie was gone and would never return. Also, the dump's short, fat pervert, Gordy Gardenia, was not divine or God.

I quickly made up my mind that I wasn't messing up my first night with Keesha, to baby sit my delusional grandmother who didn't give a crap about me. I would call my mother and let her deal with it. I was going home to my first night of forever with Key.

CHAPTER THIRTEEN

Light at the Tunnel's End

After my strange encounter with my grandmother and her gnomes, I made my way to Snuff's mobile home and my new life. On the way, I called my mother and told her she would have to deal with my grandmother's momentary lapse into the fringes of insanity. She seemed pleased. I didn't understand why. Perhaps, my grandmother had driven her crazy her whole life. Perhaps, the thought of my grandmother being permanently committed, was a long welcomed relief. When you have a crazy person in your family, they can wear you down emotionally. I think that was the state of my mother.

My grandmother's commitment only lasted three weeks. My grandfather managed to rally enough strength to catch a taxi and go sign her out. Neither I, nor my mother, were pleased with his action. However, the three weeks gave me a chance to move in with Keesha, without anyone suspecting that I was up to anything. When my grandmother did return home, I told my mother that I had moved in with my girlfriend in the city and she would have to check on her and stay with her when needed. I explained to my mother that I was seeing to my grandfather. She was going to have to pick up the slack and see to my grandmother.

Easter rolled around and I just had a couple of months left to go. Keesha and the boys were hidden out in Snuff's trailer, and I was in survival mode. I was counting down the days till we split.

A day or so after checking my grandmother out of the nursing home she was in, my grandfather slipped into a coma. I never got the chance to question him further about who Gracie's mother was. Everything just sort of took second seat, after my first night of forever with Keesha. In her arms and playing with the boys in my free time was where I wanted to be. I popped in on my comatose grandfather, but I didn't spend hours. As far as my mother and grandmother were concerned, I was living with my new girlfriend in the city, running my grandfather's routes before and after school, and taking the hauler home with me there each evening. I had entered a two month grace period I called Heaven. My nights in Keesha's arms were unbelievable. Every moment in them, I fell more in love with her. I also bonded with and became daddy to her boys, Tank and Tag. I was living in the lull just before a great storm. I was unprepared for what lay ahead.

My grandfather never woke from his coma. The one thing I did feel good about was that I had taken the time to visit him on a regular basis. In doing so, I had met my super hero, Dr. Mayo. Our brief encounter and conversation had changed my perception on life. He gave me the courage to 'test the gods' and extract from them what I wanted. Having Keesha in my life was the result of my paying attention to his instructions. My mother climbed out of her bottle, sobered up, and spent a lot of time sitting with my grandmother when she was in the nursing home. I think she was trying to make peace with my grandmother. My grandfather, in his comatose state, clung to life a lot longer than the doctors predicted. They said he would die the end of January. He lived till the week before my graduation in May. When my schoolmates were giddy about the prom and prom dates, I was grieving the loss of the only family member that had ever been there for me.

All winter and spring, I drove my grandfather's trash route. I no longer turned the money over to my grandmother. I paid her bills and then the rest I used to support my new family. Keesha was pleased that I turned all of my weekly wages over to her, to buy groceries and clothes for her and the boys. Life was good for the three of us. I had a fair size stash of money put aside for us to go to California on. Whatever Key didn't use for the week, she added it to the stash. I ran my last trash route the day before my graduation. However, I still drove the hauler. It was our only mode of transportation till I rented us a car the night of my graduation. Dr. Mayo had told me not to waste my money on cars, insurances, etc. He had told me to rent what I needed, as I needed it. In California, I planned to buy Keesha and me bikes with seats on the back of them for the two boys. We were going to live the life of university students. She was thrilled with the idea, and all the new clothes she and the boys had. I think she appreciated finally having a man that would take care of her and let her be a mother. The boys thrived.

The only demand that I made on Keesha was that she keep the boys indoors during daylight hours. Snuff's mobile home and acreage were on the backside of the dump. Gordy or his dozer driver, Carlos, could see Snuff's place from the rim of the dump. I insisted she keep the shades pulled on that side of the trailer. She understood we were living in a mobile home that was supposed to be closed up for the winter. We weren't paying rent. She understood. What she didn't know was that I was trying to prevent her from coming in contact with the less than desirable people of Chester Holly's world. She was my Chet Mayo world. I didn't want the two knowing about each other.

As I said before, a week before my high school graduation, my grandfather died. My grandmother had my grandfather cremated and my mother, his only child, wasn't able to stop her. I was appalled, knowing how he felt about the issue. What was even worse, my grandmother did not hold a funeral for my grandfather. She just stuck his ashes in the Russian Gnome nesting doll and set him on top of his four televisions. I felt short changed, like I wasn't given my chance to pay my last respects. No wake was held either. My grandmother just went on with her life, like nothing out of the ordinary had transpired. I hated both her for it. I did not enter my grandmother's trailer again. Seeing my beloved grandfather's ashes sitting on top of his four televisions was not something that I could handle.

It was a sad time for me, as I approached my graduation. However, I put on smile and tried not to show it in front of Key. She was not aware of the fact that my grandfather had died, or that my crazy grandmother was alive and lived just the other side of the dump. Prom happened, but I did not go. I couldn't take Keesha in fear of my grandmother or mother finding out about her. I let my grandmother and my mother think I took my fictitious city girl-friend. When my mother asked to see my prom photo afterwards, I told her it would come in the mail in a couple of weeks. She bought my lie. I was just trying to survive and protect Keesha, my tuxedo girl, till I got my diploma and we kissed Gardenia goodbye.

In Key's arms at night, I was secure and the time flew by. The days were what dragged. However, my final week of classes, trash hauling, and studying for finals did end. To my surprise, my parents and grandmother were suddenly planning on attending my graduation. I was in a panic and did not want Key meeting them. I had been very careful about keeping my two worlds separate. I knew my prejudiced, red neck stepfather would say something off the wall to her concerning her skin color, and probably ask her why she was trying to stick me with her two little black bastards. That was who my stepfather was. My grandmother would make insinuations that a waitress was beneath me, and that Key was a whore for being one. My mother would probably get drunk and who knew what she would say to Key. I felt I had to protect Keesha from them. So, I didn't tell Key what night my graduation was.

In an effort to throw a little extra money into our flight Kitty, I had been running some extra late night trash routes. In my stupid young thinking, I saw it as the perfect cover to get thru graduation and Key not knowing about it. I decided to leave Snuff's trailer in my trash hauler coveralls and then change into my graduation clothes at school, pretending to run a late route. Before leaving out, I told her to pack everything that was important to her and the boys, that we would be leaving that night. I lied to her and told her that I didn't plan to attend graduation, and had made arrangements with the high school office to mail me my diploma to the university in California. I would make the one last trash run, return the hauler to my boss across the dump, walk across the dump, and then we would order out a rental car and leave somewhere around midnight. My plan seemed logical to me, to keep my two worlds from colliding on my last night in Gardenia.

Keesha seemed really edgy before I left out on what was supposed to be my final trash run. At one point, she went into the bathroom and threw up. I thought she was nervous concerning our upcoming flight into the night. I was a little on edge myself. My not telling her about graduation, and not taking her to it, was a selfish decision that would end up costing me. My grandfather fell out of favor in my grandmother's arms. I was about to follow in his footsteps.

I ignored Key as I put on my coveralls. I was nervous and antsy myself. I had a Valedictorian speech to give, and I wasn't used to being up in front of my classmates. I was the dump kid who always stood in the back of every line formed. I ignored Keesha's moodiness and left, telling her I had about a two or three hour trash route to finish before returning the hauler to my boss. There are some things a man has to do in life, or so I thought. Keeping Keesha from meeting my parents and grandmother was one of those things. I didn't dream that she knew I was attending my graduation. She followed me to the hauler as I left out, like she was waiting for me to tell her something. I kissed her by and told her to finish packing, that I wouldn't be gone long.

As I drove away from Snuff's trailer, I got a whiff of odors from the dump. It was spring. However, Gardenia did not have the scent of flowers. Now, that snowy weather was over, the smell of rotting garbage was getting bad. In the winter, the dump froze and the smell somewhat subsided. The warm days of spring had brought with it the stench of rotting garbage.

"Tonight is the last night, Chester." I muttered as I left Keesha standing in the driveway of Snuff's trailer. "Tomorrow, this time, you will be three states away and free of this smelly life forever. Your new life as Chet Mayo is about to be born."

Surprising to my fellow students, I was the valedictorian for our senior class. I was the only 4.0 student in my graduating class. My classmates, who had turned their noses up, at me the dump kid, were shocked. I received twenty seven college scholarships, and so many trade school scholarships that they could not all be presented to me. I walked away with practically every scholarship and award that was offered for the year, including two full Ivy league scholarships, cosmetology and barber school scholarships, truck driving scholarships, etc., etc. I had purposely applied for every scholarship that the cheerleaders and football studs had applied for, as well as every scholarship that the snooty kids of my class desired. They had ignored me and belittled me my whole life, when I couldn't help who I was. It was my night to get even. I smiled and waved at each of them, when it was announced that I had been given their coveted choices. There were some red mad faces in the crowd at my graduation. I had tested them as gods, pushed their buttons finding out what scholarships they were all applying for, and then extracted payment where it hurt them the most.

~   ~   ~

After my graduation ceremony, my mother, step father, and grandmother cornered me and insisted on taking me out to a restaurant to eat. I couldn't refuse them, without them suspecting I was up to something. They asked me where my city girlfriend was. I told her she was in the hospital with an emergency appendectomy. They just smiled and seemed to accept it. My step-father arrived late for my graduation; just in time to see me receive my diploma. He seemed a little edgy and he was hot, sweaty, and smelly for some reason. However, being smelly wasn't unusual for a trash hauler. I assumed he had put on his dress clothes without taking a shower. Maybe he had driven his route till the last minute.

My stepfather had invited his single, ditsy, blonde eighteen year old niece to accompany them to my graduation and then out to eat afterward. She worked in a chicken processing plant. Although she was very blonde and pretty, she had quit school after turning sixteen. She was not my type, nor invited by me. After my graduation, she was the proverbial motor mouth and talked non-stop. At the restaurant, she went on and on in detail about her job gutting chickens in the processing plant. She left nothing to the imagination. The removal of chicken intestines was a twenty minute subject I couldn't get her off of. I tried numerous times to change the subject to something more appropriate for my graduation dinner. She was relentless in returning to the subject. I sat and pretended to eat, knowing that Keesha was waiting for me, with her suitcases packed. I was already late returning to her. I needed to get the meal over, and get out of there. It seemed like it took my mother and motor mouth forever to eat.

My grandmother, who had attended my graduation, had made an excuse to keep from eating with us. She had gone home in a taxi. I didn't think much about it. I wasn't particularly liked by my grandmother, not to mention that my mother and she were always at odds. Her leaving early was just one less headache I had to deal with.

I had hoped for a quick in and out meal. However, it had not turned out that way. We had been in the restaurant a good hour and a half and my mother and motor mouth were still picking at their food. I sat nervously wanting the evening to end. At least motor mouth kept my parents from noticing how fidgety I was. I still had to order a rental car. Midnight was the cutoff time for getting one delivered. I had to return to Key by eleven. My family was totally oblivious to my eyeing my watch. Motor mouth was sucking up all the attention and the air in the room. That was okay with me. My only concern was how slow they were eating.

My mother and stepfather didn't seem to have a clue that most high school graduates did not hang out with their family after graduation. Graduation parties were going on all around the city. I was stuck in a trucker's diner listening to motor mouth. My party didn't' start till I got home to Key. Our party would begin when we got in the rental car and kissed Gardenia goodbye.

My stepfather's cell phone rang. He smiled from ear to ear, seeing who it was calling him. I thought that was odd, when he told my mother that it was my grandmother.

"Are you home?" My stepfather asked. He then paused and replied to whatever my grandmother was saying on her end of the conversation. "You did well. The Klan won't forget."

I was relieved when he suddenly stood and grabbed the ticket from the table. My mother and motor mouth immediately put down their forks and stood. Then they walked away from the table. I was embarrassed when my stepfather walked out of the restaurant without leaving a tip. I felt bad for the waitress, but I couldn't make a show and pull money from my own pocket and pay the tip. That was something that might push my step-father's buttons and set him off in a demeaning rant and rage. I didn't want that, or have time for it. I just wanted to get out of there and the night to end smoothly.

If my stepfather thought a waitress was slighting him for anything, including her returning his flirting, he didn't tip. I immediately thought of Keesha and how she had tried to keep her boys housed, fed, and clothed on tips as a waitress. Jerks like my stepfather were waitresses' nightmares. They took up their time, and money out of their pockets. I did not respect my stepfather. I put up with him because my mother for some reason felt safe with him. I had never understood why she hung on him twenty-four hours a day. It was rare that she even visited my grandmother without him.

At ten minutes to twelve, on the outside of the restaurant, I managed to ditch my family. It had seemed as though they were purposely trying to delay my getting away from them. I was really aggravated with them, but didn't show it. I was too close to kissing them goodbye forever.

My family had spoiled my plans to leave at midnight. It was now ten minutes till twelve, and too late to order the rental. I would have to wait till morning to leave. Pissed, I drove my grandfather's trash hauler back to my grandmother's trailer and parked it in her driveway. I left the keys in it, so she could find them. Then I checked to make sure I had my new cell phone and my diploma. I had them. Then I retrieved my backpack from my grandfather's tool shed. I had visited my grandmother earlier in the day and had packed a few personal possessions stored there. I was sure I had everything I needed from my grandmother's place.

One personal possession that I was taking with me was the canvas portrait of Miss May Belle. I had removed it from its frame earlier in the day, rolled it, and put it in my back pack when my grandmother wasn't looking. She had been busy having coffee outside with Gordy. I couldn't leave the portrait of Miss May Belle behind. The portrait was a keepsake, a reminder of a wonderful Christmas Eve I had spent with my grandfather. I was sure that my grandmother would trash it, once she discovered it in the back of my grandfather's closet. The portrait of Miss May Belle was going with me to my new life in California. She would hang on my wall, next to a photo of my grandfather.

I cut across the smelly dump heading for Snuff's place. I was aggravated that it was too late to order a rental car. However, it was just a little hitch in my plans. I would overcome it. My family thought I was going out with friends and stay out all night celebrating my graduation. That gave me a little leeway to pack Keesha and the boys up in the morning, and escape before the trash haulers started their day and my grandmother discovered the keys in her hauler. I was underage, seventeen. I needed to get over the state line before my family discovered I was gone. I feared my stepfather would send the state police for me. I wondered if Gracie had suffered my frustrations, when she was trying to runaway.

As I walked, I revamped my plan and checked off all the new details in my head. A rental car would be delivered to Snuff's trailer somewhere around five thirty A.M., after I called at five. I had a map of U.S highways in my back pack. I had my driver's license and insurance card in my new billfold. I had given my old one to Tag. I was sure that Key had done her part and the boys were bathed and ready to go. We would load them into their car seats in their pajamas, to save time. I had my stash of cash hidden at Snuff's place in my grandfather's billfold. Only Keesha knew where it was, and how much was in it. I had begged my grandmother for my grandfather's worn out billfold. Keesha and I had hid it and our money in one of Snuff's old work boots in his closet. My new plans seemed workable to me.

As I walked, I couldn't help but notice that a burning flesh smell permeated the dump's air. I decided that Gordy was possibly doing some night burning, possibly getting rid of a steer or other dead animal that had been discarded in his dump. Dead animals were supposed to be taken to the rendering plant. Sometimes the haulers discarded dead animals, they had found in trash bins on their routes, in Gordy's dump. The rendering plant charged for taking dead animals. Trash haulers were out to make and keep every dime they could get their hands on. Gordy often complained about dead animals being left in his dump illegally.

The stench of the burning flesh, mixed with the rotting garbage smells was stomach turning. I had always hated warm weather when the dump came alive and reeked with its obnoxious odors. The smell of the burning flesh was about to make me puke. It was awful.

As I walked towards Snuff's trailer, I thought I had the bull by the horns, as they say. I was in love with the most beautiful woman in the world, had two sons, and had over six thousand dollars saved to start my new life in California with. I had saved practically all of my part time wages for the last four years. Keesha had been very frugal in what she had spent. I think the amount had increased to close to seven thousand dollars. I wanted to whistle as I walked, due to my being so excited. However, I refrained from doing so, in fear the sound would alert or wake up Gordy Gardenia. He might think I was some picker in his dump stealing something.

As I neared Snuff's rusty trailer, I observed that all of the lights were out. That was strange. However, I told myself that Key had probably turned the lights out to get Tank and Tag to go to sleep. Maybe she had fallen asleep with them. Reaching Snuff's door, I let myself in. I then flipped on the living room light. The trailer had an eerie, strange, empty sound.

"Key . . ." I called lightly heading for the bedroom that we shared. I didn't want to wake the boys up.

Key did not answer. I headed down the mobile home's long skinny hallway and stopped at the door to the boy's room. I peeped in hoping I hadn't awakened them. To my surprise, Tank and Tag were not in their beds. With my heart jumping into my throat, I quickly made my way to the bedroom I shared with Key and opened its door praying the boys were asleep in the bed with her.

The trailer was too quiet. Keesha reclined with them on our bed sometimes, when she couldn't get them to go to sleep.

"Key . . ." I called softly and then turned on the light when I didn't get an answer.

I then grabbed the door frame in a panic. She was not there and neither was Tank or Tag. The beds had not been slept in.

"Oh God no . . . !" I screamed and ran to the front of the trailer trying to make sense of their absence. That was when I spotted my old billfold and Tank's military cap lying on the kitchen table. I ran and moved them about to see if there was a note lying with them. Maybe there had been an emergency and she had called a cab and taken the boys to the hospital ER for some reason. I had once told her to call a cab, if she ever needed to take the boys to the doctor for any reason. In a panic, I scanned all flat surfaces looking for a note. There wasn't one. I spun around and looked beside the front door. Key had put her packed suitcases earlier in the day there. She knew we were leaving. They were gone. Not wanting to believe what I was seeing, I then ran back to the bedroom we shared and opened the closet door. There was nothing of hers or the boys there. Then I rammed my hand down into an old work boot of Snuff's where Key and I kept our stash of money. My grandfather's billfold, containing close to seven thousand dollars, was there. I didn't know what to think. The only explanation for her and the boys' missing clothes was that she had left me. I didn't know why.

When it finally sunk in that I had lost the only person that had ever loved me, I sat down on the end of the bed and bawled like a baby. She was everything to me. After a couple of hours sitting in the dark crying, I got up realizing that my life with her had come to an unexpected end. I grabbed my backpack and put my grandfather's billfold and cash in it. Keesha had not taken any of the money. That bothered me. Thinking of her out there somewhere with my boys, without money for food and other necessities, hurt me deeply. I would rather her have taken the money. I was a man. I could make more. It was my place to take care of her and the boys, even if she was temporarily at odds with me. At least I prayed it was a temporary thing and she would come back or call me.

Morning came. With my heart residing somewhere in the toes of my shoes,

I walked back across the dump to Rosa's place. I knocked on her door and asked her to rent me a room and hire me for the summer. She agreed to do so. I could not leave Gardenia without Key. I had to give her a chance to make her way back to me. I was not a kid anymore. I also decided I was never driving for my grandmother or family again. I might not be leaving for California, but I was leaving them in my dust.

After several days of thinking about what might have caused Key to leave me, I decided it had to be the fact that I had not invited her and the boys to go with me to graduation. Somehow, she had found out that I had fibbed to her about having the school office mail me my diploma. I had been a stupid young jackass that had made a bad decision. That choice had cost me.

Several weeks passed. Keesha did not call, write, or return. At that point, I was sure that Dr. Mayo's advice would be to pick myself up by the seat of my pants and test the gods again, even if one goddess had struck me with a lightning bolt. Down deep, I knew that Key was gone for good. I just didn't want to admit it. I was in love with her and just couldn't let go. My graduation dreams of kissing Gardenia goodbye had turned into my worst nightmare. Winning twenty seven scholarships meant nothing in comparison to losing her. She was my goddess of love.

Rosa welcomed me with open arms. I started driving for her as well as became her boarder. My mother and grandmother were furious. I didn't care. I was an adult, out of school, and tired of hauling trash to support all of them. I hadn't made it to California yet, but I was slowly becoming Chet Mayo.

I felt like a zombie driving Rosa's trash route for the first few weeks. Broken hearts don't mend easily, or quickly. I missed being in Key's arms at night and the boys throwing their arms around my neck and hugging me. All I could do was just keep putting one foot in front of the other and telling myself that I was still going to California and become a detective at the end of summer. That was all I had to hold on to, while I waited and hoped that Keesha would call. I drove two trash route shifts everyday to keep busy. It was the only thing that kept me from coming unglued mentally. I knew that Keesha was my soul mate, the only woman I would ever truly love.

During my fifth week of driving for Rosa, I gave a lot of thought to Dr. Mayo's theory of testing the gods. I had tested the goddess Keesha beneath the Christmas Eve mistletoe and got a kiss from her in payment and three months in her arms. Losing my payment had been unexpected. I wondered if Dr. Mayo ever got hurt when he tested the gods and goddesses of his world. I had been loved by my goddess and then half destroyed by her abandonment of me. I came up with a conclusion. I had forgotten one of Dr. Mayo's instructions. He said after testing the gods, you should run. I had latched on to my goddess Keesha with a death grip, instead of running.

After several weeks had passed by with no word from Keesha, I decided that I would never let myself become emotionally involved with another woman. I told myself that I would kiss them beneath the mistletoe and then run like hell, never looking back. I decided to be a one date man, when I got to California. I would be a 'kiss and run' man and never date any woman more than once. I never wanted to ache again, like I had over Key and the boys. I entered survival mode, and shut my heart down.

CHAPTER FOURTEEN

My Grandfather's Missing Ashes

The middle of July, my grandmother was abandoned by my mother who had once more climbed into her bottle for some reason, and hadn't come out. My grandmother, being without a driver, groceries, and other items she needed, tried to make up with me. She invited me over for dinner. I agreed to it, but stated that I would bring fast food. I hadn't forgotten the fake flower coffee filters.

Knocking on her door, I found she was not at home. I took my key and entered, like I always had when I was living with her. Stepping inside, a change in the appearance of the living room snagged my attention. The Russian gnome nesting doll that held my grandfather's ashes was missing from its perch on the top of his four televisions. I glanced about the room to see where my grandmother might have moved my grandfather's ashes. I didn't spot them anywhere. I told myself that she had probably taken them out to Mt. Pleasant Cemetery and had them either buried, or placed in their building for urns. I wished, in the moment, that she had told me. I could have gone along and paid my last respects. My grandfather had always been more like a father to me. I had lived ninety percent of my life beneath his roof. My mother had been really bad about dumping me on my grandparents.

Walking over to the table, carrying fast food for two, I recalled my grandfather once telling me that my grandmother was a wild card and unpredictable in what she chose to do at times. Fear gripped me as I also recalled my grandfather saying that he feared his ashes would end up in Gordy's trash dump. I now shared his fear.

Even though I had showed up with fast food for dinner, my grandmother was gone. It annoyed me, but I had grown up with her craziness. I left her share of the fast food on her kitchen table and then walked across the road to Rosa's mobile home, entered, and sat down at her table to eat my dinner. Even though I rented a room from Rosa, she did not cook for me, clean up after me, or do my laundry. She was my landlord and my boss, not my woman; as she put it. After leaving dirty dishes in the sink once, I learned my lesson. When I went to crawl in bed that night, I found them in the middle of my bed. There are many lessons a young man learns when he first embraces adulthood. Key made a man out of me, and Rosa taught me to clean up after myself.

Rosa was a naturalized Hispanic citizen. She and her husband had entered the U.S. legally and worked for my grandfather when they were very young and first in the states. They had saved their money and purchased their own trash hauler three years after arriving with one suitcase. Rosa's husband was dead now, but she still ran their trash service and hired drivers for their seven routes. She was better off financially than my grandmother and grandfather ever was. That was a thorn in my grandmother's side. She saw Rosa as being less than her. Rosa, being extremely gorgeous, pushed her buttons. My grandmother and mother were not especially beautiful women.

Rosa paid her employees well. Those coming to her needing jobs were loyal to her. She was willing to settle for a little less profit in order to keep her trucks moving. In the long run, her seven trucks were making her wealthier than the other haulers in Gardenia who paid minimum wage and couldn't keep drivers. Rosa was a gorgeous, raven haired, Hispanic woman who had a way with men. She used her brains and her charms to be the goddess of her world. She flirted with her drivers and competing haulers. All the men in Gardenia were her gods and she tested them. Most of the time, she got what she wanted. She was equally as good at running like hell once she got her 'Banana Crème Pie' payments. She was a female version of Dr. Mayo.

I was sitting at her kitchen table eating my fast food when she returned home from driving one of the routes herself. One of her drivers had taken the day off due to his first child being born. Rosa was not afraid to get her hands dirty when needed.

"Chester, you are looking good! What is up?" She asked eyeing me, my French fries, and soda.

"Sit down and share my fries." I replied grinning at her. "Grab a glass and I will pour you half of my drink."

Rosa was older than my mother. However, you couldn't tell it. She had the figure of a model and looked to be in her twenties. My love for Keesha was the only thing that kept me from succumbing to her flirting. I was missing the nights of passionate love making with Key. I was sure that Rosa would take me to her bed in an instant, if she got the chance. I just wasn't sure that was what I wanted. My heart still longed for Keesha and the boys.

"Your step-father told Carlos that you are a man now." She replied opening an upper cabinet and removing a drinking glass. She then handed it to me for part of my iced soda. "Your stepfather is not happy about who made you a man."

I bit my lip and then handed her the glass of soda. "Did Carlos tell you who, he thinks, has made me a man?" I asked in reply. I was pretty sure that I had kept Keesha and the boys a secret.

"Your stepfather told Carlos that the hermit told him that you had a black tuxedo girl stashed at Snuff's place, till graduation night."

"How did the hermit know I had a girl at Snuff's place?" I asked.

"The hermit was picking in the dump late one evening and spotted you and her carrying groceries in from your grandfather's trash hauler."

"He told my stepfather?" I asked in disgust. I had gone to great lengths to keep Keesha a secret.

"He told only your stepfather, as far as I know. Your mother's man does not like women with color in their skin. He does not like me."

"What else did the hermit tell him?" I asked beginning to boil on the inside.

"The hermit told your stepfather that he walked over to Snuff's place to wish you good luck on your graduation night. You were gone. He talked to the tuxedo black girl who came to the door and told her all about your family's graduation plans, including a blonde girl being your date after graduation."

"I am going to kill that damn hermit!" I replied angry and biting my lip. Now, I knew why Keesha had walked on me. She thought I had gone to graduation with motor mouth.

"The hermit said the tuxedo girl burst into tears and was very angry. He said he left quick and returned to his dump picking."

"Oh god . . . ," I muttered in disgust, knowing that the mentally challenged man had spoiled the only good thing that had ever happened to me.

At that point, I decided Keesha must have called a taxi, right after her talk with Wolf Dog the hermit. She was already packed, with her bags by the door for our trip. Even though I was mad enough to kill the hermit, I knew that I would have to keep my cool and see what I could pump out him. Maybe he had some clue as to where Key had gone. He was the last one to see her. Maybe he watched her leave from the dump rim.

"Tell me about your black tuxedo girl, the one that has made a man out of you?"

"She is a black waitress that I met on Christmas Eve. It was love at first sight for both of us. I kept her hidden out, because I didn't want my family saying off the wall things to her. I am lily white and she is ebony black. You know what prejudiced, red neck, crazies the members of my family are."

"Your tuxedo black girl has rubbed your white sheet stepfather and grandmother very raw. Your stepfather cannot be a white sheet, if his son sleeps with skin of color. Your grandmother sees skin of color as less than her. Did you take a white skinned girl to your graduation, disrespecting your girl with ebony skin?" Rosa asked eyeing me and not smiling.

"My stepfather invited the girl. She was just there the night of my graduation. I was trying to protect my black skinned girl by not taking her to my graduation. I now regret that. The hermit spoiled the only good thing that has ever happened to me, damn him."

"You should know that your family is not happy with you, Chester. You have embarrassed your white sheet stepfather. He is from a long line of white sheet, night men. A man cannot move up in their society, if his son sleeps with tuxedo girls."

"Why are you telling me this, Rosa?"

"Be happy the hermit got to your tuxedo girl before your stepfather did." She replied.

"Are you telling me that my stepfather intended to hurt or frighten Key?"

"Your stepfather has tried to hurt and frighten me. He once showed up in front of my trailer, many years ago, demanding that I leave your grandfather alone. He didn't stay long." She laughed. "It was a very hot night for him."

I grinned in spite of the fact that I was angry with the hermit. She had a twinkle in her eye that said, "Ask me more?"

"How hot was his night?"

"I walked right up to him in his white sheet, pulled my lighter from my pocket very quickly, and set his white sheet on fire. He forgot fire safety rules; you know . . . drop and roll. He fought the flaming sheet trying to get it off. I then laughed as he ran away screaming from his burns. He is a little man who hides in a wine bottle and behind white sheets. It takes a cat woman like me to send a white rat running back home and into his bottle. Your stepfather now fears me! I yelled after him, that night, it would be his mobile home that burned to the ground, with him in it, if he ever tried again to mess with me. I shake my lighter at him to remind him occasionally."

"I have always wondered how my stepfather got the burn scars on his face and arms. Good for you, Rosa! The jerk made my childhood miserable." I replied. "He was always playing ghost in a sheet and scaring the pee wad out of me when I was three or four."

"A white sheet is once again at my door making demands." She replied eyeing me and eating my last French fry. I thought it best I tell you, before I set the sheet on fire."

"What is my jerk of a stepfather up to now?" I asked in disgust.

"It is another member of your family that wears the white sheet. Your stepfather fears me. He has not forgotten the pain from his burns and knows I will do it again. It is your mother that has put on the sheet."

"My mother is on your case?" I asked in shock.

"Your grandmother tells me that she is going to whoop my ass, if I fool with you. She knows you are now a man. Are you worth getting my ass whooped for, Chester Holly?" She asked smiling from ear to ear.

"I understand she once wanted to whoop your ass over having an affair with my grandfather." I replied winking at her. At times a little of my Chet Mayo surfaced. "My grandfather was an experienced man in the bedroom. I am not. In my opinion, you should remember the good times with him, but forget about me. He was worth getting your ass whooped over. I am not."

Rosa laughed. "I like you Chester Holly. You are not afraid to tell me what you think. You wink at me, like I flirt with the men on dump road. I push their buttons and you push mine. I get whatever I want from them and run. You push my buttons, but you run without taking anything from me."

"You are a goddess, Rosa. Before Keesha, I was one of the males on dump road standing, admiring, and fantasizing about you. However, in the present moment, I still desire to push the buttons of my ebony skinned Keesha goddess. It is her love and arms that I want to keep and sleep in forever."

"It is good to have at least one male that does not want to tie me to the post of his bed. I need such a friend." She replied. Then she smiled adding. "Your grandfather was a wonderful man. Like you, he did not want me. He was my friend. However, your grandmother did not see our friendship. She imagined there was more between us."

"She does have a wild card imagination." I replied.

"Did you know that it was not your grandfather that your grandmother wished to whoop my ass over? It was another man, one that she was having an affair with." Rosa replied with a twinkle in her eye. "Your grandmother always treated me like I was Hispanic trash and beneath her when Ricardo and I first arrived in the states and drove for your grandfather. She hates me because I have become the goddess in the dump and once slept with her lover. He chose me and not her."

"My grandmother had a lover and you took him from her?" I asked getting into a story I hadn't heard before.

"When I was young, my Ricardo had an affair. I caught him in bed with someone. To get even, I chose a man and had an affair, a man much richer than my Ricardo. I wanted to show him that I was able to move up and on without him. Your grandmother was about forty-three back at that time and was pregnant with a late life child. I thought her baby belonged to your grand-father. She was pregnant by the rich man I was using to get even with Ricardo. She caught us toying with each other behind the man's trash hauler. My skirt was up and his pants were unzipped. She burst into tears and ran home to her trailer. It is him that she later in the morning threatened to whoop my ass over."

"I am pretty sure I know who you are speaking about." I replied in disgust. Apparently, Gordy Gardenia had been sleeping with my grandmother and Rosa at the same time. That was disgusting.

"Your Grandmother was not a happy woman. She tried to whoop my ass back then, but she didn't get the job done. I pulled my metal nail file and told her to bring it on. She ran from me. Now, it is you that she wants to whoop my ass over." She replied laughing and winking at me. "The rich man was not worth getting my ass whooped over. However, you might be one day."

"In my opinion, a man who has had experience with only one woman is probably not worth pulling a nail file for."

"I like you Chester Holly. I can see that you are a faithful man to the woman you love. Your tuxedo woman was lucky to have you. I am sorry she walked on you. Do you want me to whoop the hermit's ass for you?"

"I will take care of Wolf Dog! He cost me!" I replied.

"You have not heard from your woman since your graduation?"

"Not a word . . . ," I replied with a wave of depression sweeping over me.

I then rose and threw my fast food mess in the trash. It was my intention, to head down to the hermit's place, confront him about spying on Keesha, and ask him if he saw her leave in a Taxi, or did someone give her a ride. She was out there somewhere and I had to find her and make things right with her.

"Are you sure your woman walked away after the hermit left. Snuff's woman disappeared a little over seventeen years ago from that same area. He has never been able to find a clue as to where his woman or his unborn child disappeared to."

"I intend to study criminal law and be a detective, Rosa. I will find her."

"Your ebony skinned woman is not the only woman missing, Chester. There are many missing women from our county and those surrounding us. Will you take the time to find them too?"

CHAPTER FIFTEEN

The Hermit's Murder

Leaving Rosa's mobile home, I walked a quarter of a mile down dump road heading for the hermit's place. Rosa had called him Wolf Dog for years, and the nickname had stuck. Wolf Dog the hermit was a picker who rode the back of Rosa's trucks and emptied cans. It was the first of August. Keesha had been gone for two months. I had not received any sort of communication from her. Rosa telling me about the Wolf Dog's encounter with her was the first clue I had as to why she had left me.

As I walked, I tried to calm myself. I knew that the hermit was mentally challenged. If I got him rattled, he might come unglued and clam up on me. I needed to know what he had said to Keesha, as well as whether she had left in a taxi or with someone. She could have ordered a taxi or approached one of the neighbors beyond the dump for a ride. The hermit was my only hope of finding her again. Two months had not numbed my feelings for her. She was that special someone that only comes along once in a lifetime.

The summer sun was just starting to lower in the sky. As I neared the end of the dump road where it turned out onto the highway, I saw that there were flashing lights in front of Wolf Dog's place, as well as yellow tape and a crime scene investigator's van. They had not been there when I returned from my last run for Rosa. A small crowd was gathered at the yellow tape. Most of them I didn't know. I assumed they were reporters or possibly neighboring farmers from across the highway. My mother was standing with them. I sped up my pace and joined her in the group of onlookers.

"What is going on?" I asked taking a spot next to her.

"Wolf Dog is dead. A man came to buy a wolf pup from him and found him." She replied.

My mother's eyes were bloodshot, but she was at least sober. I assumed she was coming down off of something. She seemed real fidgety.

My heart sank into my shoes. The hermit had just died, taking with him possible information I needed to find Keesha.

"Wolf Dog didn't look sick to me yesterday. I watched him leave out and return riding the back of one of Rosa's trucks." I replied. "He waved at me."

"He has been murdered, Chester. The man who found him, stood next to me here for awhile, till the sheriff took him beyond the trailer to question him. He whispered to me that Wolf Dog's head is missing."

"What . . . ?" I asked thinking I had to be hearing her wrong.

"Someone has cut off his head and taken it with them." My mother replied in a low voice.

"Holy crap . . . !" I replied turning to watch the forensic team go in and out of the hermit's filthy trailer where he had slept with at least a dozen dogs every night of his life. I could just imagine the nightmare they were having, trying to collect evidence. "Who would want to kill him, much less take his head? He is a harmless, mentally challenged, garbage can picker."

"A man doesn't get his head cut off for no reason, Chester. Someone had to be really angry to chop off his head with a meat cleaver."

"His head has been chopped off with a meat cleaver?" I asked in unbelief.

"A pink handled one, Chester," She whispered, looking me directly in the eye giving me a keep your mouth shut look.

I didn't say anymore. My grandmother was notorious for painting the handles on her brooms, mops, and hand tools. She painted them pink so my grandfather, a macho man, would not run off with them. She had a pink handled meat cleaver in her kitchen. My grandfather had been a deer hunter and she had on many occasions helped him butcher what he brought home.

Thinking about her meat cleaver, I thought about the two stolen valuable serving pieces I had seen in that same drawer, a huge sterling silver spoon and fork. Until now, I had forgotten about them. I had heard that sociopaths took souvenirs from their victims. Surely, I was reading more into what I was thinking about, than there really was. My grandmother had major screw loose, but surely she wouldn't decapitate a man and take his head for a souvenir.

"How long has the hermit been dead, Mom?"

"An hour or so, maybe . . . ," She replied leaning in to whisper again. "There was still blood oozing from his neck when the man found him. I ran over here when I heard the sirens. The man, wanting to buy the wolf pup, was white as a sheet. I got one look at the body before they roped us all off. He was hanging upside down from his trailer light fixture. All of his blood was running out of his neck onto his floor, and his twelve wolf dogs were licking it up."

At that point, I gagged and wanted to barf.

"Don't have such a wimpy stomach, Chester. Living in a dump, it looks like you would be used to seeing messes." My mother stated seeing I was about to puke. "I couldn't even set a mouse trap when you were little. You would throw up if you saw one caught, and it a little bloody. You are not five years old anymore."

"It is not everyday a man hears about someone having their head chopped off and dogs licking up their blood." I retorted taking a deep breath to try to keep from puking in front of her and the others standing behind the yellow tape.

My mother didn't say anything more. She returned her attention to the activity around Wolf Dog's trailer. Standing there, my mind drifted back and I relived the last two hours. I had taken fast food to my grandmother, but she had not been home, after inviting me for dinner. That would have been about the time that the hermit had died. I hoped I was wrong. At the same time,

I didn't remember my grandmother and the hermit ever having cross words or any type of argument. Where was my grandmother, if she wasn't with my mother? I didn't know whether I should express my concerns to my mother or not. For once, in months, she looked like she was sobering up. I didn't want to send her running once more into a bottle.

"Gordy . . . !" I heard my mother mutter to herself. I wondered what she meant.

After the coroner took the headless body away, I walked my mother back across the road to her place. I tried to not think about the name she had muttered when we had been speaking of the missing head. I had too much to think about. Dealing with Key being missing was all my emotional state could handle. I didn't want to consider that my mother was insinuating that she thought Gordy was the head snatcher. Besides, Gordy was around seventy eight. The hermit was in his forties. It wasn't feasible that Gordy could have overpowered the hermit and cut off his head. Also, the hermit was at least a head and a half taller than Gordy.

As I walked back toward Rosa's trailer, one of Rosa's Hispanic drivers, Carlos, caught up with me and matched my pace. He had also walked down from Rosa's, when he saw all of the flashing lights. Carlos lived in a travel trailer behind Rosa's mobile home.

"Some chicken plucker did that." He stated striking up a conversation with me. "That dude was hung by his feet, like he was a chicken on a poultry processing line. His head was whacked off with a machete or something. I used to work in a chicken plant. Cutting chicken heads off was not a pleasant, or easy job. It took an expert to do such a thing."

"You saw the headless dude?" I asked recalling that my mother had said she got a quick peek before the county sheriff had showed up.

"I peeked over your mother's shoulder, as did a couple of others who arrived before the sheriff. I know a plucked chicken when I see it. He was killed by someone who has worked on a processing line."

Suddenly, motor mouth popped into my thoughts. Then I dismissed the thought of her as fast as it had come. There were thousands of people who worked in poultry processing plants. A skinny, wimp of a girl like her couldn't chop or slice off a man's head with a machete. She probably weighed a hundred and ten. Besides, I doubted if she even knew the hermit.

"Did you know Wolf Dog?" I asked Carlos.

"Not personally. However, I have run him out of Gordy's dump a few times when I was running the dozer. The hermit liked to walk the high rim of the dump looking thru binoculars. I have caught him eyeing Snuff's trailer with binoculars a few times. He always runs when he sees me."

"What do you think he was looking for with his binoculars?" I asked pumping Carlos for information. The hermit was dead. I wouldn't be getting any information out of him.

"I think he watched women. He may have had the mind of an eight year old, but his body was that of a grown man, and I am sure he had his attractions."

"When was the last time you caught him eyeing snuff's place thru his binoculars?" I asked hoping it wasn't Key he had been watching. I had warned her about keeping the blinds pulled.

"I have only been working for Rosa for a couple of months, the same as you. Before, I worked for Gordy for eighteen years running his dump dozer and burning whatever he wanted to get rid of that he wasn't supposed to have in his dump."

"Dead animal bodies . . . ?" I asked.

"Yea, animals and other crap illegally dumped."

"Why are you working for Rosa?"

"Gordy let me go last May, stating he was thinking of retiring and closing the dump. He told me his health was failing, and it was just a matter of time till he had to lock the dump's gate and call it quits." Carlos replied.

"Tell me more about the hermit and his eyeing Snuff's place thru binoculars. When did you say that happened?" I asked fishing for details.

"I ran Wolf Dog out of the dump the first time, around the time Snuff's pregnant girlfriend disappeared. He watched her. I also caught him standing on the high rim of the dump watching Granny Mabel, just after her husband died. Several times, I have caught him trying to look in Gordy's windows at Gracie with his binoculars. Last spring about Easter time, I caught him on several occasions looking thru his binoculars at Snuff's place. I figured he was planning to steal something. Snuff was in the north settling his aunt's estate at the time. His trailer should not have had any one in it, other than you or your grandfather checking on it."

"I have the Key." I replied. "I was there at times, checking on the place. My grandfather wasn't able to, due to his being in the nursing home."

"Maybe Wolf Dog was watching you, Chester. Who knows?"

"Did you ever catch the hermit doing anything illegal in the dump?" I asked, remembering the awful burnt flesh smells, the night I walked across the dump heading to get Keesha and kiss Gardenia goodbye.

"The guy didn't have enough sense to do anything illegal. I think he just had a fascination with women and satisfied his sexual appetite by window peeping with binoculars. He was just a kid in a grown man's body."

"Tell me about the last time you caught him in the dump with his binoculars?"

"It was the morning after the kids in town graduated high school. I remember the date because my cousin's daughter graduated. I spotted Wolf Dog on the rim of the dump with his back to me. He was piddling with something that looked like clothing. I slipped upon him and scared the pee wad out of him. I grabbed him by the arm, and he came unglued. The man cried like a baby and wet his pants. I let the dude go. I didn't intend to scare him that bad. I picked up the clothes, he had picked from the dump, shoved them in his arms, and told him to get out of the dump and stay out of the dump. He ran like crazy, taking with him the women's clothes."

"What kind of clothes were they?" I asked trying to pump him further.

"Clothes are clothes. You know trash haulers are always dumping used clothes in their loads. The dump is full of them. When something rips or tears, people in the city throw them in their trash cans. To the best of my memory, he was holding up a pair of smaller size women's jeans and T-shirt of some sort. Those are common items in the dump. I bulldozed hundreds of them under every day."

"Were the clothes new looking or old?"

"They didn't look real dirty or worn." Carlos replied. "Wolf Dog was holding them up to himself, like he was thinking of putting them on."

"Do you think Wolf Dog might have been a cross dresser?"

"That is possible. Maybe that is why I was always running him out of the dump. Maybe he was looking for women's clothing to wear." Carlos replied.

When we reached Rosa's place, we parted company. Carlos headed for his travel trailer, and I entered Rosa's mobile home with the intention of going to my room and trying to make sense of all the things my mother and Carlos had told me concerning Wolf Dog's murder and his obsessions.

"I am glad you are back. Have you heard the news?" Rosa asked flipping her cell phone closed. She had been talking to someone.

"Are you talking about Wolf Dog's murder?" I asked.

"Yes . . . Granny Mabel just called and told me about it. One of her sons is home for a few days. He walked down to the end of the rode to see what was going on. He called her on his cell phone and told her to stay inside and lock her doors. He told her that someone had just murdered Wolf Dog less than an hour before. She called me and told me to lock my doors. I was about to do it, when you walked in. Does the sheriff think a murderer is hiding somewhere in our dump community?"

"There were flashing emergency vehicle lights when I left here earlier. Carlos saw them and beat me down to the dump road entrance. I walked down, not too far behind him. My mother was there and a crowd was gathering. I thought Wolf Dog was possibly ill, and being sent to the hospital. My mother informed me that he had been murdered."

"One more murder . . ." She replied not smiling. "How many more will come up dead or missing around here, before the sheriff realizes that there is something going on in Gardenia and its dump?"

"I think law enforcements' attention has definitely been snagged tonight. Wolf Dog's head was missing." I replied. "What did you mean when you inferred more than one person was dead or missing."

"I forget that you are just seventeen, Chester. Your family has probably shielded you over the years from the gruesome newspaper and television reports concerning this county's missing. If I had children, I would not let them listen to such things."

"Tell me what you are talking about." I replied pumping her.

"Seven women and one man that I know of have come up missing over the last seventeen or so years. The first was Snuff's woman. One was a lady trash hauler who owned her own truck. Another was an elderly black lady who disappeared from a nursing home. Your grandfather's Miss May Belle was her daughter. Recently, three door knockers have disappeared. Also, there is a missing minister and his pianist."

"Miss May Belle had a mother that disappeared?" I asked in shock.

"Yeah, about the time your grandfather started getting serious about her and wasn't coming home regularly to your grandmother."

"Okay . . . tell me about the others?"

"The Baptist minister and his pianist disappeared from the little church that sits on the road behind the dump. Everyone believes they just ran off together, except me."

"When did that happen and why do you doubt their running off with each other?"

"They disappeared when you were about five. Gracie attended their church's Sunday school. The pianist picked her up on Sundays. Gordy was alone and I think he just wanted Gracie out of his hair, so he could do what he wanted on Sunday mornings. Anyway, she and the minister came up missing. The congregation believed they ran off together. The minister left a wife and four children behind. However, I don't believe that theory. The pianist and I knew each other. She was one of my trash customers. I picked up her trash every Wednesday. The pianist was a closeted, Baptist lesbian. I doubt very seriously that she ran off with her homophobic minister. She had a steady lady lover."

"I get your point." I replied mulling over in my mind what she had told me. "What about the others?"

"They all have some minor tie to Gordy Gardenia." She replied eyeing my reaction.

"I know about Snuff's girlfriend's disappearance. Before my grandfather died, he insinuated that it was possible that she just walked away because Snuff did not put a wedding ring on her finger. My grandfather thought she might possibly be a single parent somewhere, choosing not to include Snuff in her or her baby's life for that reason. He refused to marry her."

"That is possible, Chester. However, how do you explain the missing door knocking women?"

"They probably annoyed the hell out of some illiterate sociopath, with their incessant door knocking. He, possibly now, has them chained to his bed and they read their literature to him every night." I smirked.

Rosa grinned. "I would chain you to my bedpost, if I could get by with it. You could read your detective novels to me every night."

It was my turn to grin. "If I wasn't so madly in love with my tuxedo girl, I just might chain myself to your bedpost." I returned. "You sure know how to tempt the devil out of a guy."

"Should you fall out of love with your tuxedo girl, tap on my bedroom door some night. You might find yourself falling in love with a hot tamale girl."

"I will keep your offer in mind." I replied.

"Is it true you plan to become a private detective, Chester?"

"I plan to get a degree in criminal law and then open my own detective agency, or go to work for one out in California. Why?"

"Could I hire you to do a little snooping for me, before you leave the end of August?"

"What kind of snooping?"

"My Ricardo's cremated ashes are missing. Someone broke into this trailer and took them about two years ago. I think I know who has them. I just don't know why he would take such a thing?"

"Most break-ins are by kids and teens. Maybe one just didn't realize what he was taking."

"The man that has taken my husband's ashes is not a teen, Chester." She replied eyeing me seriously. "Ricardo's ashes are not the only ones that are missing. A thief has been stealing urns of ashes from the mortuaries in the city. There was a story about it in last weekend's newspaper."

That caused a little bit of panic in me. My grandfather's ashes were not in their usual place in my grandmother's trailer earlier, when I took her fast food for dinner.

"I guess I missed reading about the missing urns and ashes. You want to tell me more?" I replied.

"Gordy Gardenia was once married to a young girl that was the daughter of an undertaker."

"What does that have to do with missing ashes?"

"Have you ever paid any attention to that huge metal building that Gordy Gardenia has attached to the back side of his mobile home?"

"Not really. It probably houses dozer parts or broken down trash haulers. Why?"

"There are no outside doors or windows, Chester. There is no way to get a dozer or trash hauler into it. The only way to get into the metal build is thru Gordy's mobile home. The outside of the metal building has no doors or windows. Sometimes, I hear strange noises coming from there."

Rosa's place was on the same side of the dump road and next to Gordy's.

"What kind of sounds?" I asked getting serious about what she was trying to tell me.

"I hear pecking, like a woodpecker, sometimes . . . other times there is crying and sad mortuary music."

"That is a little creepy! Maybe Gordy just has a taste for sad music and he has a woodpecker problem."

"I want you to find out what is inside Gordy's building. I think the crying I hear is my Ricardo trying to tell me where he is."

I grinned and then bit my lip. Not only was my grandmother nuts, Rosa was a little off the wall herself.

"What are you going to pay me for my snooping services?"

"If you find my Ricardo's ashes in there, and bring them back to me, I will give you half a year's wages. That would be a nice little bundle for you to start a new life in California on. His ashes are that important to me."

I smiled from ear to ear. That amount added to the six thousand I already had was quite a small bundle.

"You have yourself a super snoop." I replied reaching out to shake hands with her.

Rosa took my hand. "You won't be sorry you are helping me, Chester. Your tuxedo girl could be inside that building. She could be the one playing the mortuary music."

"I doubt that, Rosa. Keesha was not a musician. However, she had other charms that kept my interest."

Rosa grinned, getting my meaning.

"Gracie suddenly disappearing is also a mystery." Rosa added. "She may have found my Ricardo's ashes and was frightened by them. Maybe that is why she ran away."

"Do you want to enlighten me as to why you suspect Gordy of stealing ashes?"

"The last time I slept with him, back when your grandmother was pregnant by him, he wanted us to make love in a coffin, with me on the bottom. The coffin was in the closet in his bedroom. I was frightened and told him to go shower first. He had just returned home from a trash route. While he was in the shower, I sneaked out of his mobile home and ran home to Ricardo. Had I stayed and climbed in that coffin, I think he would have closed the lid on me, and I would now be one of the missing."

"Gordy likes to make love in a coffin?" I asked in disbelief. I had heard a lot of rumors about Gordy, but this was a first.

"Gordy is crazy, Chester. I was just having an affair with him to get even with my Ricardo for having one with a lady trash hauler. You don't always think straight when you are young. My craziness almost got me killed and buried in a wooden coffin. I never told Ricardo. It has been a secret that I have never told. Now, I am telling you."

"I believe you, Rosa. There is darkness in Gordy's eyes that I have never been able to explain. My grandmother thinks he is a god. I have tried to tell her that he has a screw loose."

"I am glad you believe me, Chester. I have made a lot of money here in Gardenia in the trash hauling business. I want to go home to Mexico in the next few years. I can live like a rich woman there on what I have earned here. I cannot go home without Ricardo's ashes. It would be disrespect. We came here together, and we must go home together."

"I need something to keep my mind off of my missing ebony girl. I will snoop for you. Just so we don't have any misunderstanding between us, if I find a way into the metal building and find Ricardo's ashes and bring them back to you, you will give me half a year's wages in cash."

"That is right!" Rosa replied with a serious look on her gorgeous Hispanic face."

"What do I get for wasting my time? The building could just hold all kinds of furniture and junk that Gordy has rescued from his dump."

"Nights in my bed till you leave for California and two month's wages." She replied flashing her flirtatious, feminine smile at me. Then she half whispered, "We will keep the two weeks of love making a secret. I wouldn't want to have to use my nail file on your mother or grandmother, should they call wearing white sheets."

"It is a deal." I stated knowing that I would take the two month's wages, but not the two weeks of love making. It was Keesha's arms that I longed for. However, I have to admit, Rosa was tempting the hell out of me.

"Wait right here!" Rosa demanded.

In a moment or so, Rosa returned with a small digital camera and showed me how to use it.

"Take photos, Chester, of anything you see that might be questionable. Bring out Ricardo's ashes, if you find them. We will send the sheriff back, if you find ashes or bodies other than his."

"Now, you know I won't start snooping till tomorrow morning. When Gordy is busy collecting early morning dumper's fees, I will circle in behind his place from yours and try to find a hole of some sort to look thru into his building. I will also be late starting my trash route. I don't want docked for the time I use to snoop."

"That is agreeable." She replied. "Be careful, Chester!"

CHAPTER SIXTEEN

Snuff's Secret Lady

The next morning, I waited till the trash haulers lined up on dump road to empty their first loads for the morning. Gordy never trusted anyone to collect his dump fees. He did that himself. Leaving Rosa's trailer, I intended to make a quick jaunt across the road and see why my grandmother had stood me up for dinner the previous evening. Her lights were on, so I knew she was home. Maybe she just forgot I was coming the previous evening. My grandmother was elderly and had not exactly been with it the last few years. Walking to the shoulder of dump road, I spotted a familiar truck in the line.

"What are you doing at Rosa's place so early in the morning?" Snuff's voice yelled from a couple trucks back in the line.

I grinned, waved back at him, and then walked down two truck lengths to have a quick morning chat before the line of haulers started moving. Gordy hadn't opened his dump gate yet.

"What are you up to this morning, Chester?"

"When did you get back?" I asked ignoring his question. I really didn't want to explain why I was now living at Rosa's place.

"I've been back about three days or so. Do you notice anything different about me?" He asked pulling out the front of the clean coveralls he had on. "I think I have a secret woman friend. I returned home and every stitch of my clothing had been washed, bleached, and pressed. Look at these white socks!" He stated pulling up the leg of one of his coveralls to display the top of his white socks.

"You do look a little ironed and pressed." I replied grinning. "Did your secret woman iron your underwear?" I asked ribbing him. I knew that Keesha had washed, bleached, ironed and cleaned up all of his clothing to pass the time while we waited the two months to leave for California.

"Believe it or not, Chester, she did iron my underwear and mended the holes in my socks."

Keesha had been a cleaning freak. I grinned knowing she had done it. My own coveralls were not dirty during the few months we were together. She washed and dried them every night. Now, they hadn't been washed in a week. I looked like all the other old bachelor haulers who didn't have a woman to tell them to take a bath or change their underwear.

"A secret lady friend isn't a bad thing, Snuff. You look pretty sharp this morning, and you definitely don't smell like garbage. I would say you smell like bleach and fabric softener. The smell suits you." I returned laughing.

"I wish she would return. I would hire her to keep house for me. My place and things haven't smelled so good since my woman disappeared seventeen or so years ago."

"Maybe she will return some day." I replied grinning and secretly hoping so.

"Have you heard about Wolf Dog?" Snuff asked dropping the subject of his clean clothes and trailer.

"I walked down to the dump road entrance when the emergency vehicles started flashing their lights last night. It was pretty gruesome." I replied.

"That is what the news at ten said last night. I was busy catching up on business in town, and missed the excitement." Snuff replied spitting on the ground. He chewed.

"Can I ask you a question about the dump? I am just a kid and I haven't been around for part of Gardenia's history."

"Sure . . . Chester! However, I don't think you are a kid any longer. Your grandmother told me, when I got back, that you are living with a girl in the city. She said you are a man now."

"I don't think it takes sleeping with a woman to make a kid like me, a man. I think it takes honesty and integrity. Those two items I am working on. Hopefully, when I have them mastered, I will be a man." I replied.

"You are sly with your tongue, Chester. You would make a good politician." He replied slapping me on the back. "Now, what was it about the dump you wanted to ask me?"

"Were you around when the building behind Gordy's mobile home was built?"

"My family has always owned the farm behind the dump. Yea, I was around. Why?"

Why did Gordy build it with no doors or windows? It is a huge building and the only access is possibly a door opening out of the back of Gordy's mobile home. Mobile home hallways are narrow. There is not much he could carry down a narrow hallway and store there?

"The building used to have an entrance door on the side facing Rosa's trailer. Gordy took the door out just after my girlfriend disappeared. He said he was tired of kids messing in the cemetery inside."

"Cemetery . . .?" I asked in shock.

"There is a little cemetery inside the building called Heaven's Gate." Snuff replied.

"Why would he construct a metal building and enclose a cemetery?" I asked.

"The people who sold him the land for the dump had a small family cemetery they wanted preserved. If Gordy wanted the land, he had to agree to preserve the graves. Gordy built the building over the little cemetery, which was demanded as part of his real estate contract. The former land owners visited the indoor cemetery fairly often, till about fifteen to twenty years ago. They then died off and the little cemetery was forgotten. About the time you were born, Gordy boarded up the outside entrance door. He covered the opening with sheet metal, and dug up the cement walk that led to it. He did it to keep neighboring kids out. There was a rash of cemetery vandalism back at that time. Kids were stealing marble vases, the kind you find on tomb stones."

"Were there any urns of ashes taken?" I asked seeing a possible connection between Ricardo's missing ashes, possibly those of my grandfather, and those from the mortuaries in town.

"They caught a couple of dump kids stealing urns, back then. Those boys would be men in their late twenties now. I do remember they spent six months in juvenile hall for the thefts."

"Rosa's husband's ashes have been missing for about two years. Do you think it might be possible that one of those boys is now stealing ashes again, even though he is a grown man?"

"Men's habits and wants don't change much, Chester. I played with toy trash haulers when I was a little boy, and now I play with the big ones. A thief with an interest in cemetery items, as a child, could collect them as an adult. I had a cousin who had a thing for stealing the signs off of ladies rooms. His house was covered on the inside with them. He stole his first one when he was ten. He had a heart attack at sixty-three, and died while trying to lift one from a highway rest area, women's facility. A zebra can't change his stripes. Maybe men can't either."

"I get what you are saying to me. Do you remember the boys' names?" I asked.

Snuff grinned and spit again. "I don't remember their names, but they were two of Granny Mabel's sons."

"I think I may have solved Rosa's missing ashes mystery. Do Granny Mabel's urn stealing sons visit her out here in the dump?"

"I'm sure they do, Chester. Mabel is their mother. Ask Gordy. They used to drive him crazy with their cemetery antics before he closed up Heaven's Gate."

"Thanks Snuff, I will." I replied and then quickly asked. "What did the boys do with the urns and ashes when they were young?"

"They were using the urns to water their pit bull dogs in. The best I recall, the newspaper back then said they just dumped the ashes out on the ground wherever they found them, because the urns were too heavy to carry with the ashes in them."

"I am going to hate telling Rosa about what you have just told me. However, one of those two boys has probably taken up his old childhood hobby of urn stealing."

For some reason, Gordy was really late opening the gate. All of the drivers had shut their trucks down and were standing outside of them smoking and waiting. Snuff and I continued talking, but he changed the subject.

"I have been meaning to talk to you about something, Chester. Would you hear me out on a subject that I am sure you are tired of hearing about?"

"What is it Snuff?" I asked knowing it was the water rights issue.

Snuff lived just a few feet out of Gardenia's town limits. All those who originally bought a plot of land from Gordy to park their trucks and mobile homes on had gone together to drill a community well. Gordy wouldn't let anyone hook on that didn't originally buy plots from him. He had always been the self proclaimed mayor of the community and no one bucked him for fear of losing their dumping rights. The other nearest refuse dump was a hundred miles away. Although Gordy refused water to anyone beyond the dump cluster of mobile homes, he allowed any trash hauler to dump in his refuse because that was a steady source of income for him. Snuff could dump his trash but he could not have Gardenia community water.

"While up north, I followed a story in their local newspaper about a newly elected young mayor who took over a little town that was dying. He pushed a lot of buttons and breathed new life into his little town by changing a lot of the old ways. The oldsters, who were dying off, had to stand back as he and the younger citizens of the town implemented new ways for the town to grow and attract business. The senior citizens were not happy about the changes, but the young mayor was voted in by the younger citizens and that was that."

"What does that have to do with whatever is on your mind?" I asked.

"I am forty-seven. Your grandmother and Gordy are older than me. Mabel is their age. Rosa is the youngest of us older Gardenia citizens and then you and Gracie, if she were here. If you called for an election and ran for mayor of Gardenia, you could change the way things are done in Gardenia concerning water rights, and other issues."

"You are outside the town's limits, Snuff, just like my parents are. I couldn't just up and automatically give you and my parents water rights, if I were mayor." I replied.

"You are not getting my point, Chester. A new mayor could propose a bill to annex my land and your parent's land. Three votes would be all it would take to be elected mayor and then get whatever bills you wanted passed. There are just five adult voters in this dump town, Mabel, your grandmother, Gordy, Rosa, and Carlos."

"And just which of the five would even consider voting for annexation. They are all scared of Gordy. He has ruled this dump all his life and threatens to revoke dumping permits, if anyone crosses him on any issue."

"Granny Mabel's husband is dead. She has a new occupation to support her-self and no longer needs dumping rights. You just have to figure out what her buttons are, push them to make her vote for you, and then call for a vote on the annexation of my and your parent's property."

"Who else would vote for me?" I asked out of curiosity. He was sounding like Dr. Mayo.

"Rosa thinks Gordy has stolen her husband's ashes. She would vote yes on anything that she would see as getting back at him. She is convinced Ricardo's ashes are in Gordy's cemetery building. He won't let her in to look. Promise her to have Gordy investigated for illegal activity in his closed up building, and she will vote for you. She has tried to convince all of us haulers that he has a woman or something caged in his building that cries."

"I gather she has told you about her theory, concerning Gordy being some sort of casket pervert?"

"Rosa has driven Gordy crazy sending nut cases to his place to try to find a way in his building. Gordy says she is trying to harass him because they once had an affair and he dumped her. He says he broke it off with Rosa, because he met Gracie's mother and fell in love. He says Rosa was mad and threatened to be his worst nightmare. Who knows what the actual facts are. In case you haven't figured out all of this town's history, Ricardo did have an affair. What you might not know is that Ricardo was a gay man."

"Ouch . . . I didn't see that one coming." I replied biting my lip.

"Rosa is slick. Years ago, she promised me that she would tell me where my girlfriend had disappeared to, if I broke into Gordy's building and looked around for her. What has she promised you?" He asked with a sheepish grin. "Don't feel bad, Chester, half the men in this dump line have either slept with Rosa, or been used by her."

"I see . . .," I replied thinking how I had almost been one more nut case added to her list.

"Were you in the cemetery building before Gordy closed it up?"

"In it and out of it . . . I was younger back then. Gordy hired me to help him remove the door and put the outside sheets of metal on. There was nothing in there but a dozen or so ancient tombstones. The grass was dead from lack of sun. There was nothing in there but a square section of dirt about twenty feet square with a dozen or so dusty tomb stones standing. Gordy cut the trees in the cemetery before he erected the building."

"Were there any urns of ashes in there?"

"No." Snuff replied once more spitting tobacco about four feet out into the road. There were a couple of metal barrels in there with lids on them. I figured they were for trash. You have to put the dusty, dirty, fake flowers somewhere when they have outlived their usefulness."

"Does a second door, in to the metal building exist? Is there an opening in Gordy's mobile home?"

"Both of Gordy's mobile home doors open out the front of his trailer." Snuff replied. "Check it out the next time you are up at the dump gate. You can see the front of his trailer and both doors from there."

"Thanks, Snuff. I owe you one. Tell me more about your mayor thing." I replied feeling that I owed it to him to listen, since he had saved me from some humiliation.

"Right now, there are only five legal voting residents in Gardenia. Whoever runs for mayor, just needs to push the buttons of three to get elected. Mabel, because of Gordy calling the law on her boys for urn stealing, is one. Rosa is two, because he dumped her, Carlos is three. Gordy let him go last summer after eighteen years. Carlos lets on like their parting was amicable. I know better. Gordy promised to one day turn the dump over to Carlos, and let him run it. The other two voters are your grandma and Gordy."

"So, you want someone to run for mayor and then get an annexation bill passed which would make you and my parents legal residents and voters."

"It is that simple. I will help you run for mayor and pay your campaign expenses. I get annexation and water rights in the long run. My farm cistern is too shallow to provide enough water for washing my trucks. All I want is water rights . . . and maybe the opportunity to run for Mayor someday, just to make Gordy squirm."

"You sly old dog . . .," I replied laughing. You have this all figured out.

"Chester, you are the smartest person in Gardenia. Your mother told me about your twenty-seven scholarships and walking away with practically every senior award made. You are the one to help me pull this off. You don't have to stay mayor of Gardenia. You can resign after your first term, or after you get me and your parents annexed."

"I am only seventeen, Snuff." I replied trying to get around any further discussion. "I am not old enough to vote, or of legal age."

"There are no laws in Gardenia stating how old you have to be to run for mayor, Chester. Gordy has just always been the law. He is a man, not a town. You file a petition with the county calling for a town election and then run for mayor. There is nothing wrong with being the youngest mayor in our state. You definitely have the smarts to fill the office."

I broke out in a laugh. "You aren't kidding, are you?"

"No! Think about it, Chester. If you were mayor of Gardenia, you would get invited to all of those big wig county functions, and interact with our state representatives and senators. You would be on the social invitation list of all the other mayors in the state. It would mean respectability for you, in the world beyond this dump. You are smart enough to pull this off, Chester, and get major clout for your trouble."

"But Snuff . . . I don't plan to live in Gardenia much longer. I plan to leave in a little over two weeks. I have accepted a scholarship to the university in California. I plan on kissing this place good bye. That has always been my dream. I can't hang around here. I have my future to think about."

"Being mayor is the first step to your future, Chester. Who do you think the people in California would most likely open their arms wide too, a former trash hauler or a former mayor? Stating that you have been the mayor of a town, somewhere in the Midwest, looks better on a job application than saying you hauled trash."

"You are pushing my buttons, aren't you, Snuff? Do you know a Dr. Mayo by any chance?"

"That name sounds familiar. I just don't know where from."

"I am not giving up my chance to go to college, Snuff. I have worked hard to earn my scholarships."

"This is the information, or computer age, Chester. Start your university classes on line. Take what classes you need to stay in good standing with the university, till you have the title of mayor secured. Your education is important, but opportunities in life are important too. Being a former mayor, a few years down the road, will get you in a lot of successful people's doors that an education won't. Rich people entertain and do business at parties. They invite mayors, governors, senators, and presidents. Your being a genuine mayor, of a town Called Gardenia, will get you in the door of a lot of rich people."

"I get your point, Snuff. You don't know what you are asking me though. I have lived and dreamed of the day I could kiss this place good bye. I don't have any friends, due to being the smelly dump kid that none of my classmates have ever wanted anything to do with. I am lonely, Snuff. I have been looking forward to making college friends."

"There are a lot of lonely people in this world, Chester. When you were being snubbed by your classmates, did you bother to look around and ask yourself if there was another kid in the same position? Gracie needed a friend. I watched you for years snub her at the school bus stop. You had a chance for a friend. You just didn't take it."

"Damn it, Snuff . . . I know you are right about everything, including Gracie. I didn't discover that Gracie needed a friend, till it was too late."

"This is a presidential election year, Chester. Your name will be on the ballot with the big boys. Opportunities don't come along every day like this. You must push life's buttons when they present themselves."

"I will talk to you tonight about it. The gate is opening. Look for me about nine. I am driving two shifts for Rosa to keep my head on straight and let the summer pass." I replied, knowing that Snuff knew my button was my desire to be respectable in life.

Snuff slapped me on the back and then left me standing. He jumped up in the driver's seat of his trash truck, and joined the line of garbage haulers that were starting to move thru Gardenia's dump gate.

Standing on the shoulder, watching the line of trucks move, I thought about a letter I had received from Zeke's Feet Detective Agency the day before. They had turned down my application to work for them. The letter was friendly, but said they only hired women and professionals. The women part I ignored. Suddenly, the title of mayor seemed appealing to me. In my thinking at that moment, I decided the title would give me a little clout or professional appeal. Being turned down by Zeke's Feet was not to my liking. I was more than a dump kid and a high school graduate. I was Chet Mayo and I was on my way up in life.

My new mission in life became to push Zeek Feet's owner's buttons, till he hired me. My grandfather had asked my grandmother out 57 times before she said yes, not that they were the perfect match. I would fill out 57 applications if I had to. I was now a button pusher and I intended to extract a job as a private eye from Zeke, whoever he was. It was a matter of pride, the difference between being a fish gutter and a surgeon, as Dr. Mayo put it.

I had to give Snuff credit. He was one smart old dude. He was also right about my education. I could choose beginning college classes that were offered on-line. He was also right that I needed to embrace my opportunities when they were presented, because opportunities were fleeting moments. I might not ever be presented with another opportunity to be mayor of somewhere.

CHAPTER SEVETEEN

Maturing and Waiting

Instead of making my way to Gordy's metal building covered grave yard to snoop around, I headed for Granny Mabel's place instead. My plan was to check out what her pit bulls were drinking from. Snuff had indicated that two of her sons, when they were small, stole urns and used them to water their dogs in. Following up clues was what being a private detective was about. Maybe her sons still liked to water their dogs from urns, even though they were now adults.

As usual, the pit bulls went to lunging on their chains and Granny Mabel burst out her front doors with the intention of throwing rocks at me.

"Wait!" I yelled at her. "I am here to talk to you about giving you some fruit jars!"

My grandfather had told me that the way to get along with Mabel was to give her jars when you found them in your dump loads. She needed new ones all the time to put her moonshine in.

Granny Mabel dropped her handful of rocks. "Well, come on up here. I don't want to talk business in the middle of the road." She yelled and then she told her pit bulls to shut up. They immediately returned to their normal sleeping positions on the ends of their chains.

As I walked past them, I paid attention to their watering dishes. Some were plastic bowls and some were coffee cans. Scanning as far back as I could see, to the position of the farthest dog, I spotted a tall vase like object. It looked heavy like an urn, but it had no lid. I wanted to get a closer look at it, but I didn't dare walk amongst the pit bulls to do so.

"Well . . . where are the jars?" Granny Mabel asked eyeing me as I stepped upon her mobile home's tiny wooden porch.

"I am driving for Rosa now. I was wondering if you would like to have jars when I find them. My grandfather and I shared the pint of special water you gave him on Christmas Eve. I promised him, before he died, that I would keep an eye out for them for you."

"Woody was my friend. I am happy to know you shared his special water, and that he thought about me on his death bed. That makes me feel really good. My ungrateful sons only ignore me and bring me misery. Do you know what it is like to have five sons and all of them gays?"

"You have five gay sons?" I asked.

"Yeah . . . it must have been something in the water here in the dump. I didn't make them that way." She replied displaying a hint of uneducated ignorance.

"Where are your boys and what are they up to?" I further asked, knowing that two of them had spent time in juvenile hall for stealing urns with ashes.

"I haven't seen the older three in about two years. They are too busy to mess with the likes of me." She replied.

"What about your younger two boys?" I asked knowing they were the ones I was interested in.

"One is in prison for stealing a hearse. He said it was just a prank. The police wouldn't believe him." She replied pulling a pack of cigarettes from her pocket and offering me one. I turned it down.

"What about your youngest?" I asked as she took a drag off of her smoke.

"He was here earlier, but left in a hurry for some reason. I could tell by the look on his face that he was up to something. Fifty is missing from my purse and I know that he has skipped out on the law. I won't see him again for months. He is supposed to go to court this week for stealing flags off of graves. I have never understood what his fascination is with grave yard and dead men's things. I won't see him again till the law catches up with him, and he ends up in jail or prison again."

"I am sorry about that. If you ever need anything lifted or chores done, yell at me, I will help you if I am around."

"Well, that is nice of you Chester. My knees are killing me today. Would you mind watering my dogs? I'll give you a mustard jar of my special water!"

"Keep your special water, Mabel. I don't need to be paid for helping you. Where is your outside water faucet, and how do I get past your pits?"

"They are pussy cats. If they growl at you, just show your teeth and growl at them back. They will run with their tails between their legs." She replied demonstrating by showing her teeth and growling at a pit that lay near her.

The dog immediately jumped up and ran off, with its tail between its legs. The pit put space between itself and Mabel, stretching its chain as far as it would go. I smiled thinking of all the times I had run from her and her dogs. To push the dog's buttons, and make them cower, was the simple showing of your teeth and a growl. I was amused. There was a lot I didn't know about pushing buttons. It occurred to me that those about me were each teaching me different, valuable, button pushing lessons. I was smart enough to make note of them. Mabel had just taught me how to get past her dogs. The vase like thing in the far weeds would be my payment, when I pushed the dog's buttons when Mabel wasn't looking.

After talking with her for a few minutes, and telling her that I was thinking about running for Mayor of Gardenia, I showed my teeth, growled, and proceeded to water her dogs. When I came to the dog in the back, I stooped down to pet it. That gave me an excuse to look closely at its watering dish. It looked like a marble cemetery vase. However, there was no lid and it contained stale water. I tipped it over to pour out the old water. When doing so, I discovered a metal plate on the bottom of it. I wiped the mud off and was shocked to find that it had an identification metal plate on its base. Ricardo Mendez was imprinted on its copper identification plate, along with his birth and death date. Mabel's son had taken Rosa's husband's ashes. I looked to see if Mabel was looking from the window. She wasn't. I took the heavy urn and stuck it inside of my summer coveralls top. Then, I left after finding a tin can to put water in for the Pit Bull. I immediately walked back to Rosa's trailer looking for her.

~   ~   ~

After leaving Granny Mabel's place, I returned to Rosa's mobile home where she was answering the phone and getting her drivers organized for the day. When I entered, I motioned toward the bulge in the front of my coveralls. In shock, she immediately hung up the phone and told the two drivers that were waiting for their assignments to wait outside. You could tell from the expression on her face that she knew what was beneath my coveralls. The two drivers didn't pay me any attention. They were happy to step outside and grab another cigarette before starting their day.

"Is that what I think it is?" She asked walking over to me and poking my coveralls front with one of her highly polished, perfectly manicured red nails.

"Before I show it to you, Rosa, you have to understand that the lid is missing and there are no ashes in it. I don't want you to go berserk on me, when I tell you where I found it."

"I know where you found it. Gordy had it." She replied with a hint of anger in her voice.

"No . . . it was another man that had it." I replied unzipping my summer weight trash hauler coveralls and pulling the dirty marble urn out. I turned it upside down so she could see the metal plate on the bottom.

"Oh . . . Mother Mary . . ." She stated in shock looking at it. You found him. Where are his ashes and the lid for it?"

I then proceeded to tell Rosa the story about Granny Mabel's youngest two sons and their thefts of cemetery urns and other items when they were about ten. I then told her that the youngest had been in and out of jail for crimes of that nature his whole life, and that he had been living off and on for the last two years with Mabel. I then told her where the urn was and what it had been used for the last couple of years.

"I am sorry, Rosa. You are not going to find his ashes. There is no telling where the fruitcake dumped them. He may have just dumped them outside your trailer door here, two years ago, to make the urn lighter to walk away with."

"Gordy didn't have my husband's ashes?"

"No . . . Snuff told me about the two boy's history and I went to Mabel's place and discovered the urn in the mud back where her pit bulls are chained. No one has ever discovered the urn, because no one goes near her dogs in fear of being attacked."

"I owe you, Chester. Do you know how many men I have hired to sneak around and look for Ricardo?"

"I have a pretty good idea, Rosa." I stated grinning. "However, I am the man, your super-snoop. I got the job done. I believe you are going to owe me a little bundle to add to my stash. Have it ready for me at the end of the day."

"Are you collecting on the nights in my bed too?" She shot back winking at me.

"I am a one woman man, Rosa. If I ever come to your bed, it will be because I want to be there, not because I am extracting payment from you."

"I like you, Chester Holly. You are a respectable man."

~   ~   ~

Rosa bonded with me over the incident of finding the urn. She had Ricardo's urn to take home to Mexico with her, and she was thankful for that. I did notice a few days after returning the urn to her, that she had all of her drivers smoking and putting their ashes in the urn just outside her trailer door. She was taking ashes home to Mexico to Ricardo's family, one way or another. I noticed that she smoked quite a few cigars that week, herself. On one of my trash stops that week, there was a metal pan with ashes from a barbecue grill. I rescued them. That night, when she was asleep, I finished filling her urn for her from the grill ashes. A man has to do what a man has to do, when it comes to the women in his life. She needed ashes to save face with Ricardo's family. I gave her ashes.

~　　　　　~　　　　　~

A couple of days after my dump road discussion with Snuff about running for Mayor, I went with him to the county commissioner and filled out the paperwork to call for an election in Gardenia for a mayor. During that time, I started on-line college classes. Keesha did not return, write, or call. Heeding Dr. Mayo and Snuff's brilliance, I revamped my plan to flee Gardenia. I saw myself leaving Gardenia with respectability, rather than going somewhere else and finding it.

Thirty days later, after approaching the county commissioner, a hearing was held and three of the five residents of Gardenia voted to have the election. My grandmother and Gordy Gardenia were furious. Snuff and I then filled out the paperwork, and I was placed on the November ticket as an independent candidate for mayor. Gordy, on hearing that I was officially running for mayor, filled out last minute paperwork and barely squeaked under the deadline to get his name on the ballot running against me. He also ran as an independent candidate. Neither of us had the Democratic or Republican endorsements to run otherwise. However, we were on the ballot with the big wigs as Snuff called them.

The election in November went just as Snuff had predicted. There were five legal Gardenia voters. Rosa, Carlos, and Mabel voted for me. My grandmother voted for Gordy and Gordy voted for himself. I was too young to vote for anyone. I thought it was quite ironic. I became the youngest mayor in the state . . . Mayor Chet Holly.

I attended my freshmen classes on-line and continued to drive for Rosa. At that point, I started to dream bigger dreams. Dr. Mayo had been right. We only get out of life what we dare to walk up and take from it. Opportunities are sometimes the gods we must test. Running for mayor was one of those 'Test the Gods" moments.

Keesha did not return. No matter how hard I tried, I could not get over loving her. She was always in the back of my mind, as were her boys, my sons. I had been madly in love with her, and that love just would not go away. I had my first semester of college classes in when I was sworn in as Mayor of Gardenia the following January, on the same day a new president was sworn in. Gordy Gardenia attended, but he was red faced and visibly pissed. My grandmother did not attend. However, my mother sobered up and was there for my swearing in, all smiles. That pleased me. I had always wanted her to crawl out of the bottle and see who I was and be proud of me. She bought me a special fountain pin as a gift to commemorate the day. I treasure it.

In February, I drew up a petition asking the town to consider annexing Snuff and my parents' places which were just outside of Gardenia. Once again, three votes to two, the measure passed. I thought Gordy was going to have a cow. He locked his dump down for a month to get even. Rosa just laughed and sent her trucks the extra hundred miles to dump elsewhere. Drivers from the city were annoyed, but they didn't really matter. What mattered was that the citizens of Gardenia no longer feared Gordy.

My elected term in office was for two years. Those two years started the January day I was sworn in. Snuff had been right. I was invited to all kinds of social events and parties thrown by the wealthy and big wigs of the state. I attended functions and was invited to dinners that my snooty high school classmates could only dream a life time about having an invitation to. Somewhere during my time of running and becoming, I honed my button pushing skills and became Mayor Chet Holly Mayo, not Mayor Chester Holly. Keesha had made a man of me in bed. Being mayor matured and made me a man in other ways.

The last fall of my second year as mayor of Gardenia, I once more looked forward to leaving Gardenia and following my dream to attend the university in California. I had taken on-line college classes as well as attended year round a junior college that was about forty miles from my home in Gardenia. I purchased myself a motorcycle and rode it to classes. I had worked hard for Rosa to support myself, never slacked in my duties as mayor, and studied hard.

I continued to be a 4.0 student. As a mayor, I am not sure how I rated. However, I did my best to see that the little town, at the very least, saw themselves as someone, not just dump dwellers. My mother climbed out of her bottle and supported me in whatever I chose to do as Mayor. My grandmother did not. She lived and breathed Gordy Gardenia, and continued to refer to me as the good for nothing bastard kid that she had to raise.

Gordy found my grandmother a driver for her hauler, a homeless man from the city. He did not pull in the money like my grandfather or I did. Karma sometimes bites you. My grandmother was in its teeth. She was squeaking by.

The hermit's murder remained unsolved for the fall and then the two years I was Mayor. I was shocked to find out that the hermit was Gordy's son. None of us knew that. He claimed the body and had it cremated. As it turned out, the hermit's mother was the funeral home girl that Gordy had dumped my grandmother for. The hermit's mother had been just as mentally challenged as him. Apparently, Gordy had married her for her family's money. Her inheritance was what he bought the dump property with.

The hermit's mother had been a recluse and stayed inside the trailer never speaking with anyone. After her parents died, Gordy had stuck her and the hermit in the mobile home and forgot about them. No one in the dump had paid any attention to the hermit or his mother, because they lived in such filth. Not even my grandmother knew that the hermit's mother was Gordy's legal wife. That left the residents of Gardenia questioning Gordy's story about having a young wife in the city, the mother of Gracie.

I wasn't on speaking terms with my grandmother during my two years as mayor. I wasn't sure what her reaction was, when she found out that Gordy had a wife in the dump. She had delusions that Gordy was going to marry her. The hermit's mother was in a nursing home in the city, paid for by Gordy. He couldn't legally marry anyone. I am sure that my grandmother had to of been shocked and disillusioned. Gracie never returned or kept in touch with anyone.

After Snuff's place was annexed into the town of Gardenia, I moved in with him. He never suspected that I did so, because I wanted to be near my memories of Keesha. My heart just would not let her and my sons go.

~ ~ ~

It was mid-December. I had less than a month left as Mayor of Gardenia. A knock sounded at Snuff's mobile home door. It was late and dark outside. I was sitting at Snuff's table filling out my 56th application, trying to get hired by Zeke's Feet Detective Agency. I was leaving for California the first week in January to finish my college years at the university in California. I was also sitting and making a list of what I felt I wanted to take with me. I did not run for a second term as mayor of Gardenia. I had accomplished what my grandfather and Snuff had asked of me. I was looking forward to the spring semester and the life of my dreams. I was finally about to kiss Gardenia goodbye. This time, I wasn't running away in the middle of the night. I had matured and was leaving as a man. I was nineteen, going on twenty.

A second knock sounded. Snuff was in the rear of the mobile home showering, so I got up to answer it.

"Rosa . . . what are you doing out this late and in the cold. It is six degrees out there." I stated pulling her inside and closing the door behind her. I then hugged her, and offered to help her off with her winter wrap.

Over the previous two years, Rosa had become very important to me. As Mayor of Gardenia, I always had my weekends filled with invitations of various sorts that required a date on my arm. Rosa had accompanied me everywhere from local charity balls to dinners in the governor's mansion. She was a gorgeous Hispanic woman, and turned heads wherever we went. Rosa and I understood each other. Much to my mother and grandmother's dismay, I took Rosa up my ladder of success with me. She was my companion and date for all social events. Rosa charmed the hell out of men/gods where ever we went. She pushed their higher class buttons, and I reaped many benefits from her ability to test the gods.

"I have to talk to you, Chester. The crying and the mortuary music have started again. I am not crazy, Chester. I want you to come with me now and hear it."

"It is probably just the wind howling. Maybe there is a piece of tin loose on one of Gardenia's mobile homes and it is making a whistling sound." I replied, reluctant to go back out in the night air. I had just settled down after having a long day running two trash routes. Heavy snow was supposed to start falling at any moment and I was looking forward to crawling in bed with a good novel. Books were still my best friends.

"It is not a loose piece of tin, Chester. Get your boots on. I am not giving you any choice. You are going to come and listen. You are mayor of this town. If demons are about to invade, exiting from Gordy's metal caged building, I don't want to be the one that didn't warn our town they were coming."

I laughed. Rosa never ceased to amuse me.

"What do I get for coming to listen to your crying voices and mortuary music?" I asked grinning.

I wasn't a seventeen year old kid anymore. Keesha had been gone for two and one half years without a word from her. I was considering starting to date. I was no longer the smelly dump kid. As mayor, I saw myself differently, and those around me also saw me differently. I had many invitations from young, politically motivated women my age around the state. I just had never felt comfortable in letting Keesha go. Also, the pretty, wealthy, political girls always reminded me of the cheerleaders and snooty girls from my high school years, who had turned their noses up at me when I was a dump kid. I was ready to love again. I just couldn't let myself love the types who had once ridiculed me and put me down. I was comfortable with Rosa being my constant companion on the weekends. However, there was nothing between us.

"One night with me . . ." Rosa replied smiling and handing me my jacket from its hook by the door.

"You know that I never take you up on that type of payment. How many nights do you owe me now for different favors, fifty or so?" I asked laughing, and taking my jacket from her. I then sat down to put on my boots.

"Would you rather that I promise you 25 times in my bed for coming to listen to my crying and the mortuary music?" She retorted pulling my stocking hat from the coat rack and haphazardly sticking it on my head.

"You know that I am leaving for California in three weeks. I don't have time to collect the 25 times or the fifty others." I replied to annoy her.

"It is not my fault that you are such a poor lover, that you fear crawling in bed with me and disappointing me with your lack of experience." She shot back to annoy me.

"I am not a seventeen year old boy anymore, Rosa. If there is no crying in the wind or mortuary music, I am staying the night at your place and collecting some of what is due to me." I stated winking at her.

"You are a tease, just like me Chester. You could have crawled in my bed long ago, you have not. I know about your tuxedo girl and your commitment to her. Maybe I have seen you as a safe companion, one that lets me be faithful to my dead husband. This is Rosa that you are talking to." She replied winking back.

Rosa was in her fifties, but you couldn't tell it. She was one gorgeous Hispanic woman on my arm on the weekends. She was serious clout. I had moved out of her trailer, because as a man, she had tempted the hell out of me at times. There had been times I had wanted to crawl into her bed, in spite of my love for Keesha.

"I am not kidding this time, Rosa. You are going to pay up tonight, if I don't hear your music and crying in the wind."

"I should be so lucky." She shot back. "You are all talk and campaign promises, Mayor Holly."

"Maybe it is time for me to put up or shut up." I replied winking at her.

"Maybe it is time for me to make you put up or shut up." She retorted winking back.

There was no getting the best of Rosa in a conversation. That was why all the men loved her and wanted her. She teased the devil out of them.

"I dare you to make me tonight." I replied standing after getting my snow boots on. I leaned over and kissed her on her cheek. That was usually as far as it ever went between us. "Give me just a moment. I want to walk back and let Snuff know where I am going."

"Well, hurry," Rosa replied. "Sometimes the crying and music don't last long."

I walked back to the rear of the trailer and shouted in Snuff's open bathroom door telling him where I was heading and why. He stuck his head out of the shower and listened.

"Be careful, Chet. Wolf Dog's death has never been solved, and three more women around the county have come up missing since you have been mayor.

"I will just be at Rosa's place, Snuff. She is spooked from wind blowing on a piece of loose tin or something. I think I will spend the night over at her place, just to pacify her."

"Is that what they call love making now-a-days, pacifying a woman?" He asked laughing.

"There isn't anything between Rosa and me, except friendship. However, don't expect me home. I think I am ready to give in to Rosa's flirting. She has been my companion for two years. I think I am ready to let Keesha go."

Snuff and I had a common bond. We both had girlfriends that had discarded us and disappeared. Snuff had become my best friend over the past two and one half years, and Rosa had become my companion. There was a lesson I learned during my term as Mayor. Friends do not have to be the same age as you. In high school, the seniors only ran around with other seniors and so on down the ranks. As Mayor Chet Holly, I had discovered a sea of people that wanted to be my friends, and they were all ages. Snuff and Rosa were in their fifties. Granny Mabel was in her seventies and Carlos was thirty-six. I was nineteen, almost twenty. Once upon a time, I had wanted to kiss Gardenia goodbye and never remember my dump town or its people ever again. Now, the same dump people were my friends. I was going to miss them when I went to California.

Snuff grinned. "Don't you think she is a little old for you?"

"What is age, Snuff? Rosa has stood by me since the day I moved out of my grandmother's place. I feel more comfortable with her than girls my age. I trust Rosa."

"You have a screw loose, Chester. You can have any girl you want, if you let yourself. God knows they flock after you, now that you are the state's most famous young mayor."

"That is just it, Snuff. They flock after me now. I want to be with a woman who accepted me the way I was before I became famous in this state as its youngest mayor. Rosa has always accepted me. I think I am going to take her up tonight, if she asks me to come to her bed."

I then returned to the front of the trailer and to Rosa who was nervously waiting.

"I heard you tell Snuff that you were going to take me up tonight, Chester. You know that your mother and grandmother will wear white sheets and try to whoop my ass when they find out." She stated flirting with me. Flirting was who Rosa was.

"Carry your lighter, Rosa. Old white sheets sometimes need to be burned."

"Are you worth getting my ass whooped?" Rosa asked as we exited Snuff's mobile home. She had asked me that once before, years prior.

"I don't know, Rosa. I think I told you two or so years ago that I have only been with one woman. I may be a total dud in the love making department. My girlfriend back then did leave me. However, I am a fast learner and a 4.0 student. You could teach me to love you the way you want to be loved." I replied as we tread the heavy snow to get to her vehicle. She handed me her keys.

I then drove Rosa back to her place. There was no crying in the wind or mortuary music. However, there was eventual howling in the wind in Rosa's bedroom. We slept together for the first time. I tried not to think about Keesha, as I found pleasure in Rosa's arms. I was nineteen going on twenty. It was time. Keesha had made a man out of me when I was sixteen going on seventeen. At nineteen going on twenty, Rosa taught me what it was like to satisfy a woman and then her satisfy you. I spent a remarkable night in Rosa's arms that led to two weeks of nights in her bed. I was happy. However, there is always a happy lull before a storm.

It was New Year's Eve and Rosa and I had made our presence known at several parties thrown in the city at various wealthy individuals home. As usual, Rosa had charmed the devil out of everyone at the parties. However, I was the lucky young fool that she gave herself to. We had purposely returned home about an hour before midnight. We wanted to celebrate the New Year's arrival together in privacy. I was less than a week away from leaving for California. I had my plane ticket purchased. We wanted the time together, to say to each other all the things left unspoken, and spend one last magical, momentous night in each other's arms.

It was about five minutes till midnight and we were both lying stark naked watching the ball about to drop on television to mark the New Year. Suddenly, I heard what sounded like crying in the wind, only there was no wind outside. Then I heard the faint sounds of canned, religious, elevator music. The music was eerily sad sounding.

"What is that?" I asked sitting up straight in Rosa's bed and turning the volume down on the television using the remote.

"That is the crying I have been telling you about for almost three years." She said sitting up, with a frightened look crossing her face.

"Do you hear sad religious music?" I asked straining my ears. "Is that the mortuary music that you talk about hearing?"

"That is it, Chester. The demons are late coming this year. The night of the living dead and Halloween were two months ago. Why are they choosing tonight to haunt me?"

"That isn't demons, Rosa. You stay here in this trailer and lock the doors. I am going to follow the sounds and see where they are coming from." I stated jumping up and forcing one leg quickly into my dress pants and jumping about trying to force my other leg in. I was trying to hurry. I then thrust my arms into my black dinner jacket, ignoring putting on a shirt.

I was no longer a dump kid, even though I still drove two trash routes for Rosa. I was a mayor, a politician, and I dressed appropriately for occasions such as New Years Eve parties.

With dress pants and dinner jacket haphazardly put on, I ran barefoot down Rosa' mobile home hallway toward the front door. I slipped my bare feet in my black dress shoes and then grabbed a work coat from the coat rack by the door that belonged to Carlos. In the moment, I couldn't recall where I had discarded my overcoat, when Rosa and I had returned after an evening of parties, dancing, and socializing. Rosa and I had practically torn each other's clothing off just inside the door and down the hall way heading for the bedroom in a frenzied moment of wanting each other. Carlos' work coat had to do in the moment.

"Take these, Chester . . ." Rosa stated handing me a flash light and a small digital camera. "I want to see what that demon looks like, if you catch up with him." She stated, while standing stark naked helping me get into Carlos's jacket and stocking hat. I was in a hurry. She had always told me that the crying and music never lasted long.

I quickly kissed her on the lips and then opened the front door and headed out into the winter night to follow Rosa's crying in the wind and mortuary music. To my dismay, the sounds stopped just as I stepped out of Rosa's door. I stood and waited a moment or so for the sounds to start again. They didn't do so. Then I turned around and reentered Rosa's trailer, knowing that I could not follow sounds that were not being made.

"Do you believe me now?" Rosa asked, helping me back off with Carlos's work coat and then out of my clothing that I had quickly put on.

"I believe you," I replied, taking her in my arms and resting my head on top of hers. "I think we should put a sweat suit and tennis shoes on my side of the bed, just in case the sounds start again."

"You were definitely a little slow in getting your naked butt back in your tuxedo pants and jacket," She laughed. "Not that I have not enjoyed watching your naked butt dance around in a frenzy trying to put clothes on."

About that time, gun shots and fireworks sounded outside. We knew the ball had dropped and it was New Year's.

"Happy New Years Rosa . . . !" I said turning her face up to mine. I then kissed her passionately and she returned the kiss. We celebrated the moment, standing in our birthday suits just inside her mobile home door.

To my dismay, my kiss under the mistletoe with Keesha, replayed in my mind at the same time. I just couldn't get away from my memories of her, no matter how hard I tried. When spring and high school graduation time rolled around once more, three years would have elapsed since she disappeared. At that same time, I would be entering my senior year in the summer semester at the university in California I had plane reservations for January fifth to fly to California. Gardenia's new Mayor, Rosa, would take office on the sixth of January. She had beat Snuff in the mayor election. Gordy, who had failing health, according to Mabel, did not run. Gordy and my grandmother did vote in the election. However, they were wild cards and no one knew which candidate they voted for, or why. There were ten legal registered voters in Gardenia's second mayor election, due to annexation and a couple new drivers moving in and living in travel trailers behind Rosa's mobile home. There were ten registered voters in the election. Rosa got six votes and Snuff got four.

CHAPTER EIGHTEEN

Reflections in the Mirror

The next morning, New Years Day, I was a little spooked due to having heard the crying and the sad music, that Rosa called mortuary music. Ignoring the fact that my grandmother and I had not been on the best of terms for a couple of years or so, I decided to check on her. We were civil and spoke to each other in public, but there was no actual relationship between us. She was cold, distant, aging, and slowly turning into a withered up, hundred pound prune that really needed to be in a nursing home. My grandmother was just in her sixties, but looked in her nineties and like death warmed over. She had not aged well. I blamed it on her living in the shadows of the dump and breathing its toxins her whole life.

Leaving Rosa's place, after fixing her breakfast and serving it to her in bed, I walked across the dump road and stepped upon the porch of my grandmother's mobile home. I tried my key and it worked. It was the same key I had used growing up. My grandmother had never changed the locks. That surprised me. I let myself in and stepped inside.

"Grandma . . . ," I yelled. "It is me, Chester."

There was no answer. I decided that she might have stayed at my mother and stepfather's place the previous evening, to wait the New Year in. Maybe she just hadn't made it home yet. I eyed my grandfather's four TV sets which still set stacked in the living room. He would have celebrated New Year's Eve by watching the ball drop on four screens. He had been a character. I had loved him, and he had been a father to me. I had not loved my grandmother. I felt a little guilty about that. However, my grandmother never let me get close to her. She always pushed me away and continuously hurt my feelings calling me a bastard child.

I had eaten some salty bacon with Rosa before walking over to my grandmother's place. My mouth was really dry. I decided to grab something from my grandmother's refrigerator to alleviate the problem, possibly a soda. I walked over to the fridge, opened its door and looked to see what there was. There wasn't any soda, but there was a gallon of milk. My plan was to just to pour a small amount into a juice glass to drink and wash the saltiness from my mouth. As I pulled the gallon jug of milk from the refrigerator shelf, I gasped seeing something that had been missing.

"Oh God . . . !" I stated, placing the gallon of milk on the kitchen cabinet. I then reached to the back of the top shelf of the refrigerator and pulled out something very familiar.

My grandfather's ashes, in his Russian gnome nesting doll urn, had been in the refrigerator for possibly two or so years. I quickly placed the gnome on the cabinet top and grabbed some paper towels from a holder on the kitchen wall and went to wiping water condensation and mold from the container. Part of the urns paint came off with the wiping.

"I am so sorry, grandpa. Not only did she cremate you in Hell's fires, she then buried you in the North Pole and froze your cremated ass off."

I spent at least thirty minutes cleaning up the outside of the urn using spray cleaners and a whole roll of paper towels. I didn't dare look inside the gnome to see what was growing there. IF there was anything growing inside, it had to be my grandfather's righteous indignation at how poorly he had been treated in death and burial. After cleaning the urn the best I could, I returned it to its perch above the four televisions, with the intentions of taking him and his urn with me later, when I left. It was time to stand my ground with my grandmother and see that his ashes were buried in Mt. Pleasant.

In spite of my total shock and churning stomach, from having to clean up a molded burial urn, I had solved one mystery. My grandfather's missing ashes were found, and they had not been discarded in Gordy's dump. That was a relief. I remembered my grandmother stating that her lost baby's ashes were in her button box in the top of her closet. When I fell apart after Keesha was gone, I had forgotten about them. Rising, I made a quick trip down the mobile home hallway and entered my grandmother's bedroom and then opened her closet door. There was no button can on her top shelf. I was relieved. Maybe that had been one of her delusions. At least I would not have a second urn to clean up.

I returned to the kitchen and seated myself at the kitchen table. It was a quiet place to think for a few minutes. I had solved my grandfather's missing ashes mystery. I wished that the origin of Rosa's night sounds would be equally as easy to solve. Rosa swore the sounds had been coming from the metal building that covered the forgotten, tiny, family cemetery. Before leaving for California, I decided I had to somehow get in that building and look around, to appease Rosa and to set my own mind at ease.

I didn't believe in hell or demons. I did believe that there were crazies like my grandmother and Mabel's son who pulled all kinds of off the wall crap, frightening normal people into thinking they were demons.

I waited for about an hour, but my grandmother didn't return. Taking my grandfather's ashes, I walked across the dump to Snuff's place. I would leave my grandfather's ashes there, till I made arrangements for their burial. I also needed to finish making the list I had started the night before, concerning last minute details that needed to be taken care of before I boarded my plane. Also, I had some last minute packing to do.

It was New Year's Day and Rosa's trash haulers weren't moving. Gordy's dump was closed for the holiday. It was a rare free day for me. I knew that Rosa would stay in bed till noon after eating the breakfast I made her. I had things to do, and people to say goodbye to. It was the first day of January and I was catching a plane to California on the 5th. I smiled thinking about Rosa. She had deserved breakfast in bed. Boy, had she deserve breakfast in bed!

~   ~   ~

Entering Snuff's place, I hung up my jacket on one of the hooks by the door, set my grandfather's urn on a bench there, and then prepared to head for my room to put on some clean jeans and a sweat shirt. I had on my dress pants and dinner jacket from the night before. As I reached my bedroom door, Snuff stuck his head out of the bathroom. His face was all lathered up. He was in the middle of shaving.

"You better get the lead out, if we are going to get there on time." He stated and then withdrew his head back in the bathroom.

I hurried to the door, "Be where on time . . . ?" I asked sticking my head in the bathroom door. My necktie was loose around my neck and its two ends were hanging down on my half buttoned white dress shirt.

"Your stepfather's birthday party . . ." He stated between swipes with a razor. "New Year's Day is his birthday."

"Damn it." I replied in disgust. My mother had made a point of ensuring that I said I would be at her trailer for his 50th birthday party lunch. I had forgotten in all of the excitement of New Year's Eve and the discovery of my grandfather's ashes. I now knew why my grandmother wasn't at home. She was at my mother's place, probably helping to get the party together. My grandmother liked my stepfather, but hated her own daughter. I never understood my grandmother's bond with him. He was a mean, crude, rude, red neck. He had been my stepfather since I was two. I was not fond of him.

"How late are we?" I asked pulling off my tie and quickly unbuttoning my shirt.

"We were supposed to be there ten minutes ago. I fell asleep in my chair out front and just woke up. I called your mother and told her that you had a little mayor business and that you and I would be twenty minutes late."

"Thanks Snuff." I replied. "Can I share the bathroom with you?"

Sure he said, moving over to the second sink and continuing shaving. "How was the mayor business you have just returned from taking care of?"

I grinned. "Well, I served her breakfast in bed this morning. Does that give you any clue?" I replied putting toothpaste on my brush in an attempt to do a quick brushing. I still had that salty bacon taste in my mouth.

Snuff laughed as he glanced up at my reflection in the full wall mirror above the twin sinks. I stood bare chest, trying to do a quick clean up. I didn't have time to shower. I started to brush my teeth and took a look at my red eyes in the mirror as he eyed me. I hadn't gotten any sleep the night before. I glanced at Snuff who seemed to be staring at my reflection in the plate glass wall mirror.

"Is something wrong?" I asked seeing how seriously he was eyeing me.

"Look at your reflection in the mirror, Chester, and then look at mine. What do you see?" He asked in a scary, serious voice.

I spit out my mouth of toothpaste, rinsed real quickly, and then stared into the mirror at myself and then into the mirror at him.

"Well . . . what am I supposed to be seeing?" I asked eyeing our two reflections. Snuff in ways was an older version of me.

"Don't move!" Snuff stated scooting past me quickly and exiting the bathroom.

In a moment or so, he returned with a snapshot. He handed it to me. "Who is in that snapshot?" He stated handing me a black and white cameral snapshot.

"It is me when I was about sixteen or seventeen." I replied looking at the photo of myself wearing jeans and no shirt. "I don't recall when this photo was taken, or why it is in black and white, but it is me. Why do you ask?"

"That photo isn't of you, Chester. It is me when I was sixteen. Look in the mirror, Chester. Take a really good look at our reflections and tell me what you see. I may be crazy, but I know what I am seeing." Snuff replied in a serious tone I had never heard before.

I looked back into the mirror and Snuff removed his shirt and stood bare chest staring into the mirror.

"Oh my god . . ." I muttered suddenly realizing what he was getting at. He was just an older version of me. We had the same facial features, chest features, and the same long fingers and tiny black mole on the back of our left hands. I was in shock and didn't know what to make of it. I had red hair. "What color hair did you have when you were young?" I asked still not wanting to believe what I was seeing.

"I had red hair, the same color as yours." He replied, as he suddenly held to the edge of the vanity in front of him.

I eyed my own red hair in the mirror.

"I . . . think you might be my kid, Chester. I don't understand how. The doctor said my missing girlfriend and I were going to have a girl. I looked into the mirror when you started brushing your teeth and saw myself in your reflection. Maybe, I am just grasping at straws wanting to solve the mystery of my missing girlfriend. Maybe I am reading into things, what isn't there."

"I am shocked as you are, Snuff. Look at this mole on the back of my hand. You have the same identical one. Tell me that I am the one that is hallucinating." I stated holding the back of my hand over for him to look at. He crossed my arm with his left and compared them. His hands and long fingers were just older versions of mine.

"Who has your mother told you is your father, Chester?"

"My mother got pregnant when she was fifteen and ran away. She didn't return, till I was about two. My grandmother and mother have always refused to tell me who my father is. I have asked, begged, and demanded. They have always refused to tell me."

"You have to belong to me, Chester. You have to be the baby that my girl-friend was two days overdue with, when she walked along the dump rim and disappeared. How the doctor made a mistake telling me you were a girl, I don't know. However, you are the spitting image of me, when I was sixteen. How did your mother end up with you?" He asked in a shocked voice. "If I am your father, your mother has to know what happened to Jennifer. I have driven myself crazy looking for my missing girlfriend, your mother."

204

"Let us not make accusations, till we have our blood DNA tested. We could just be two men who are look-a- likes. Doctors don't usually make gender mistakes. Yours did tell you your baby was going to be a girl."

"I don't know what to make of it, Chester. Are you willing to give blood and have the test tomorrow morning? We don't have much time, with you leaving for California on the 5th."

"I am willing, Snuff. To be honest, I would be thrilled to find out you were my father. I have begged my family to tell me who my father is. They have always refused to tell me."

"If you are my son, Chester, I am going to be one proud man."

"My family has never been proud of me, Snuff. To find out that you are my father would make me one proud man. They don't come any better than you. I won't confront my mother till we are sure. I don't want any trouble with her or my stepfather, if it turns out that we are just look-a-likes."

"I have waited this long, Chester. I can wait on the results of a DNA test. If you are my son, I am locking this place up and going with you to California. If you are my son, I want to be a part of your day to day life, and follow your accomplishments. I missed out on your youth. I don't want to miss out knowing you as a man."

"You're the best, Snuff. You are already my best friend. You can go with me to California if you want, whether you are my father or not."

"I feel the same about you, Chester." He replied.

We both then decided not to attend my stepfather's birthday party, in fear we might let it slip what we suspected and about the DNA test we would be taking the following day. We didn't want to spook my mother into climbing into a bottle, or into disappearing.

In the back of my mind, I doubted that Jennifer was my mother. I had a nagging suspicion that Snuff had possibly slept with my alcoholic mother when she was fifteen. Maybe Snuff had played around on his Jennifer, although he had never admitted it. My grandfather had stated once, that he thought Jennifer had walked because Snuff wouldn't commit to her. Was it possible that my mother, pregnant at fifteen, was the reason? Jennifer's baby was supposed to be a girl.

New Year's Day passed and became history. The following morning, Snuff and I took time off from our trash routes, met at a doctor's office, and gave blood to be tested. I hoped, as much as he did, that I was his son.

~ ~ ~

After Snuff and I left the doctor's office, we both went our separate way. He had his trash route to run for the day, and I was driving a route for Rosa. About noon, my stomach was growling. I parked my trash hauler along the curb in front of Mc Dee's fast food to grab something quick to go. I was late running my route, due to the visit to the doctor for blood tests. I was also out of route on the far side of the city where the factories were. As I was standing in one of two lines waiting to order, I glanced over and Motor Mouth was standing in the other.

"Chester . . ." She stated smiling. "I am here on my lunch break. If you aren't meeting anyone, would you like to eat with me?" She asked like she was really glad to see me.

"Sure," I stated. My stepfather was her uncle. I couldn't ignore her.

"If you get your food first . . ." She stated. "Grab that back booth, where it is quieter, so we can talk."

"I have to eat in a hurry. I am running behind time on my route." I stated to let her know I would not be sitting with her long, or had the time for lengthy stories about chicken processing. I was sure that she would talk about chicken guts the whole time we ate, embarrass me, and annoy those seated around us.

"I am short on time too," She replied.

I got thru the line first, so I claimed the back booth for a quick visit. I would eat my food after I got back outside and in the hauler. Talk about chicken guts and food just didn't go together. I was sure that was how our lunch conversation was going to go. I hadn't forgotten my graduation night dinner. I opened my straw and popped it into my soda, as she sat down with her sack of food and soft drink.

"What's up?" I asked trying to get to the point of any conversation with her, and then excuse myself as quickly as possible.

"I have an apology to make to you, Chester. It is long in coming."

"What do you have to apologize to me about?" I asked.

"How long has it been, since you graduated from high school?" She asked unwrapping her burger.

"It will be three years the end of May, why?"

"I am older now and realize that my uncle, your stepfather, used me to delay you going home after graduation. He purposely asked me to come along that night, and paid me fifty dollars to monopolize the conversation, and talk about the chicken plant. He said he needed to stall you, while your real gift was being prepared. I was young, stupid, and did as he asked. At the time, I had my eye on a red handbag that cost about fifty. I saw it as any easy way to obtain it. Anyway, I now realize there was no gift being prepared for you." She stated pouring ketchup on her fries.

"I am not sure what you are talking about. No, there was no gift after the dinner." I replied.

"Back at that time, Chester, I didn't know your stepfather and my father were white sheet men. I happened to pick up the upstairs phone receiver, a few days after your graduation, and heard my father and your stepfather laughing and talking about some black girlfriend of yours. I heard my uncle, your stepfather, state that he had scared the pee out of your black girlfriend, while you were walking down the aisle at graduation."

"Oh . . . God," I muttered thinking of Keesha and her two little boys. Rosa had told me how my stepfather, wearing a sheet, had tried to frighten her. "What did you just say?"

"I am really sorry, Chester. I had nothing to do with what happened to your girlfriend that night. I was just a stupid young girl, who was making an easy fifty to buy a red purse."

"Why would my stepfather want to scare my girlfriend?" I asked in shock.

"Your stepfather was about to move up in rank in the Klan and couldn't do it because you, his son, was dating and sleeping with a black girl. He was furious when the Klan confronted him with it. He purposely was late to your graduation. It is my understanding, from bits of conversation I have heard since then, that he raped her, beat her, and then started in on her two little boys. He then showered, changed clothes, and made his way to graduation. Afterward, your grandmother did her part by offering her a ride with the intent of getting rid of her."

"Are you positive about what you are telling me?" I asked in total shock with my heart dropping into my shoes.

"Your stepfather watched from the dump rim for you to leave for graduation. When you were gone, he put on his white sheet, walked down from the rim to Snuff's place, and scared your girlfriend. He then had his way with her, with her two little boys watching. Your grandmother and some man with a name like Gorman got rid of your girlfriend and her two little boys afterward. Anyway, that is what I have heard my father insinuate. I am sorry, Chester. I was young, stupid, and didn't know they were using me."

After almost three years, I had just heard my first clues as to what had happened to Keesha.

"Do you know where my grandmother and the man with a name like Gorman took my girlfriend back then? Did they put her and the boys on a bus or take them to an emergency room?" I asked trying to keep my voice calm. I needed to know what she knew. Alienating her, by yelling at her, would not get me any further information

"I don't know Chester. Only your grandmother, or the Gorman man, can tell you that. All I know is that it was a white sheet thing. Your stepfather was getting back at you, because you had cost him his promotion in the ranks of the white sheets."

"Thanks for telling me this, I owe you one." I stated trying to remain calm. I might need more information from her. I didn't want to alienate her.

"There is something else I have got to tell you, Chester."

"What is it?" I asked hoping for a clue as to where Key was.

"Your stepfather didn't just scare and rape your black girlfriend. When she couldn't get up to defend her two kids, he then beat the two little boys till they were unconscious. Afterward, he went into the trailer and gathered up what things he thought belonged to her and the boys, to make it look like she packed and left you. He carried those possessions up into the dump and set them afire."

I bit my lip to control my anger. Motor mouth was being up front with me. I had to give her credit for that. Then, I thought about Rosa. I had been sleeping with her for a couple of weeks. Now, I was finally on the verge of having a clue as how to go find Keesha. I blushed, feeling like a cheating husband.

"Why are you blushing Chester?" Motor Mouth asked.

"The V in your neckline is a little low." I whispered lying. "I'm sorry, I peeked."

"Maybe I should pull it a little lower." She whispered back, smiling from ear to ear. "I have never had a mayor peek down my blouse. Do you like what you see?"

Then, I really blushed.

"I have got to go. I am running really late on my route. Call me sometime." I stated quickly and then got up, not knowing quite what to say.

"You can definitely expect a call from me Chester." Motor Mouth replied, flashing me a flirtatious grin.

As bad as I hated to admit it, she did have a pretty smile. Also, I had to give her credit for being gutsy enough to admit her part in the disappearance of Keesha. That alone said she was a good person.

As soon as my trash route was over for the day, I was going to have a long time coming confrontation with my grandmother. I wasn't my grandfather. I was not going to roll over like a dog and forget what she had taken from me. After her, it was my stepfather that was going to get the brunt of my anger. He had raped and beaten Keesha. I was his son. It didn't get any more demeaning than that. I was so angry.

There was one good outcome from having lunch with Motor Mouth. There was the possibility that Keesha was somewhere in another state afraid to contact me. I would find her and make things right with her. At the same time, I didn't know how I was going to tell Rosa I wouldn't be sleeping with her anymore. Rosa had been my constant companion, and had hung on my arm at every major event for the last two going on three years. We were seen as a couple around the state. How could I tell her that my time and nights with her had been wonderful, but I wanted to go find Key? I loved Rosa, but I was in love with Keesha. She was the other half of me, my soul mate.

~   ~   ~

After putting in my day running my route for Rosa, I returned to Snuff's place to clean up and then go confront my grandmother. Letting myself in, I was surprised to find Snuff sitting in the dark crying like a baby.

"What's wrong?" I asked flipping on the living room light.

"She is dead, Chester."

"Who is dead?" I asked seeing that he was beyond distraught.

He didn't say who, but he held up a very soiled, torn, and rotted maternity top. "It is hers. I picked it out for her myself."

Then, I realized that he was referring to his girl friend Jennifer, who had disappeared.

"Where did you get it, Snuff?" I asked taking it from him and turning it around and over looking at it.

"Do you remember me telling you that the county hired me to tear the hermit's health hazard trailer down?"

"What does that have to do with this maternity top?"

"I started tearing the mobile home down a couple of days ago. It was one awful mess with fleas, roaches, and mice droppings everywhere. There was also dog poop six inches deep in the corners. Anyway, I was removing and loading everything out of his bedroom into a dumpster. I was about to throw Wolf Dog's pillow into it, when the scrap end of a woman's garment fell out of its pillow case. It was this maternity top. Wolf Dog's pillow was black with dirt and body oils. I honestly don't think the pillowcase had been washes for fifteen or twenty years. That maternity top was inside the case. Your mother was wearing it, the day she took a walk and never came back."

"Did you look to see if there was anything else belonging to her, in the trailer?"

"I tore that place a part, Chester, thinking there might be some clue as to what happened to her and the baby she was carrying. There was nothing there, but the maternity top you are holding. The hermit had it stuffed inside of his pillow case. I don't know what to make of it. The hermit would just have been a fourteen or fifteen year old kid when she disappeared. Your mother, Woody's girl, and he were about the same age. How did he come up with Jennifer's maternity top, and why did he have it hidden?"

"Did you call the sheriff and show him the top?"

"The sheriff photographed it and then went his way. I don't think he believed me, that the top is hers."

"Do you think someone beheaded Wolf Dog because he might have seen what happened to your girlfriend?" I asked. "He became more sociable and talkative when he became a picker and started riding the backs of our trucks to make himself a living."

"I have asked myself the same thing, Chester. At the same time, I asked the hermit numerous times over the years, if he knew what had happened to my girlfriend or had heard anyone talking about it. I have asked everyone in the dump area that on a yearly basis trying to get information. Wolf Dog has never given me any indication that he knew my Jennifer. I just don't understand how he got the top and why he hid it. Now, he is dead. I will never know the answer."

"I am sorry Snuff. I really am. It could be possible he just found it in the dump and kept it for some reason." I replied seating my-self on the couch beside him and handing him back the rag of a maternity top. "I need to tell you something, Snuff, about a girl that I was once in love with. You aren't the only one that has a missing girlfriend."

"What do you mean?" He asked in reply.

I then told Snuff all about my secret tuxedo girl named Keesha and her boys. Then I replayed my conversation with Motor Mouth concerning my stepfather beating and raping Keesha. I couldn't hold back my tears.

"So, my secret cleaning lady was actually your lover for three months, and I might actually have a couple of grandsons out there somewhere?"

"She was more than my lover Snuff. She was that special someone you only meet once in a lifetime. I did something really stupid. I thought she walked out on me because she was mad at me over it. I didn't have any clue that she had been assaulted and my boys subjected to cruelty. I have spent three years hoping she would get over being mad at me, and call me."

"There is something weird going on in and around Gardenia, Chester. Women disappear, a mentally challenged man gets his head chopped off, and the night winds make crazy noises."

"You have heard the night sounds that Rosa speaks of?" I asked in shock.

"Yeah . . . I have heard them. They sound like voices crying and a distant stereo playing sad, religious, mortuary music." Snuff replied getting up from his position on the couch. He took the maternity blouse, lovingly folded it, and then took it to the kitchen and put it in a gallon size plastic zipper bag for safe keeping due to it being in such dirty and fragile condition.

"When did you hear the sounds last," I asked, "And which direction did they come from?"

"I heard them on New Year's Eve. It was a few minutes before the neighbors' fireworks and guns were shot off signaling the New Year. I was out side with my own gun getting ready to shoot it off. That is when I heard it. It seemed to float over the dump coming from the dump road. I thought at first the crying was some man beating a wife somewhere. Then the crazy music started."

That settled it in my mind. The sounds had to be originating from Gordy's place. I was at Rosa's place on New Year's Eve and heard the sounds. Gordy's metal building was between Rosa and Snuff's places. Gordy was up to something, but what? I was sure that my grandmother knew the answers. She was always hanging out at his place, now that my grandfather was gone.

CHAPTER NINETEEN

The Confrontation

I had just showered and put on clean jeans and a T-shirt in preparation to go to my grandmother's place to confront her, when a knock sounded at Snuff's door. Snuff had disappeared into his bedroom with a bottle of whiskey, just prior to my getting into the shower. I knew he was going to get drunk. Finding Jennifer's maternity top had brought home to him the reality that his girlfriend was dead. You can live with hope. Thinking she was alive somewhere, raising his baby as a single parent, had kept him going. Hope had kept him looking for her. Now, his hope was gone. In the back of my mind, I prayed that Keesha and the boys were alive and well, that my grandmother had just driven them to another city or state and kicked her out. All fools dream.

I walked to the door in bare feet. I hadn't managed to get my socks on yet. Once there, I opened it. The icy wind, suddenly blowing in the door, made me shiver.

"Mom . . ." I stated in surprise, seeing who it was. "Come in and get out of the cold. If you are here about me missing dad's party, I had good reason." I quickly spit out.

"Don't worry about that, Chester. I think your stepfather has left me. He didn't even show up for his own birthday party."

"He what?" I asked in shock.

"He didn't show up for his own 50th birthday party. All his white sheet friends were there, his brother, and niece that works in the chicken plant. Needless to say, I was a little embarrassed. To be honest, I am happy he has left me. I am free now to clean up my act and move on with my life."

"You are happy my stepfather has left you?" I asked in shock. My mother had always stuck to him like glue, including going out with him of a daytime on his trash hauler.

"I don't have any reason to be afraid anymore, Chester. It is time for your stepfather to go his way and I mine. He just beat me to the punch."

"You have always hung on him like glue, mom. I don't get it."

"I needed the protection of the white sheets, Chester. The person I have always been afraid of didn't dare mess with them or chance my telling them what I know."

"Do you want to fill me in on who you have been afraid of? This topic is new to me, Mom."

"That is why I am here. I am no longer afraid of my past. I want to make things right with you and with Snuff." She replied.

"You have a beef with Snuff?" I asked in shock.

"No, it is him that has a beef with me, but he doesn't know it."

Snuff's bedroom opened and Snuff stepped out quietly with the intent of using the bathroom facilities. Hearing me and my mother speaking about him, he walked up the long mobile home hallway heading for the living room and stood in the shadows of the hallway listening.

"Does it have anything to do with who my father is?" I asked fishing.

"Before I start, Chester, I want to tell you that I am really proud of you and what you have accomplished; in case I have failed to tell you so. Being the mayor of a town, at your age, is really something."

"That is the nicest thing you have ever said to me, mom. Thank You!" I replied with my eyes tearing up. I then hugged her. I was nineteen years old and hearing my mother, tell me for the first time, she was proud of me.

My next expectation was her telling me that she had slept with Snuff when she was young, and that I was his kid. There was no other explanation for my looking just like Snuff. However, I was a little antsy about it. She would have been pregnant with me the same time Snuff's girlfriend was. Snuff was my best friend. I just didn't want to face the fact that he might have had two pregnant women on the string at once, and one of them a fifteen year old, my mother. That would make him a pervert.

"Chester . . . I have something really awful to tell you and it concerns me and Snuff. I just don't know where to start. I have kept my secret hidden since I was fifteen. Before you leave for California, I have just got to get it off my chest, so I can move on with my life. Also, there is the possibility I will be sent to jail for what I need to tell you."

"Mom, wait till I finish putting on my socks and make us a pot of coffee. Both of us may need the caffeine." I replied pointing for her to be seated at the kitchen table. I then headed for the coffee maker. I needed a moment to think, and decide what questions I wanted to ask her concerning my conception and about my stepfather's assault of Keesha and the boys. I might never get another chance, if she crawled back into a bottle for any reason. I already was pretty confident that Snuff was my father. What I didn't know was where Key and the boys were.

When the stout coffee finished trickling thru, I poured us both a mug full and then sat down across from her. She immediately wrapped her hands around her mug, like her hands were extremely cold.

"All right mom . . . I am ready for whatever it is that you want to tell me! If it is about the black girl I was dating in high school, I already know about dad and his white sheet night of frightening her." I stated trying to sound as calm as possible, non-threatening, and baiting her at the same time. I had read enough detective novels to know to keep my cool.

"You know about that night?" She asked with a shocked expression on her face.

I just shook my head yes and took a drink of my coffee.

"Your stepfather's rape of her and his attack on the little boys is one of the things I have come here to talk to you about." She spit out thinking that I already knew.

At that point, I knew what motor Mouth had told me was the truth. I bit my lip and tried to remain calm. My mother had used the words rape and attack. My gut was in knots, knowing what had happened to cause Keesha to leave me.

"Yes . . . I know mom." I stated forcing myself to talk to her in a quiet civil voice. "A member of the Klan slipped around and told me." I lied, knowing my stepfather's niece was my informant.

"Do you know what my mother did to her afterward?" She asked eyeing me.

"I am pretty sure I do." I stated trying to give a vague answer. "Do you want to tell me your version of what happened? You said you want to get it off of your chest."

"I had barely climbed out of the bottle and was half sober when you graduated high school. Your grandmother and stepfather planned the restaurant thing afterward. Your grandmother purposely didn't go with us to eat. Your stepfather had already done his thing. It was your grandmother's job to see that she was disposed of. I rode with your grandmother in a taxi to graduation. Your stepfather drove himself and arrived about forty or so minutes after us. You were already giving your speech. He was hot, sweaty, and looked like he had changed his shirt and pants before coming. God as my witness Chester, at the time, I didn't know what he had done. I was still tipsy."

"What did grandma do to my black girlfriend?" I asked taking another drink of my coffee and trying to act normal. Inside, I was seething mad.

"Your grandmother went home that night to her trailer in a taxi. Someone met her there and drove her around to Snuffs' place. She pretended she was lost and knocked on Snuff's door asking for directions and then offered your frightened hurt black girlfriend a ride into the city to the emergency room. She gladly accepted the ride. I found out about the graduation night happenings a day or so later while listening to your stepfather brag on the phone to his brother about what he had done. Your stepfather thought I was across the dump road checking on the hermit. Sometimes, back then, I shared plates of food with the hermit, when I had it."

Once again, her words confirmed what Motor Mouth had told me.

"Go on . . ." I said forcing myself to remain calm and non-threatening.

"I heard your step father laughing and talking about raping your girlfriend and beating her two kids till they were unconscious. I couldn't tell you, because I had problems of my own. The man, I was terrorized of, was still roaming about Gardenia and I didn't dare go anywhere without your stepfather. I needed your white sheet stepfather for my protection."

"Did you have anything to do with the rape or beatings?" I asked. "I want to know mom."

"God as my witness, Chester, I was half drunk the night of your graduation. I was not part of what happened. The only thing I am guilty of is keeping my mouth shut till now. However, I have had good reason to do so."

"I believe you, mom." I stated trying to hold back my anger. My alcoholic, red neck, loser of a stepfather had raped the woman I loved, not to mention he had beaten Tank and Tag. I was furious on the inside. However, I knew that I might not ever get the chance to hear what she had to say again, and she had not told me yet that she and Snuff had slept together and produced me. I wanted to hear her say it. Forcing myself, I once again replied in the calmest voice I could muster. "Whatever you have done or not done, I forgive you mom."

My mom smiled at me. I forced a smile back. Looking into her eyes, I saw that she was telling the truth.

"I am tired of living a lie and crawling in bottles to forget, Chester. I am tired of living with a man I don't love, just so that I don't have to fear Gordy

Gardenia. I am tired of covering for my mother who has serious mental issues."

"Tell me whatever it is that you are trying to tell me mom. When I leave Gardenia in a couple of days for the university in California, it will be too late. I want to leave with no secrets between us." I replied once more trying to pump her and at the same time wondering why she was afraid of Gordy Gardenia.

"It is bad, Chester, really bad." She stated trembling and holding to her mug of hot coffee.

"Whatever your fear concerning Gordy is mom, you can just forget about it. Mabel told me last week that Gordy has a fast growing lung cancer and the doctor has given him two or three weeks at the most to live. Gordy's dozer man is collecting the gate dump fees, and a hospice nurse is calling on Gordy. He has been in bed really ill for several days now."

"That is the best news I have heard my whole life. May he die in torment and rot in hell forever." My mother suddenly sputtered showing anger that I had never seen her display before.

"I share your sentiment. Gordy is not my favorite person either. He toys with grandma. I also know that he has a thing for young girls. You have a right to fear being around him." I replied and then added lying and baiting her. "I know what Gordy did to you."

"You know about Gordy?" My mother questioned with trembling in her voice.

"Yes, I know about Gordy and Snuff." I replied vaguely still trying to bait and pump her for her secrets.

"I have made myself sick trying to think of some way to tell you who your father is. I have always wanted you to know. I just couldn't tell you, as long as Gordy was in his prime and capable of killing me or you."

At that point, I was confused. What did Gordy have to do with my birth, or her sleeping with Snuff? What she was saying didn't make sense. There was no reason for Gordy to have ill will at her, because she chose to sleep with Snuff and get pregnant by him.

"Do you want to tell me about Snuff being my father? I know you and Snuff's girlfriend were both pregnant at the same time. Do you want to tell me your version of how Gordy fits into this soap opera? Grandma has told me her version." I lied.

My mother once again looked shocked. She then sputtered, "You know about Gordy and your real mom?"

I didn't know what she meant by the words she had just spoken. Did she just infer that she wasn't my mother? That was a surprise comment I hadn't expected. I was just fishing with the Snuff being my father comment.

"Oh . . . god . . . ," I muttered realizing I had opened up a whole new can of worms. I was Snuff's son, but not by my mother.

"I know everything, mom. I understand." I replied once more forcing myself to remain calm and once more baiting her. "I just have one question. Why did grandma beat you just before you ran away when you were fifteen, and how did you end up with me? There are a few of my puzzle pieces that I haven't been able to put together yet. I would rather hear your version. In my book, you are my mother."

"I was young, stupid, and fifteen, Chester. I thought I was in love with a man who was much older than me. He seduced me, slept with me on numerous occasions, promised to marry me, and buy me a big house in the city which was what I dreamed about back then. I wanted to escape the dump. I got pregnant by him and was really excited about it. I thought he would be too. After taking a home pregnancy test late one evening, I went to his place to tell him. The sun had just gone down. I let myself in and walked back to his bedroom. I heard panting noises and a woman screaming. I thought Gordy had his bedroom TV on." She stated suddenly pausing and biting her lip, like she wondered if she should go on.

"Go on, Mom," I stated in as calm a voice as I could muster, realizing that it was Gordy Gardenia that had seduced her at fifteen and gotten her pregnant.

"His back bedroom door was open. I just walked in all excited and then in total shock stopped dead in my tracks. He was on top of a naked, pregnant woman who was fighting and trying to get away from him. She was in labor and getting raped, Chester. Seeing me pop in so unexpectedly, he yelled at me and then took his fist to her and knocked her out. I started to run, but he caught me and cornered me in the hall. He pushed me up against the wall, threatening me. He then proceeded to slap me and send me sprawling back into the bedroom and onto the end of the bed at her feet. You just came sliding out of her at the same time. In fear, I yelled telling him not to hit me that I would help him hide her body and not tell about what had just happened. Her eyes were rolled back in her head. His hit killed her. I was desperate. He walked over to the closet, to grab a blanket to roll her up in. He was ignoring you totally."

"I see . . ." I stated reaching over and putting my hand on top of hers, realizing that she had been a young stupid girl who had been a victim of Gordy.

"I grabbed you, pulled the rubber band from my pony tail, tied off your umbilical cord with it, and entered survival mode. I didn't have anything to cut your cord with." She stated and then half gagged. "I bit the cord into with my teeth, because I knew I was going to have to make a run for it, or the two of us would not live to see the next morning. I had blood all over my mouth and you were screaming. I grabbed your mother's maternity top which was discarded and wadded up beneath her knees where Gordy had ripped it off of her. I quickly wrapped you in it. I knew, if I made it home to my father, we would be safe. I had to think quick and run."

Suddenly, I saw my mother in a whole new light. No wonder she had stayed in a bottle her whole life and clung to my stepfather for safety. She had confronted a rapist and murderer and had lived to tell it.

"What happened next, mom?"

"When he picked her body up, which he had rolled up in a blanket, I darted down the hall with you in my arms and out the front door. He dropped her dead body and then stumbled over it, trying to chase me. I ran like crazy for mom and dad's place and ducked behind dad's trash hauler to hide as soon as I got there. When I peeped and looked back, he wasn't behind me. I assumed he was probably doing something with the pregnant woman's body."

"Did you see him exit his trailer with my real mom's body?" I asked trying desperately not to spook her.

"When I didn't see him following me, I placed you in the seat of dad's trash hauler, thinking you would be safer there, than inside should Gordy come after me. I ran to mom and dad's trailer and frantically opened the door and entered totally out of breath. Mom was there, but dad wasn't. I was in a panic. In total terror of Gordy coming after me, I told mom quickly what I had walked in on and seen. I also told her about me being pregnant with Gordy's baby. I blurted out everything in one breath. At that time, I did not know that my mom was in love with Gordy, and that she too was having an affair with him and was also pregnant by him. Your grandmother went bezerk hearing that I was pregnant by Gordy. If your grandfather hadn't walked in the door, I think she would have beaten me to death."

"That explains the coldness between you and grandma. I am sorry she wasn't there for you." I replied still trying to remain calm and civil. "What happened next?"

"Mom didn't know that I had you outside in the truck. I didn't have the chance to tell her. All she cared about was the fact that I was pregnant by Gordy and that I was a conniving little bitch who was trying to take him away from her. I honestly didn't know, Chester, that mom had a thing for Gordy at that point in time. I was just barely fifteen and still wearing a ponytail. My instinct had been to run home to the person I trusted the most for help. Mom turned out to be a second nightmare."

"Go on . . ." I replied.

"When dad pulled her off of me, I bolted and ran from their trailer, grabbed you from the hauler, and ran to the only other person's mobile home that I thought Gordy wouldn't look for me in. I ran for the hermit's place and knocked like crazy. He let me in. I told him that I had just given birth to an Eskimo baby and asked him if he would like me to show it to his dogs. You know how he has always been obsessed with anything having to do with Alaska, Eskimos, or husky dogs."

"He did see himself as a Yukon man." I replied simply. "Go on."

"Wolf Dog let me in all smiles. I showed him you and then asked him if I could wash you in his sink and get some milk from him for you. I told him that I was going to name you Wolf Dog after him. He was delighted to have my attention and produced a small doll like bottle that he fed pups with. I washed it, filled it with milk, and fed you after bathing you. I then asked him if he had anything that I could wrap you in, like a blanket. The maternity top, I had you wrapped in, was soaked with blood. Wolf Dog produced a nursing home lap blanket, like old people cover their knees with in wheel chairs. I diapered you in a tea towel he had and then wrapped you in the knee blanket. I did the best I could in the dazed, frenzied state I was in."

"In my opinion, mom, you did well by me. What happened next?"

"I then let the hermit hold you, while I washed my face and tried to get the blood off of the front of me. After I was presentable, I asked him to borrow a big sloppy tote bag that had belonged to his mother. I told him that I was going to Alaska to visit my baby's father, and if he would let me have a few things that I needed, I would send him back a real Alaskan wolf pup. He agreed. I took the big tote and poked holes in the sides of it and then put you in all wrapped up in the wheel chair lap blanket. I needed to run with you, and I didn't want anyone seeing me running with a baby. I was at the hermit's place for about thirty minutes."

"Did Gordy try to find you in the trailers in the dump?"

"After putting you in the tote, I peeped out and saw Gordy stop his pickup in front of mom and dad's trailer in the distance. When he went inside, I immediately exited the hermit's trailer and ran for the highway and the spot where all the kids waited on the school bus. It was dark. I quickly scooted down an embankment and crawled into a round drain pipe beneath the road. It was dark and I stayed there till the following morning. I am sure that Gordy drove the roads and looked for me all night. When I heard the school bus coming, I crawled up out of the drain pipe and boarded with my big sloppy tote. I was a dump kid. No one paid any attention to the fact I look dirty. When I got to school, I walked directly to the cafeteria, swiped a couple little cartons of milk for you, and then hurried out the back door of the school. I hitched a ride south with a truck driver."

"Wasn't the driver suspicious of you having a new born with you?" I asked.

"Every time you started to whimper, I would stick the dog bottle in your mouth. He thought I had a puppy with me in the tote. I never took you out. I rode with him three hours south. I slept in another drain pipe for the night, and then my next ride took me all the way to the white beaches of Florida. I kept you safe in that tote for several weeks. I lived behind dumpsters, alleys, and in drain pipes with you for weeks. I stole milk for you, and I ate out of trash cans."

"You were pregnant, mom. What happened to your baby, Gordy's baby?"

"I lost my baby, probably from stress and not having enough to eat. I survived Chester. I did what I had to do for you and me to survive."

"Why didn't you go to your school principal, or the police in the city?" I asked.

"I was barely fifteen. I entered survival mode after my mother beat me. No one was killing you or me. If I couldn't trust my mother, I wasn't about to trust a stranger. The principal, in my thinking at that time, would have just called my parents to come get me. My mother had just tried to beat me to death and Gordy wanted to. I was traumatized."

I glanced up and saw Snuff standing in the mobile home hallway behind my mother listening. Apparently, he had been there for a spell. He put his fingers to his lips telling me not to let my mother know he was there. Apparently, he had heard the whole story. Like me, he wanted to hear the ending. His nineteen year old mystery was suddenly being solved.

"What did you do with the bloody maternity top, mom?" I asked knowing that Snuff had found it in Wolf Dog's trailer.

"I was in a panic. I just left it. It was too bloody and wet from her water breaking to take it with me. I had to keep you dry. I suppose Wolf Dog burned it. He was heating his trailer with a wood stove back then."

"Did you know who the pregnant woman was, mom? It will not affect the feelings I have for you. You are my mother. You saved my life."

I watched Snuff in the background cupping his hand over his mouth to fight any sounds he might inadvertently make. I could see the horror in his face. He had loved Jennifer, like I had loved Keesha.

"I never saw Snuff's girlfriend but once, she was sitting in his hauler. However, I am pretty sure the pregnant woman in Gordy's bed was her. The pregnant woman's face was bloody and bruised from where he had been slapping and beating on her. He was yelling at her to lie still while he was panting and raping her when I walked in. She couldn't lay still, Chester. She was in labor. I am sure she was Snuff's girlfriend."

"I already know most of this." I replied with my hand on top of hers. "You were a victim, mom, just like Snuff's girlfriend."

"I am sorry, Chester. I just couldn't tell you who you were all these years. When I returned here from the south, I told my mother that I lost the baby belonging to Gordy and that you belonged to a guy in the south who was in prison. I told Gordy that you were a girl, and that I had put you in one of those baby doors down in Texas. He never got a look at you when you were born. He was busy getting a quilt to roll your mother up in."

"You lied about my parentage to keep me safe."

"Gordy thinks the pregnant woman's baby was a girl. I purposely told him that, when he called and threatened me when I returned. I told him that you were a girl and that I had stuffed you in a baby give away door. I stayed in the city, till I met and married your stepfather. I stayed clear of the dump."

I got up from my place at the table, walked around and put my arms around her. She was my mother. I loved her in spite of everything. Snuff remained silent in the hallway listening with tears rolling down his face, and with his hand cupped over his mouth to silence himself.

"Mom, do you have any idea where Gordy might have disposed of Snuff's girlfriend's body?"

"The dump or the cemetery behind Gordy's mobile home is my guess. I don't know for sure. I have stayed away from Gordy for good reason all of these years. I have never allowed myself to be alone with him, and you now know why."

"Do you remember what color of blanket he wrapped her in?"

"It was white, one of those hospital type blankets they put on beds. Gordy rescued it from the dump and mom had bleached it for him. I remember her washing and bleaching it a few days before the rape and murder." She replied.

"Going back to my girlfriend, mom, do you have any idea where grandma took Keesha and my boys the night of my graduation? The two boys are mine, mom. I am their father." I lied trying to get empathy from her, by convincing her I was the biological father of Tank and Tag.

"The two boys were yours?" She asked in shock. "You were only sixteen going on seventeen."

"I had been dating Keesha secretly since I was thirteen, mom. I was young and experimenting with sex. We met at school. She lived with her parents in the housing project. I felt they were better off there, than in the dump. I fathered Tank when I was a little past fourteen and Tag when I was fifteen." I replied lying again. "The two boys are your grandchildren. I love them mom and want to find them. They deserve to know me."

"All I know is what your stepfather eventually told me. He did his white sheet thing and then your grandmother dropped by with someone driving her, pretending to be lost. They gave your girlfriend a lift. I would like to think your grandmother took them to the emergency room. However, you know that probably was not on her agenda. I dare say your grandmother, and whoever was with her, may have further beaten them and dumped them over in the next state. They may be alive, Chester, and just too scared to return to you. I honestly don't know what happened to them. I was half drunk that night."

Suddenly, thoughts of Gracie crossed my mind.

"I have one last thing to ask you mom. Who is Gracie? Everyone talks about her young mom who lives in the city, but no one has ever met or seen her."

"Gracie arrived on the scene after I run away, Chester. I don't know who she is. She could be Gordy's by some young girl he seduced, or she could be kidnapped. I honestly don't know. Only she can tell you what her story is, if she ever comes back."

Once again, I felt guilty for all the years I had ignored Gracie as we stood and waited for the rural bus to take us to school. She had probably needed me for a friend, and I had ignored her.

For the first time, I saw in my mother a woman who cared. Snuff stepped back down into the dark hallway as she rose to leave. I knew that he was thinking the same thing as me. We couldn't afford to go off on the one person that had voluntarily solved our mysteries.

After my mother left, Snuff and I decided we would go to the sheriff after I questioned my grandmother and we had all of our ducks in a row. I also wanted to know who drove my grandmother that night. I wanted everyone brought to justice who had a part in taking Keesha and the boys from me. Snuff wanted the same for Jennifer.

Wolf Dog's murder was still a mystery. Why would anyone string him up like a piece of poultry and cut off his head? I did now know why the maternity top was in his pillowcase. My mother had left it behind the night she ran away with me. Wolf Dog, the hermit, had probably seen it as a souvenir of a special time when a friend brought her new born baby to see him. Maybe his pillowcase was his special place for keeping things. He did have the mentality of an eight or nine year old.

CHAPTER TWENTY

Letting Go

The following morning, I rose early and headed for Rosa's place to tell her I would be a little late starting my route. A heavy snow had fallen overnight. There was at least eight inches on the ground and on the dump road. It was my last day running my route. I just had a couple days left, till I caught my plane to California. Trash men were like the mail men. Rain, snow, or sleet didn't stop us from making our rounds.

I had plans to take Rosa to dinner after our work days were completed. She was boss, receptionist, and fill-in driver for her trash service. She was a strong woman who ruled her world, and that included me. I actually liked her telling me what to do. Maybe I was making up for all the years that my grandmother and mother didn't pay me any attention. Maybe I was seeing Rosa's bossiness as love. Whatever it was, I had liked belonging to Rosa for the few weeks that we had slept together. Now, it was ending suddenly and I wasn't sure how she was going to take it. I had never told her about Keesha and the boys. I was dreading telling her.

I walked up the snow covered steps to her porch, opened the door, and walked in like all the other drivers did in the morning to get their route assignments. Carlos was ahead of me. I stood impatiently as he chatted with her in Spanish and then collected his keys and hard hat. Finally, he quit running at the mouth and left.

"You weren't in my bed, last night, Chester." She stated grinning. "Have you already traded me in for a California college girl that I don't know about?"

"I wanted to be in my best girl's bed. However, I was doing a little detective work last night." I replied trying not to go in to detail.

"If you want to do some snooping, you should sneak over to Gordy's back building and put your ear to it. I have been hearing crying all morning and I think it is coming from there. Just before Carlos came in, I could swear I heard that mortuary music play for a few minutes and then it stopped as suddenly as it started. There is something weird going on over there this morning, Chester. I will pay you two months of nights with me, if you will just sneak over to the back of his building and put your ear to it and listen."

"You know that I am leaving on a plane in a couple of days. Just how will I collect on the two months' of nights with you? Besides, there is eight inches of fresh snow on the ground and probably drifts behind that building. Do you want to make an abominable snow man out of me? Snow men make very cold lovers."

"How about one night with me, tonight, and I cook dinner for you." She replied knowing she had offered me less.

"Will one night be better than two months' of nights?" I asked winking at her.

"You tell me tomorrow morning, when you wake up not wanting to leave me." She replied winking back.

"Why don't you just be my boss, tell me I am on company time, and then command me to go stick my ear to Gordy's building till you tell me to stop?" I asked laughing. "I was in love with her, but I loved Keesha more. I just didn't know how I was going to back away from Rosa, without hurting her."

"Here is my digital camera. It takes moving pictures. I want you to go over there and find a hole in the big building and let it record whatever is going on inside. I heard the crying in the wind and the crazy music just before Carlos came in. You are on my payroll. I am relieving you of your route this morning. I will run it for the next two hours. I have to know what is going on over there."

"What do you think is going on over there?" I asked wondering why she was so interested in snooping and peeking in the metal building.

"About ten years ago, I knocked on the side of his building because I was hearing strange, loud, bird sounds coming from there. The next morning, I found a chicken on my front lawn with its head cut off. It was a warning to stay away. It is no longer bird sounds that I hear. I hear crying in the wind and mortuary music. I want to know what is causing it, so I can get a court order to make him stop whatever is going on in there. I think he is raising chickens and maybe black panthers. Black panthers cry like women."

"You found a chicken on your lawn with its head cut off?" I asked thinking of the hermit.

"Yes, and it was wearing one of my company logo ball caps." Rosa replied grinning. "The cap was just to let me know I was being warned. Where I am from in Mexico, there are black magic priests and priestesses who cut the heads of chickens off, and leave the body as a warning of the impending death of those opposing them. It is what they do with the head that frightens me the most."

"I am biting," I replied smiling. "What do they do with the head?

"They put in on a stick and pretend it is alive and that it watches, serves, and guards the gods."

Rosa never ceased to amuse me. I laughed, and then she laughed.

"All joking aside Rosa, I need to walk across the road and have a short talk with my grandmother about something before I start my day. My mother thinks it is time for grandma to go into a nursing home. I need to talk with her about it briefly. Then, I will be your snowman and go find a hole to see what Gordy is up to."

"Your grandmother has many angry, crazy, buzzing bees in her head. Be careful that she doesn't pull one from her ear and place it in yours. I would hate for you to hear her buzzing and pull the craziness she does. She has always been crazy in her beehive. She is unpredictable. She will not enter a nursing home willingly."

"If I ever go crazy like her, Rosa, just run over me with one of your trash haulers, and put me out of my misery." I replied.

"Your grandmother will think you are trying to separate her and Gordy. She still thinks that she is young and that Gordy Gardenia is going to marry her. Be careful. I would hate for my new lover, the mayor, to end up like a chicken with his head cut off and then thrown on my lawn. I personally think it is your grandmother that has killed the hermit."

"What did you say?"

"You heard me. Haven't you ever asked what your grandmother's parents did for a living?"

"Actually no . . ." I replied thinking for a moment. "My grandmother has rarely ever spoken of them."

"Her parents owned a chicken processing plant in the city, sixty or so years ago. Your grandmother cut her teeth on a playpen in the office, and played with chickens for pets. Her parents never sent her to day care or a baby sitter. She was raised in the processing plant, and wandered about it till she started first grade. Your grandfather told me about it one time."

"I hope your theory is wrong. However, that would solve one of Gardenia's mysteries." I muttered knowing how crazy my grandmother was. "I know this might freak you out, but do you think my grandmother hated the hermit for any reason?"

"Haven't you ever wondered who the hermit's father is Chester? Have you ever wondered why Gordy always personally made sure Wolf Dog had a job as a picker on the back of someone's trash hauler?"

"Just spit it out what you are getting at, Rosa."

"Wolf Dog's mother was the funeral home man's daughter, the one who took Gordy away from your grandmother. Wolf Dog is Gordy's son. He has always been ashamed of his son, the crazy hermit. He did what he had to for them, but that was that."

"Why would Gordy marry a mentally challenged woman like the hermit's mother?"

I never met her, but Snuff once told me that the hermit's mother was just like him. She had enough sense to cook for herself, but couldn't read, write, or speak. Snuff said she was deaf, couldn't talk, and had the maturity of possibly a kindergartner.

"Perhaps, Gordy married her to get the funeral home man's wealth. Gordy purchased a very expensive piece of land for his dump, and paid cash for it. I doubt very seriously at the age of twenty six, that he had five hundred thousand dollars is his savings. His parent's were bankrupt florists before they died. Plus, Gordy has never worked out on a public job." Rosa added. "He had to get the money somewhere."

"I have never considered where Gordy got his original wealth from." I replied deep in thought.

"I think Gordy lived with his funeral home wife just long enough for her parents to mysteriously die in a car wreck. He then got her inheritance money and stashed her and his challenged son in that trailer. She has not been able to tell anyone, over the years, who she is. She can't speak, much less been to school and learned to read and write. Gordy has told everyone that his funeral home wife is dead." Rosa replied.

"How do you know about the hermit and his mother?"

"After the hermit's mother was placed in a nursing home, the hermit started riding as a picker on the back of my truck. He told me about his mother and how Gordy brought them things late at night when all the dump dwellers were asleep. I just put two and two together, from the bits and pieces the hermit said. After his mother went into a nursing home, the hermit showed me a wedding photo of his mother and Gordy. There was no mistaking that the groom was him."

"You should be a detective, Rosa. You are good." I replied in awe of the woman I was going to have to cease sleeping with.

"I don't have time to be a detective, Chester. In case you have forgotten, I am being sworn in as mayor of Gardenia on the sixth. I will miss you when you go to California, but don't you feel bad if I have some young, good look-ing man on my arm, like I have hung on yours the last two years. I will have lots of functions and political events to attend. It has been good between us, but sometimes life takes new paths. I will need someone to walk that path with me."

"Are you dumping me?" I asked a little annoyed. It was me that was sup-posed to be walking away from her.

"I am not dumping you till after tonight, when I pay you for snooping. You can be my special someone till you leave on the plane. When a ship sails, another enters the port to dock." She replied laughing. "Make love, Chester. Don't fall in love. I loved Ricardo and got a broken heart when I found out he was gay and had secret lovers. Now, I make love and run when the time says do so. That time has come for us, Chester. I don't want to ache for you when you are in California and I am here. It is time for both of us to run like hell from each other."

I didn't know how to reply. However, she was right. I should have made love to Key under the mistletoe, and then run like hell. My heart would not be broken, and she and her boys would not have suffered the abuse of my step-father and grandmother.

"Now, go get my moving picture of what is going on in that building" Rosa demanded grinning at me.

"Yes, Boss." I replied and headed for the door, taking her camera with me.

As I was opening the door to exit, she called, "Chester . . ."

"Is there something else, Rosa?" I asked turning and looking into her eyes.

"Should you ever want to fly home and just make love, my door will always be open to you. I am sure that your replacement will have a very tiny anchor on his ship. I like big ships with big anchors. You are a big ship, Chester . . . I have found you quite pleasing in my bed."

I laughed and winked at her. Neither of us was kidding each other. We had bonded during the two years I was mayor. We loved each other. However, she loved me enough to let me go. Love doesn't get any better than that.

~   ~   ~

After trudging thru the snow, across the dump road, to my grandmother's mobile home, I was surprised to find that she wasn't home. I wondered where she was. Then I spotted tracks in the new fallen snow. There was a single set of tracks that headed from her front porch out to the road and then up the side of dump road. Further up, the tracks crossed the new fallen snow on dump road and made their way to Gordy's porch. That didn't surprise me. She was obsessed with Gordy Gardenia, and always had been.

"What in the world is she doing, getting out in this deep snow, and going to Gordy's for?" I muttered, asking myself. "At her age, she could fall and break a hip or something."

About that time, my cell phone rang. I flipped it open. It was Granny Mabel.

"How is my shine girl?" I asked teasing her. I had kept my word and picked jars from my loads for her for the last two years.

"I am fine, Chester, and you?"

"I am leaving in two days for California to finish getting my college degree. Don't forget, you will need to call Rosa if you have any town business to discuss after that." I stated figuring she had called me to tell me that the town's pump was frozen, or that someone had been rocking her dogs. The problems in Gardenia weren't always major issues.

"I am going to miss you, Chester. However, that is not what I have called to speak with you about."

"What does my best shine girl want to speak to me about?" I asked.

After running for mayor, I had gotten to know each of Gardenia's citizens and had learned to love each of them in a special way. Fresh out of high school, I wanted only one thing, to kiss Gardenia and its dump people good-bye forever. As a young adult, I had learned that friends could be all ages and I had grown quite fond of my town's people. That had surprised me. Snuff had become my best friend. Mabel had been my shine girl. Rosa had been my lover, and Carlos had become my lunch room pal. We met and ate fast food together several days a week, as well as talked about life and politics back and forth on our truck's CBs. These same people could have been my friends, when I was a child and a teen. I was too hung up on wanting school friends my age, and missed out on years' of special moments with the characters that lived within hundreds of feet from me on the dump road. They were gods waiting to have their buttons pushed. I was oblivious to their divinity.

The hermit, till his death, became my library buddy. Once a week on Saturday, we journeyed into the city, ate fast food for breakfast, and then sat at the library table and read for a couple of hours. I taught the hermit how to read during the two years I was mayor. We shared a lot of books on the Alaskan frontier and dogs. The hermit had never attended school. My grandfather, when he was alive, suggested that I build Wolf Dog a sled on wheels, so that he could live his Alaskan dream where he was. I built that rolling dog sled. Wolf Dog drove the residents of Gardenia crazy for a while. He mushed up and down the Gardenia dump road for weeks, from sun up to sun down. He eventually tired of the toy, like any kid does, and moved on to something else.

There are always a few people who don't want to be friends with you for various reasons. My step father was one of those. I think he saw me as a threat to who he wanted to be, a man of position in the white sheets. I am sure his other reason was that he knew what he had done to Key and the boys. Gordy and my grandmother were not my friends.

Mabel's voice reclaimed my wandering attention.

"I think you need to make your way over to Gordy's trailer, Chester. It is almost nine and he hasn't opened the dump gate. There will be a backup out on the highway with loaded trucks, if he doesn't open soon."

I glanced out at the road. Sure enough, a long line of trucks with loads of garbage on were lining up on the snow covered dump road.

"Have you tried calling him, Mable?" I asked not really wanting to antagonize Gordy for the moment. I was headed for the sheriff's office later in the day to tell them what I had discovered about him being a rapist and a murderer.

"I have tried, Chester. He isn't answering his phone. I hear crying coming from over there. Your grandmother went in there a few moments ago. Gordy is either dead, or he and your grandmother are into it and she is crying." Mabel replied.

"My grandmother is always crying over something Gordy has or hasn't done." I retorted not wanting to go to Gordy's mobile home.

"Your grandmother had a good man and didn't appreciate him. I don't understand her lifelong fascination with our short, obese pig, dump owner. He has probably had fifty or seventy five young girlfriends in the last twenty years. He has no interest in or intentions of marrying our grandmother. I have tried to tell her."

"I have tried to tell her to, Mabel."

"She tells me to mind my own business and that one day she will make me eat my words, when she becomes the Queen of Gordy's Heaven."

"She tells me the same thing, Mabel. Just so you know, my mother and I are filling out papers, before I leave for California, to have her committed to a nursing home."

"It is about time, Chester. I have been a little frightened of her lately. She has been throwing chicken heads to my pit bulls. What is she butchering chickens for? The supermarket sells them cheap and they are already de-feathered, gutted, and cut up. Lately, I have been going back to the Deli and buying my chickens already fried and roasted. I have developed a taste for their lemon roasted chicken. It is really good. I have four of those, already baked, lemon birds in my freezer right now. Have you tried their lemon chicken, Chester?"

"Thanks for telling me about the chicken heads, Mabel. I will take care of that problem. To answer your question, I have tried the Deli lemon chickens. However, it is the roasted chicken with barbecue sauce on it that I prefer."

"You are just like my boys, Chester. You either want ketchup or barbecue sauce on everything."

"I haven't seen your boys for awhile. Where are they?"

"I haven't seen them either. When they are into it with the law, I don't see them for awhile. It has been about two years since I have seen the older three. The baby, the ashes stealer one, is in jail right now for stealing cemetery flags. My other younger son is working in a Taco stand down in Texas. There are warrants out for him here for turning over gravestones and stealing grave diggers equipment. He called me last weekend to tell me that he got a new tattoo on his arm of a tombstone. I keep telling that younger son that he should get his act together, and do something respectable like making and selling shine. That is where the money is."

I bit my lip to keep from laughing. Only Mabel would think making Moon Shine was a respectable occupation.

"I have got to go Mabel."

"Well, promise me you will go and check to see if your grandmother and Gordy are in to it. Gordy isn't young like he used to be. He may be losing it mentally. Sometimes crazy people hurt those about them, not meaning to. Crazy people can be mean."

"All right, Mabel . . . I will go check on my grandmother." I stated, thinking how my grandmother had once almost beaten my mother to death.

"There was crying over there a couple nights, or so ago, Chester. It sounded like Gordy and some man was into it. It was too cold to keep my window cracked very long. It was the day your stepfather left your mother. When the man quit crying, I closed my window and went back to working my thousand piece picture puzzle."

"A man was crying at Gordy's place, the day of my stepfather's birthday party?" I asked alarmed, knowing that my step father was missing. I already knew that Gordy was a rapist and killer. Was it possible he was turning to men as victims now? I was alarmed and decided I had better get with the program and sneak behind Gordy's metal building and see what I could discover to approach the sheriff's office with.

"The crying man's voice sounded like that of your loud mouth stepfather." She replied.

"Maybe you are right, Mabel. I will go and check to see what the problem is at Gordy's." I returned and then cautioned her. "Mabel, if you hear any more crying or unusual noises coming from Gordy's place, stick your handgun in your apron pocket for your safety, and then call the sheriff. Tell the sheriff I told you to do so. I am appointing you, in this moment, as our town Marshall. Do you understand?"

"I understand, Mayor Holly." She replied.

"Raise your right hand, Mabel for me to swear you in." I replied over my cell phone.

"Can I raise my left hand, Mayor Holly? I am left handed." She quickly stated.

"Raise your left hand, Mabel," I said biting my lip for a moment to keep from snickering. "Swear that you will uphold the laws of our town, do your best to protect its citizens from harm, and to call the sheriff if anything happens you can't handle."

"I swear to all of that, Mayor Holly." Mabel replied in a firm voice and then added, "Drop by later, Chester. I have a little going away present for you. You will have to drink it before you go. I don't think those air port security people will let you on the plane with it."

CHAPTER

TWENTY-ONE

The Discovery

I had just hung up on Mabel, and was about to head for Gordy's place when, I spotted my grandmother stepping off of Gordy's mobile home porch heading back in the heavy, new fallen snow. I was relieved. I wouldn't have to go and see what she and Gordy were into it about; at least not for the present. My focus was on having a confrontation with her about my stepfather's rape of Keesha and trying to bluff her into telling me what part she played in the abuse of my tuxedo girl. Afterward, I would just straight out tell her that my mother and I were committing her to a nursing home.

I walked toward her to meet her half way in the heavy snow, and then accompany her on her walk back to her trailer. Granny Mabel's mobile home sat directly across the dump road from Gordy's. My grandparent's plot of land was three plots down from the dump. My grandmother had the equivalent of about a city block to walk in the snow.

"Why aren't you out on your route or kissing Rosa goodbye?" My grandmother greeted me sarcastically, as her breathing in and out made a misty cloud in the cold air in front of her face.

"Today is the last day I am driving for Rosa. She becomes mayor in two days and I am flying out tomorrow to California where I will attend the university and finish up my last three semesters of college. I am taking an hour or so off to tie up some loose ends."

"Granny Mabel is one of those loose ends?" She asked with a hint of jealousy in her voice. She had seen me step off my shine girl's porch.

"Mabel has no one to watch out for her. Grandpa used to. I am just fulfilling my duty as mayor and watching out for those who reside in Gardenia." I replied trying to get off the subject of Mabel. That was not what I wanted to get into it with her about.

"If it wasn't for Gordy, I wouldn't have anyone. Why are you bothering to walk with me this morning? I didn't vote for you and in my book Gordy would have been a better mayor. You are just a meaningless, little, three vote, political spear that means nothing. You have had one goal in mind, to stick it to Gordy. Gordy is god in this dump town, not you. You are nothing but a little bastard, and that is all you will ever be. Gordy created this Heaven called Gardenia, not you."

I bit my lip. Even though I was now a man, it still hurt when she called me that name. Even though I now knew that she was not related to me, she was my grandmother. I had lived most of my life with her and my beloved grandfather, whom I now knew was not related to me. My grandmother, Erma, had always had a way of knifing my self-esteem. Even though her words hurt as we walked, I now knew why she hated me. She thought I was Gordy's child by her daughter. She didn't accept my mother's story that she lost Gordy's baby while in Florida. My grandmother, Erma, couldn't handle me being alive. She had been pregnant the same time as my mother, and had lost her child belonging to Gordy.

"I have always known that you don't care for me grandma. I am a man now. I accept that fact." I stated wondering how I was going to approach the subject of Keesha and my grandmother's role in her disappearance. "Here, take my arm, so you don't fall in this mess."

My grandmother, reluctantly, took my arm. "Your grandfather always used to offer me his arm. I guess you got what manners you have from him. You sure didn't get them from your mother. She'll stab you in the back if she gets a chance, Chester."

"There are things we have never talked about, that I am fully aware of. I would like for things to be settled between us before I leave. I may never come back, Grandma."

"Just what do you want to talk to me about? I love Gordy Gardenia. I have always loved Gordy Gardenia. Your grandfather tricked me into marrying him when I was drunk. Afterward, Gordy refused to have anything to do with me because he is Catholic. Is that what you want to hear?"

"That has never been a secret too anyone, Grandma. It is something else I want to talk with you about. It is about my graduation from high school." I stated wading in.

"I suppose you are mad at me for not attending that dinner afterward." She huffed.

"No, it is what I discovered after my graduation that I want to talk about. I followed you and Gordy that night." I replied trying to bait her and make her think I knew what happened. "I know what you and Gordy did. I watched."

"You peeked into my and Gordy's heaven?" She asked stopping in the deep snow with a look of disgust on her face.

"Yes, I know what you and Gordy did." I once again lied.

"That is not fair of you, Chester. You cannot peek or sneak into god's heaven. Only devils peek and sneak. I have had to take care of a lot of peekers and sneakers over the last twenty years. Now, I may have to take care of you. Don't tell Gordy, and I will let you get by with it in memory of your grandpa. He did ask me on the phone, just before he went into a coma, to keep you safe and see that you got his haulers. Do you want his haulers? I am going to meet Gordy in a few days and I won't need them anymore."

"What do you mean . . . you are going to meet Gordy?" I asked thinking the pair of elderly dump citizens were up to something.

"I am going to meet god Gordy, Chester. I am a keeper of Heaven's Gate, and Gordy is god of Heaven's Gate."

"Grandma, Gordy is really ill. Mabel told me. He just has a short time to live. His not opening the dump gate this morning is probably his first step down on his slippery slide to dying."

"Gordy will rise from the dead. I am one of the 144 thousand who have made their robes white and will reign with him. The door knockers showed me the way. In return, I have let them be one of his chosen few. I will soon be the Queen of Heaven and he will be God! We will wear robes of white and all will fear us."

I bit my lip. My grandmother was losing it mentally. She was confusing her new door knocker religion with the white robes the Klan wore. At the same time, she was hallucinating that Gordy was god. No wonder my mother wanted me to help her get my grandmother committed before I left for California. She now had more than one screw loose.

It was time to ask her about Keesha, before she totally lost it. I knew it was now or never. My stepfather and the white sheets thought people with black skin were an inferior race. This might be my last chance to find out what my stepfather, my grandmother, and Gordy had done with Keesha and her boys. My stepfather had left my mother, Gordy was dying, and my grandmother was losing it.

"I understand why you frightened my black girlfriend the night of my graduation, Grandma. I didn't understand back then, I do now. You and my stepfather were members of the white sheets." I lied trying to make her think I knew more than what I did.

"Who told you about us getting rid of her that night?" She demanded.

"I just want you to know that I have seen the light, concerning tuxedo girls. They are an inferior race. Thank you for saving me from her." I lied baiting her.

"Did the hermit tell you?" She asked with a depth of darkness in her eyes, I had never seen before.

"Yes, he told me." I once again lied.

The hermit was dead. There was nothing that she or Gordy could do to him.

"I told Gordy I spotted him up on the rim with his damn binoculars." She replied. "Gordy wouldn't let me take care of his misfit. Misfits don't go to Heaven, Chester. They just get their heads cut off and sent down the processing line, like all of the others."

I took a deep breath, realizing that it was a possibility that she had somehow killed the hermit.

"He watched from the rim of the dump that night, Grandma. He told the sheriff what he saw, but the sheriff didn't believe him." I replied still baiting her. "Now the sheriff is sitting up and taking notice."

"What did he tell the sheriff?" She asked continuing her walk in the snow toward her trailer. "How do you know about what he told?"

"I am mayor of this town, Grandma. The sheriff came directly to me and discussed it." I replied once again lying and pumping her for information. "The hermit told the sheriff that my stepfather raped my black girlfriend and then beat her boys. Afterward, he watched you come in a car with someone and my girl and her boys went with you."

"I told Gordy years ago that he should get rid of that nitwit imp of a son of his. Nitwits and black girls are devils . . . not angels. They don't go to Heaven. You just wait till I get back to Heaven's Gate. I am tossing Wolf Dog's head out of it. He is only there because Gordy insists on it. White sheets are for angels and the 144 thousand door knockers."

I didn't have a clue as to what she was talking about, except that she had made a reference to the hermit's head. Once more she was mixing in some of her new religious teachings with the Klan's white sheets, and her prejudices.

"Did you take care of the nitwit or did Gordy do it?" I asked fishing for whatever I could get out of her in her delusional state.

"Gordy creates new souls for his Heaven. He doesn't have time to get rid of devils. I got rid of his nitwit off spring, and told him about it afterward. That is when he took to his bed and started dying. He no longer had to secretly take care of his imp. He was free to die. He is doing that now. Tomorrow he will rise again, and only the ashes of our child will be in Heaven with us. Crazies don't go there."

"Does Gordy know you are the one who took care of the hermit?" I asked, just wanting to hear her say it. She was crazy and I didn't want to have any qualms on my part about committing her. I had always known she was crazy; I just hadn't realized that she was capable of taking a life.

"Gordy knows. He wasn't happy when I presented him with Wolf Dog's head for a birthday present. He told me I was insane. I told him that I was queen of his Heaven and I wouldn't put up with him filling up our heaven with children other than mine. He will get over it, just like I got over my baby, whose ashes are in my button can."

"You gave Gordy his son's head for a birthday present?" I asked in utter shock. At the same time, I realized that Gordy hadn't turned my grandmother in for the murder, due to his own history of rapes and Jennifer's murder. If he told on her, she would tell on him. Gordy had taken to his bed, and was slipping downhill toward death, because his son was dead.

"Where is Heaven's Gate, Grandma?" I asked figuring that is where I would find the hermit's head and possibly her baby's ashes that were supposed to be in a button box.

"I tried for years to get you to knock on doors and make it into my Heaven. You had a chance to go to the door knockers' hall with me and learn about God's new kingdom coming down. You are not worthy of being one of the chosen 144 thousand. Neither was your grandfather."

"What does your religion have to do with your beheading the hermit, grandma?"

"You are so dense and stupid, Chester. Everyone knows that your soul resides in your head. Only heads go to Heaven. Bodies rot in graves forever. The nitwit's devil soul head had to be taken to Gordy's Heaven. When he rises again, he will cast into the lake of fire. Only the pure and our slaves will reside in Heaven's Gate."

"Where is Hell, Grandma? Also, I want to remind you that the door knockers do not believe in hell."

"The door knockers have it almost right, Chester. However, Catholic Hell and purgatory is a necessity. I kept that part of my Catholic religion. Gordy and I burn, in the lake of fire, all the bodies of those who peek into our Heaven. I am glad you have never peeked, Chester. In some ways you were a good boy."

I was stunned with what she was inferring. At the same time, I knew she was crazy. It was possible that a lot of what she was saying was just delusions or hallucinations.

"Tell me where the lake of fire is located, Grandma. I don't want to go there. It is best I know where it is, so I won't step off in it accidentally." I replied once again baiting her in her insanity.

"The dump is Hell, Chester. Gordy throws people out of his Heaven and into it all the time. The fire door is on the backside where he has a hole dug, and has always burned dead animals. Hell's flames are lit at night. Gordy carries the key to Hell. He is god."

Then I remembered the smell of flesh burning that had permeated the air on the night of my high school graduation. I felt as though I was going to throw up. At the same time, I prayed that was not where Keesha and her boys were. The thought was unfathomable. I tried to keep myself together. This was probably my last chance to find out from her where Key and the boys were. I prayed they were alive in another city somewhere too frightened to return or call me. I prayed my grandmother had just slipped into an insane state and was hallucinating what she was telling me.

"I have decided that I want to go to Heaven with you grandma. I am glad the nitwit and my black devil girl have been taken care of by you." I lied, trying to bait her one last time. "Did you toss her into the lake of fire, the same place you cast the nitwit son's head?"

"She is a slave in Gordy's New Heaven, Chester. That is all that black people are good for." She huffed. "Her two little bastards are slaves too. She is waiting for Gordy to rise again, just like me and the others."

"Where is Hell's gate, Grandma?"

"It is hidden, Chester. Gordy will open the gate to his new Heaven after he rises. Till then, it is his and my secret."

"Just tell me one thing, Grandma. How did my black girl and her two boys get to Gordy's Heaven?" I asked once more baiting her.

"They rode In Gordy's white pickup truck." She replied simply. "Gordy says his white pickup is his disguised chariot. All, who go to his Heaven, ride in it. I helped him load her and the boys in. They were hurt and thought he was taking them to the hospital. I walked home across the dump afterward. There wasn't room for me in the chariot."

If my grandmother was telling the truth, and not hallucinating, Gordy was the only one who knew where Key and the boys were. I prayed he had taken them to the hospital. Now, I was going to have to confront him and get the truth out of him on his death bed.

I forced myself to ask one more question.

"Do the fires of Hell burn only at night, Grandma?"

"Heaven is light, Chester. Of course Hell's gate is only open at night. Gordy is too busy in the daytime collecting dump fees to keep Hell's fire going."

Either, all of my grandmother's crazy screws were loose, or I had possibly uncovered multiple murders.

Reaching my grandmother's porch, I stopped and turned my grandmother facing me. I looked her directly in the eye and stated, "I love you in spite of everything that has gone on between us over the years. You do know that, don't you?"

"I love only one man, Chester. However, I do care enough about you that I have decided to take you and Rosa with me tonight. Heaven's Gate closes tonight, till god Gordy resurrects. I will find something for you to do in Gordy's Heaven. However, you can't be mayor, run for election, or be voted in as god. Maybe Gordy will let you be a personal guard, or something. Rosa will have to be a slave. You and she will die tonight like the hermit. An angel of wrath, from Gordy's Heaven, will be sent with a sword to grant the two of you eternal lire. Don't resist, Chester. That is the only way you can get into Heaven's Gate."

I was suddenly in a panic. Rosa was on my grandmother's radar to kill before the day ended. I had to quickly move Rosa to a safe place, before I could call my mother, have her meet me to commit my grandmother, and later call the sheriff. It was possible there was a killer out there besides my grandmother and Gordy. I was shaking on the inside in fear for Rosa. God only knew who else was on my grandmother's radar, including me. I always knew my grandmother had a screw loose. My grandfather had referred to her as being a wild card. She was far crazier than either of us had ever guessed. I realized in that moment, my grandmother could have made me and my grandfather victims in our sleep over the years, had she chosen to do so. It was only by the mercies of my Grandfather's Catholic God that we were alive.

I helped my grandmother up the snow covered steps to her mobile home's tiny porch. She then turned and smiled at me. Smiles from my grandmother were rare.

"Grandma . . . I found grandpa's urn of ashes in the refrigerator. Do you recall putting them there, and why you put them there?" I asked to see if she was totally off the wall in the moment, or was capable of telling me why she had done something."

"Your grandfather was a devil who burned with fire wanting me. Even in death, he comes trying to crawl into my bed, saying that he loves me and wants me. He wants from me, what is not his to have. I am Gordy's soul mate, his soon to be Queen of Heaven. I have spent a lifetime trying to convince Gordy that it is him I love. Gordy has flaunted young angels in my face, to get even with me for marrying your grandfather. I cremated your grandfather, to show Gordy that I never intend to sleep in a casket next to your grandfather. I iced your devil grandfather, so he would not burn with want for me, and quit coming to me in my dreams. It is not your grandfather that I want to spend eternity with. Gordy's Heaven is about complete. I will rule with him, I have earned that right. I have warred with devils like your grandfather and mother. I have earned my position in Gordy's heaven. You will have to earn your place in Heaven now, Chester. I have proven myself and my loyalty to him. Yor must do the same if you want to rule and reign with him. Die willingly, Chester. It is your only hope."

"Tell me about Gordy's heaven, Grandma." I asked seeing that she was totally lost in her hallucination, mixed with reality, and her obsession with Gordy.

I knew that Gordy had always had a thing for young women. He had no interest in my grandmother who was a hundred pound frame of wrinkled flesh. Gordy had a thing for girls between the ages of fourteen to seventeen. I had no doubt that my grandmother had spent a lifetime loving and being obsessed with Gordy. At the same time, I was sure that Gordy Gardenia had not spent his life time obsessed with my grandmother.

"Heaven is all around you Chester. Gardenia is Heaven. Gordy is God here. Gardenia is the second Garden of Eden. Your grandfather was the serpent who tricked me. You and the other residents are the animals that live and reproduce in the garden. Gordy and I have dominion here. We say who lives, who dies, and who is cast out of the Garden. Gordy is Adam and I am Eve. He is god and I am his queen of heaven."

I just did not know how to respond to my grandmother. She was crazy and there was ever possibility that she and Gordy were sociopaths.

"Grandma . . . Gordy does not love you, he never has. He likes young women, the age my mother was when he seduced and used her. He is not interested in elderly, wrinkled, old ladies like you. He is a rapist, and definitely not a God. He has used you all these years, for who knows what."

"You will pay for your disrespect of Gordy, Chester. He is god and could kill you at this moment with a thunderbolt. He has a rod that can send electricity thru you. He is a god of lightning."

It was at that point, that I realized my grandmother was totally delusional. There was no trying to reason with her or get her to see who Gordy was. I helped her into her mobile home and then headed across to Rosa's place to insist she spend the next night or so in a motel room, till I managed to get my grandmother committed. I knew that I would have to have a court order to do so. She was not going to go willingly. Luckily, Gordy was on his death bed and would not be able to interfere.

~   ~   ~

Rosa was in total shock when I told her that my grandmother was the one that had beheaded the hermit, and that the two of us were the intended next victims. She immediately packed a bag and I drove her to safety. She could run her business from her cell phone till my unbalanced, delusional grandma was locked up. The first step was going to the sheriff with what I had been told by motor mouth, my mother, and my grandmother. I knew who the killers of the hermit and Jennifer were. I had never filed a missing person report on Keesha and the boys, because I thought she had left me. I had that also to do. I feared that my stepfather was also somehow mixed up in my grandmother and Gordy's activities. He was missing, although my mother thought he had just left her. I intended to file a missing person's report on him also.

I kept telling myself that there was a possibility that Key was alive and in another state afraid to contact me. I needed that to hold on to. She was my soul mate. I just couldn't let myself consider the fact that she might be dead, a victim like the hermit and Jennifer.

It was time for me to get the investigation into my grandmother and Gordy's activities started. I had pushed buttons to become mayor. Now, it was time to be a man and push the buttons of law enforcement to see that Gordy, my grandmother, and stepfather were held accountable for their crimes. I was mayor.

I had just checked Rosa into a motel on the far side of the city for her safety. After telling her to lock the door and not open it for anyone, I made my way to the motel's parking lot. The next stop for me was the sheriff's office. I was unlocking Rosa's pickup when my cell phone rang. I checked to see who it was. It was my mother.

"What is up?" I asked.

"It is the happiness day of my life, Chester. You will never believe what has happened." She stated with a jovial voice.

"Did you win the lottery?" I asked, while waiting for her to tell me why she was in such a good mood.

"Mabel just called me. Gordy Gardenia was just now carted off to the hospital in an ambulance. He has had a stroke."

"For you that is probably a good thing, mom. However, grandma is not going to see it that way. Who called the ambulance?"

"Mabel did. She walked across the road in the snow because there was sudden, extreme, loud music coming from his place. She intended to ask him to turn the volume down, because it had her pit bulls in a barking and lunging frenzy. Apparently, Gordy turned his stereo up loud to snag attention. He was collapsed in the floor, in front of it, in his living room. When he didn't come to the door, Mabel peeped in his front window and saw him lying there."

"Does grandma know?" I asked thinking about my earlier conversation with her and how she thought he was an invincible god.

"According to Mabel, she made a bee-line to his mobile home, when she heard the ambulance's siren and then saw the flashing lights at his place. Does that surprise you?"

"No, that doesn't surprise me. Mom, it is time for us to call an ambulance and see that she is committed for mental evaluation this afternoon. I leave day after tomorrow. We have got to get it done today. Gordy being unable to help her is a good thing."

"The snow is getting really nasty, Chester. Can you give me an hour or so before I meet you there? I am running your stepfather's route till he shows up. I need the money to live on. Rosa found me a picker for the back. He is a hard worker, but I don't think he has a green card."

"A couple of hours from now is fine, mom. I have several loose ends, as mayor, to tie up. Call me when you are ready to meet me."

"Chester . . .," She called pausing.

"What is it mom?" I asked getting in Rosa's pickup and starting it. Next stop for me was the sheriff's office.

"Be careful today. I have got this eerie feeling that something is seriously out of whack in Gardenia. I dreamed about Snuff's girl friend last night, after I left you. She told me to ask Snuff to open the padlocked doors to Gordy's metal building, and let her out. I know she has to be buried somewhere in that metal building of Gordy's."

"Mom . . . this may come as shock to you, Grandma has admitted to me that she killed the hermit. I have got to go to the sheriff, once we get her committed."

"That doesn't surprise me, Chester. As much as I love her, she has always been crazy. She would have beaten me to death, the night I tried to tell her about me being pregnant by Gordy. Your grandfather pulled her off of me."

"Have you heard from dad?" I asked inquiring about my missing stepfather. He had been in my life since I was the age of two.

"No . . . It has been days. I have not seen or heard from him, neither has his brother or niece."

"I've got to go mom. I have a lot to do before meeting you." I stated ending our conversation.

I had just flipped my cell phone closed when it rang again. I glanced quickly to see who it was, before heading out to have a talk with the sheriff.

"What's up Snuff?" I answered.

"I have thought about it all night, Chester. Jennifer's body has to be buried in that metal building behind Gordy's mobile home. Why else would he close off the entrance and refuse to let people in there for as many years as you have been alive?"

"I think you might just be right, Snuff. I am just getting ready to head over to the sheriff's office to ask him to get a search warrant. This heavy snow may slow a search warrant and an investigation down. It may be after Rosa takes over as mayor, before they get around to investigating. Ten to twelve inches of snow predicted for tonight isn't going to help anything."

I then proceeded to tell Snuff that my grandmother had admitted to killing the hermit and had plans to kill me and Rosa in our sleep. Then, I told him that Gordy was in the hospital, having had a stroke.

"I can't wait on the sheriff, Chester. I want to know if your mother is in there, before you leave on your plane day after tomorrow. With Gordy in the hospital, the timing is right for us to take a secret look in that building."

"The building has no outside door, Snuff. Breaking and entering isn't exactly my style."

"I was talking to one of the city drivers early this morning, Chester. He was telling me that there was a pair of outside doors on the side next to Rosa. He said Gordy covered them over with sheet metal about the same time Jennifer came up missing. The driver said he helped hold a sheet or two of metal for Gordy when he did it. The driver says the building is sort of a mausoleum, a cover for some graves that no one visits anymore."

"Breaking and entering could get us in big trouble, Snuff. I am mayor for just two more days. I want to go out of office with a clean slate. Let the sheriff handle it."

"Is there anything illegal about entering a cemetery by its front gate?" He then asked.

"No . . . cemeteries are public places." I replied.

"Well then, I am going to take my reversible drill and remove the screws in the pieces of metal that have the entrance doors to the old cemetery closed off. You might say I am going to open its gate. Do you want to meet me there and just watch me? You know . . . just to see that I am respectful of the dead inside? I think I recall having some ancient ancestor that is buried inside. I will just be making a cemetery visit."

"Okay, I'll meet you there in about thirty minutes." I replied knowing that he didn't have any ancestor buried there, but it was an excuse to legally enter.

"Chester . . . I have to know if your mother is in there. I have spent all my life looking for her. I have never stopped loving her and wondering about what happened to her and you. I can't wait till the sheriff investigates. Last night your mother came to me in a dream. She said that I needed to rescue her and the others in bondage there. I may be grasping at straws, Chester, but the dream was so real, she was so real."

I was shocked, but didn't say anything. My mother had also had that dream. I really wasn't quite sure what to make of their shared experience. It was a little spooky or eerie.

"Okay, Snuff. I will meet you there shortly." I replied flipping my cell phone closed.

CHAPTER

TWENTY- TWO

Hell's Stench

Standing in eight inches of new fallen snow, in a white out of flakes swirling about our heads, I prepared to help Snuff remove three, two foot wide pieces of metal siding that were suspected to cover the entry doors to a small family cemetery. The driver who had helped Gordy close it up had told Snuff the name of the cemetery. It was called Heaven's Gate. The name had been used by my grandmother, although I had never understood what she was referring to, in her craziness. I had no idea the cemetery existed. Its entrance doors had been sided over for nineteen, going on twenty years. I was nineteen, going on twenty.

Snuff and I did not know what we were going to find inside the closed up, long forgotten little cemetery that had a huge, windowless, metal building covering it and protecting it from the smells and blowing litter from the dump. What we suspected, was that there might be Jennifer's body and the hermit's head buried somewhere inside. Other than that, we didn't know what we would find inside. Rosa had spoken of crying and mortuary music coming from the metal building on different occasions. My best friend and possible father, Snuff, had a girlfriend that had been missing for nineteen, going on twenty years. Until the previous night, he had never had a clue as to what had happened to her. I, also, had a missing girlfriend and two sons. I shared his need for closure, although I secretly hoped that Keesha had just left me in fear and was safe somewhere.

We paused for a moment before beginning the removal of three up and down sheets of metal siding in order to gain entrance. An unbelievable, nasty smelling stench seeped from the building as we removed screws from the siding. Whatever was inside the building was dead and rotting. Unless you were standing right next to the metal building, you would not know that smells were coming from there. You would think they were dump odors. Gordy's garbage dump was just a hundred or so feet from where we stood.

"Whew . . ." Snuff stated as he covered his nose with the cup of his gloved hand. "You would think this is a hot summer day and something major in Gordy's dump is rotting."

"You are right about that." I returned covering my own nose with the sleeve of my jacket. "What does that smell like?" I asked keeping my nose covered.

"It smells like a mixture of rotting flesh, bleach, and cheap air fresheners." He replied stepping back and turning his face in the opposite direction of the building to get a breath. "Let me take a quick drag on a cigarette before we remove anymore siding, Chester. I am a little edgy this morning and I need the nicotine to calm me."

"Sure, go ahead," I stated dreading what might be inside. I told myself that the scent was possibly just from a dead skunk that might have gotten trapped in the building, died, and was rotting.

Snuff, with his back to the smell, lit a cigarette. I turned from the smell too, but kept my nose covered with the cup of my hand.

"Chester . . . I am scared of what we are going to find inside, especially after listening to your mother's story last night." Snuff stated between drags on his cigarette. "You do know that my girlfriend is not the only missing woman in this county."

"I know." I replied simply to keep from having to breathe in the stomach turning odor.

"Just to be safe, Chester, I called Mabel before coming here and told her the whole story, just in case we disappear. We don't know what is waiting us inside."

"Gordy is in the hospital dying, Snuff. It is who we might find dead inside that I fear. Keesha and her boys came up missing about three years ago, just like your girlfriend. I thought she had left me over something I did. Now, I fear she and her two sons are inside. Just like you and Jennifer, I have had no word or clue as to where she went or what happened to her, till my mother told us that story last night."

"If our suspicions are right, Chester, Gordy is a rapist and murderer." Snuff stated taking a heavy drag off of his cigarette.

"I am positive we are going to find something dead inside. I hope it is just a dead skunk that the odor is coming from."

"That stench isn't coming from a skunk, Chester."

"I know, Snuff. I am just trying to convince myself that my grandmother isn't part of whatever is going on inside. She is crazy. I just don't want her to be totally off the wall, sociopath insane."

"All your grandmother could be guilty of is tricking your girlfriend into her vehicle and giving her a ride possibly over the state line. It was your stepfather that raped and beat her." He replied. "She might have just been hallucinating about the hermit."

"I confronted my grandmother earlier. She has admitted to killing Wolf Dog and having plans to kill me and Rosa."

"Where did you say you took Rosa?"

"She is across town in a motel room. Rosa has been there for me. I am not taking any chances with her safety."

"You honestly think that your wimp of a grandmother killed the Hermit?" Snuff asked taking a last drag on his cigarette. "Wolf Dog is a head taller than her and almost doubles her in weight. It doesn't sound logical, Chester, unless she had help. He was hung by his ankles from his overhead light figure."

"My grandmother's parents owned a chicken processing plant when she was growing up. I don't know how she did it, but he was hung by his ankles like a plucked chicken ready for slaughter."

"She couldn't have done that alone, Chester. Your grandmother possibly weighs a hundred pounds dripping wet. The hermit was in his prime and strong from lifting and emptying trash barrels day after day."

"I haven't considered that," I replied.

"I suppose we will find the answers to all our questions inside. Are you ready to help me take off the metal siding?" Snuff asked turning back to the metal siding and the stench.

"I am ready." I replied with my heart in a panic. If my birth mother, Keesha, and my two tuxedo sons were buried inside, I knew that I was going to lose it.

Just as Snuff started work again with his reversible drill on the metal siding's screws, my cell phone jingled.

"Give me just a minute Snuff. It is Rosa. I have to answer, in case she is having a problem of some sort."

"Go ahead, Chester." He replied pulling a screw from the siding.

"Are you okay?" I asked Rosa putting my ear to my cell phone.

"I am fine, don't worry about me. I have a cigarette lighter in my pocket. If any white sheet shows up here, they are going to get burned."

"Just don't answer the door." I cautioned her as well as being amused with her. "White sheets don't always come wearing their linen."

"White sheet men are not what I have called to talk to you about, Chester. I have the most exciting news for you." She stated in a very upbeat voice.

"What is it?" I asked, wanting to get back to Snuff and help him with the siding. I watched him take out a second screw while I waited for her reply.

"How many times have you applied to Zeke's Feet Detective Agency, since you got out of high school?"

"I think my current count is 56 or 57. . . Why?"

"Well, Mayor Chester Holly, you have a letter from Zeke's Feet. Carlos brought me over the mail from my box. Do you want me to open it?"

"Just do it quick, Rosa. It is probably just turndown number 57."

There was a pause and then Rosa squealed on the phone. I held my cell phone out from my ear a little.

"Chester, you have an interview in June. The reply says the agency has a detective leaving the second week in June and they are looking for a replacement."

"That is great news, Rosa. God knows I have filled out enough applications. I knew that I would one day push the right button and Zeke would give me a chance. I was right."

Then there was a brief pause.

"Chester . . . I have a confession to make."

"Can it wait till I see you tonight? Snuff and I are doing something really important at the moment."

"No, it can't wait. I sort of doctored up your last application, before I sent it off. You were not getting any results, so I figured out what Zeke's button was and pushed it for you."

"You would think that it was you that met Dr. Mayo." I muttered and then said to her. "What button did you push, so I will know how to reply when I go for my interview?"

Snuff had the first sheet loose and was pulling it off the building.

"Don't be mad at me. I called out to California and talked with the receptionist. I told her I was the Mayor here and was looking for a detective. I asked her what kind Zeke hired and what credentials his detectives had on their applications. She was more than happy to tell me about her special detectives."

"Okay . . . just tell me quickly what you put on my application. Snuff and I are really busy with something important."

"Now, don't be mad at me Chester. You wanted an interview, and I figured out how to get you one. You just have to dress appropriately. I described your uniqueness on your application. The agency is looking for a certain type of individual."

"I gather I am not going to like what you are about to tell me, am I?" I replied biting my lip.

"The receptionist told me that Zeke only hires women. Anyway, I marked the gender box on your last application female and put your name down as Holly Chester, not Chester Holly." She stated quickly and then snickered.

"You did what?" I asked in total shock.

She quickly added. "The owner of the agency thinks you are the youngest female Mayor in our state."

"Rosa, if I wasn't so damn busy at this moment, I think I might be tempted to strangle you."

"I got you what you wanted, an interview. Now, you just have to dress appropriately. It took me just one application to push Zeke's buttons. I believe it has taken you 56 application attempts, and all have been turn downs." Rosa

259

stated ribbing me, laughing, and then hanging up on me before I could reply. I flipped my cell phone closed and put it in my pocket.

Snuff had all the screws out of the last two sheets of siding. I grabbed them one at a time and pulled them off for him. He had waited for me to finish my phone call, before starting on the screws in the hinges of a double set of locked wooden doors behind the siding.

"You are not going to believe what Rosa has done?" I stated in exasperation as Snuff worked on the screws.

"I know. Rosa showed me the application before she sent it off back around Christmas. She said it was a special going away present from her that you would never forget." He replied breaking out in laughter. After a moment or so, he added. "You know, the doctor told Jennifer and me that our baby was going to be a girl. I think your mother would be pleased with the name Holly."

"I think I might just strangle you and Rosa later in the day." I replied red faced.

"Are you ready to go in, Chester?" Snuff asked removing the last screws from the frame. "We are going to have to kick the wooden doors in and out of their frame. The door knobs are missing and there is a chain and padlock holding the center of the two doors together."

"If this is the only way in here Snuff, where does the crying and music come from? Gordy must have a door entering from his trailer."

"I'm sure Gordy had your grandmother lock his trailer doors before he was taken to the hospital. As we discussed earlier, this is our legal way in. We are entering to visit an ancient loved one." Snuff replied.

The stench was filtering out around the now loose door frame. It was incredibly awful. I hoped it was just a dead skunk rotting on the inside. However, the smell was worse than any skunk I had ever smelled.

"I may lose it, if Jennifer is in there, Chester. She is the only woman I have ever loved."

"Believe me, I understand, Snuff." I replied. "If Keesha and the boys are in there, I don't know how I will handle it. I have waited for almost three years for a word from her, never considering she and her two boys might be dead."

"Are you ready?" Snuff asked as huge snowflakes swirled in the sky around us. "I think a good kick or two will cause the wooden doors and frame to fall inward."

"I would like to say I am ready, Snuff." I replied cupping my hand over my nose. The stench was unbelievable.

At that point, we alternated kicks till the door fell at an angel inward. An unbelievable stench shot out the door like there had been some sort of gas build up inside. The smell was like rotted animal flesh mixed with skunk scent, rotten potatoes, bleach, and rotten eggs. I just don't have words to describe the odor. I immediately stood back and puked in the snow to one side of the doors. The odor had violently turned my stomach inside out. I couldn't help but react to it. Snuff jumped back to and went to gagging.

"Are you all right, Chester?" Snuff asked after calming his own stomach. He spit his chew into the snow and wiped his mouth on his jacket sleeve.

"Give me a minute," I shot back taking a handful of snow and washing my face with it, hoping it would calm my stomach. Never in my life had I experienced such a foul odor. Summer dump smells were bad, but they were minor compared to what we had just encountered.

"Here . . ." Snuff said handing me a bit of his chew. "Put this under your upper lip. It just might keep you from puking when we go in. I know you don't chew, but desperate moments call for desperate measures." He then put a big wad beneath his upper lip. "Concentrate on the chew and not the smell."

I did as I was told. My stomach was rolling and churning violently. I belched, my stomach wanting to react again.

"Do you want to go first?" Snuff asked pointing to the dark opening in the side of the building. All was dark inside. There were no sky lights or windows to let light in. It was like entering a dark cave.

"After you, Snuff . . . I am sure this is a moment in time that neither of us is ever going to forget. I will be right behind you."

"Hopefully, there is a light switch on one side or the other of the door. I didn't think about bringing a flash light. I will check the left side of the door opening, you check the right."

"That sounds like a plan . . ." I managed to mutter. The smell was unbelievable as we stepped into the darkness. I told myself to concentrate on the taste of the chew which was awful, but far more pleasant that the stench.

Snuff stepped past the fallen doors and made his way around them to the left to search for a light switch. I followed him and started feeling the wall on the right. Our eyes were adjusted to the white out blizzard outside. The inside of the building was total darkness. We needed light to see by.

Suddenly, feeling up and down the wall next to the door opening on my side, my hand came across a single light switch. I flipped it up and a series of over head long florescent tube lights started flickering on at the end of the building connected to Gordy's mobile home. We focused our attention in that direction. Then, the lights flickered and came on. Overhead speakers started playing religious, mortuary type music.

"What the hell . . ." Snuff stated loudly in shock as he eyed the back of Gordy's trailer and the little cemetery there. It only occupied about an eighth of the huge, mostly dark inside, metal building.

The back of Gordy's trailer had no windows in it, only a single door coming out of what had to be the back bedroom. It was evident that a window had been taken out in that location and a small door put in. We had not turned yet to look at the far end of the metal building in the opposite direction behind us.

"That is the mortuary music that Rosa has been complaining about. It plays as long as someone is in here, but turns off when the lights go out." I replied recalling how the music had played on New Year's Eve just before the ball had dropped on TV. Someone had been in the metal building briefly that night and had flipped the switch making the eerie music play. My question now was, what caused the crying in the wind?

Then Snuff and I eyed the walls above the tiny family cemetery, the back of Gordy's mobile home. Every inch was covered with white fake flowers. Also, you could smell the distinct smell of bleach coming from them.

"Those are dump flowers, Snuff. That is where the thousands of dump flowers, that Gordy brought my grandmother over the years, have gone. I now see why she has bought four gallons of bleach every week. Gordy has covered every inch of these walls with bleached white, fake flowers."

"I used to laugh at Rosa before the two of you got together. She was always insisting that at the end of the day, after all the haulers had gone home, that she heard pecking sounds coming from here. It had to be Gordy nailing down each one of those damn flowers!"

"Look over there Snuff . . . there is another way in here. Gordy has cut out his bedroom window and put a door in."

I eyed the door, but Snuff turned around to face the other end of the building.

"Turn around, look to the other end, and tell me what you see, Chester. I think I may have lost it, in the moment, and not really seeing what I think I am seeing." Snuff stated turning as white as a sheet.

I turned around to look in the direction he was pointing and in shock saw what he was referring to.

"Oh . . . Please God, no . . ." I muttered seeing at least fifty 4x4 posts secured in the ground in upright positions. On the top of each was mounted what appeared to be the skull or withered, dried up head of a human being. The chew didn't help me at that point. I heaved knowing where the stench was coming from. We were looking at the severed heads of at least fifty missing people.

"Hold it together, Chester. I have to know if Jennifer is one of them. I am just as horrified as you, but I have to know. I need you to go with me to the end, and be there for me if I lose it. Jennifer was everything to me."

I stood up and knew I had to be pale as a ghost after the second round of puking. I was trembling on the inside. It was Keesha and the boys that I had to go to the other end and look for.

"Do you see that huge white, throne like chair sitting in the middle of the staked heads?" Snuff asked as we started to walk in their direction. We were both in shock and not prepared to view a killing field and the trophy skulls of a headhunter.

"I see the chair and all the staked heads and urns on shelves behind the chair" I replied scanning everything in disbelief. Every inch of the walls of the entire building, on the inside, were covered with single, white, bleached, blooms that had been attached. There were at least fifty heads, maybe more, attached to the top of four foot sections of 4x4s. Around the foot of the huge white chair were the skeletons of children, at least a dozen of them. Behind the white throne like seat were shelves with urns of ashes perched there.

"The urns have to be the years of missing ashes from the mortuaries in town." Snuff replied. "Do you think Mabel's two sons, who steal cemetery items, have been part of whatever it is that we are looking at? They are adults."

"I don't think so, Snuff. One is in jail and the other is down in Texas. Mabel hasn't heard from her three older sons for a year or so." I answered eyeing all the skulls and withered heads. "Gordy rapes, but who is his head hunter? He would never kill his own son, Wolf Dog."

We sped up our pace heading for the first row of stakes. I noticed, as we reached the first row, that all of the human skulls and withered heads on their stakes faced the huge white chair. At that point I could see that there were at least twenty or so infant and children's skeletons in seated positions at the front base of the white chair. It looked just to be a handful from the other end. Up close, you could see that they were stacked against each other. The children's skeletons were intact.

"What kind of a monster was Gordy?" I managed to spit out asking as I eyed the group of little skeletons. A couple of them still had flesh on them and were withered, having not fully decomposed yet.

"A very smart one . . . ," Snuff replied with disgust in his voice. "He used the smells of the dump to cover the stench of his kills."

In total horror and shock, we started slowly walking the five rows of staked heads in front of the white chair, looking for Jennifer, my biological mother.

"Oh God. . ." I gasped suddenly stopping at one that was a fresh kill. It still had dried blood on its stake.

"It is my stepfather." I gasped with my stomach rolling. Once more, I turned to the side and dry heaved. My stepfather was just a head with one eye open and one eye partially closed.

"Oh shit . . ." Snuff replied. "He has only been dead a day or so. Where do you think his body is?"

About that time, a voice spoke behind us. We spun around in fright and panic, knowing we were standing in a killing field.

"Welcome to Heaven." My grandmother stated as she stood facing us wearing a white sheet like it was a robe trailing behind her. She was carrying a huge, sharp, antique military sword in her hand and was pointing it at us. "God Gordy isn't here at the moment, but he will be returning. His throne is waiting and he will resurrect in three days and claim it. All the children at the foot of the throne are waiting his resurrection. Aren't they good children?" She stated in a voice that said she was insane. "Have you come to wait with me and all his followers who are waiting for his resurrection?"

In that moment, there was no doubting who Gordy's accomplice was. There was visible dried blood on the sword.

"You are crazy Grandma!" I yelled in disgust and horror. My stomach was still churning from the stench and in shock at having seen my stepfather's head on a stake. Now, I was seeing the unhinged side of my grandmother, the side my grandfather called a wild card. "There are dead people in here that, from all indications, have been murdered and beheaded just like the hermit."

"I am not crazy!" She retorted in a harsh, sarcastic voice while banishing the sharp sword in a circle above her head like a pro. I am the keeper of Heaven's

Gate, the protector of God Gordy's Heaven. You can't enter Heaven if you are unworthy. I slay all those who try to enter unworthy. You are unworthy Chester. You have not knocked on any doors to secure your place in the 144,000 that will live and reign with God in his new Heaven and new Earth."

"You are mixing up your religious beliefs with whatever Gordy's delusions are, Grandma. Gordy is not a god and this is not Heaven. This is a killing ground. You or Gordy one is a sociopath, a head hunter."

"I have had to kill fallen angels who have wandered in here, trying to over-throw my god Gordy's Heaven. All those I have slain are now his slaves for eternity. He will resurrect them and they will work his vineyards and fields in the new Heaven and new Earth. Gods don't work their own harvest fields." She stated pointing at the huge white chair with stakes and heads facing it. "All bow before my god Gordy, or they lose their heads. The children bowed. They got to keep their heads. I just put them to sleep with poison in their soda."

I wanted to throw up so bad, I was trembling. It was unfathomable that my Grandmother had poisoned and killed twenty or so children.

"Grandma, Gordy is in the hospital and possibly dead. He is not returning from the dead. He is an evil man, a rapist and a murderer. You have killed all these people for no reason."

"Gordy is god. He will come again, and I will be the queen of this Heaven that he has created."

"Put down the sword Grandma. Gordy will not be resurrecting or return-ing here, although I do hope he burns in Hell for eternity for the atrocious acts committed in this building."

"Did you ever ask yourself what god's name is, Chester?" My grandmother asked with her sword raised and pointed at me.

"It definitely is not Gordy." I huffed, while sick as a dog on the inside from the stench and what I had witnessed. My whole being was trembling on the inside from the trauma.

"God's name is Adam and Mrs. God's name is Eve. I will be Eve when Gordy marries me in the new Garden of Eden."

"Gordy has used you all of these years, Grandma. He has never had any intention of marrying you. He never divorced his first wife. Gordy was raised Catholic. They believe in marriage forever. He chose the hermit's mother, not you. Grandpa has been dead over two years. If Gordy had wanted to make you his queen, he would have divorced her and married you right after grandpa died. You were raised Catholic. Wolf Dog's mother will be his wife, his queen, in the afterlife, not you."

Suddenly, she let out an angry screech and raised her sword and started toward us, swinging it. Snuff and I jumped out of her way, we were younger than her. Her sword came down knocking my stepfather's head from his stake. Seeing the familiar face roll across the dirt, she seemed distracted for some reason and backed off eyeing my stepfather's set eyes staring at her.

"Grandma, is Keesha and my boys in here?" I shouted in horror as Snuff suddenly fell in front of one of the skulls he had run behind to escape her sword. He had burst into tears.

"It is Jennifer, Chester. This skull has a silver side tooth. She had one." He muttered ignoring me and the fact that my grandmother was wielding a sword.

"Keep your act together, Snuff. You owe it to Jennifer to live and see that she gets justice." I yelled trying to distract my grandmother by walking away from Snuff who was vulnerable at the moment. "I am asking you one more time, Grandma. Is my tuxedo black Keesha and my two tuxedo boys in here?"

"Only white sheets go to Heaven, Chester; unless a god decides he needs slaves. Your black whore and her two little bastards were saved by Gordy to one day work his fields." She stated pointing to a row of ten or so stakes with heads positioned and chained to the backside of the huge white chair.

I ran back to the chair and circled in behind it to take a look at the ten or so heads on the stakes there. They all had one thing in common. They had been there awhile and were just skulls on stakes, with the exception they all had kinky, curly, black hair remaining in places. It was obvious that each was

African American or possibly Hispanic. The posts were chained to the white chair, like they were chained human bodies. I took a quick look down the row of heads. Turning my attention to the far end of the row, I recognized Key's hair on a skull. Next to her, on two shorter posts, were two tiny skulls that I knew had to belong to my Tank and Tag.

At that point, I looked back to check on Snuff. He was collapsed on his knees in front of the skull he had said was my mother Jennifer.

"Dad . . ." I yelled, seeing that my grandmother was raising her sword again and heading for him.

About that time a rock shot thru the air and came in contact with the raised sword. It knocked the sword from my grandmother's hand. A second rock came whizzing thru the air and caught my grandmother on the side of her chin, knocking her to the ground. I spun around to see where the rocks had come from. Granny Mabel stood in the kicked in doorway of the metal building grinning.

"You swore me in as Marshall and told me to keep an eye on the place. I have just done my sworn duty." She stated as Snuff rose from his knee position in tears and in shock. My moonshine girl had saved my father's life. It was a debt that I could never repay her. I was thankful for all the times Mabel had rocked me as a kid, practicing her aim.

I then walked down to where Key's skull sat perched on a chained post. Lovingly, I touched her hair and then the tiny skulls of Tank and Tag.

"Dad . . ." I called using the term for the first time. "I . . . I . . . I . . ." and then blacked out. The stress of finding Key and the boys in that condition was more than I could handle.

When I revived, three weeks later, I was in the psych ward of the city's hospital. Snuff was seated with his head resting on the rail of my hospital bed holding my hand. Gordy was dead and my grandmother had been arrested for her participation in over a hundred murders. She was in solitary confinement in the county jail.

~   ~   ~

My beloved Key's head, as well as the boys', had to be cremated. I claimed their ashes. They would go with me to California. I would bury them where I could visit them. They were my family and I wanted them to be close to me.

My grandmother had gone totally off her rocker when Gordy died. I couldn't get any further information out of her concerning Key. I assume Gordy helped my grandmother kidnap Key, Tank, and Tag on the night of my graduation. The smells of burning flesh that I had noticed, after my high school graduation, when I had walked across the dump, had to have been their bodies being done away with.

Snuff also entered a time of grieving for Jennifer, my mother. Her skull was also cremated. There was no body to bury. Snuff bought her the most expensive burial urn he could afford. I did the same for Keesha, Tank, and Tag. I spent all of my savings.

My mother quit drinking and doing drugs after Gordy was dead. She had my stepfather's head cremated and buried his ashes next to my grandfather's in Mt. Pleasant Cemetery. She also buried the ashes of Grandma's stillborn baby there. The button can filled with the baby's ashes and buttons were on the shelf behind the white throne, with multiple urns of stolen ashes.

My grandmother was sentenced to life in prison. The metal building was torn apart by law enforcement in order to excavate for bodies and ashes of the missing. My grandfather had said my grandmother was a wild card. He just never suspected how wild. It is a wonder he had lived to be an old man and die of lung cancer.

One hundred and seven sets of human remains, heads, or ashes were found. The victims included my Keesha, Tank, Tag, my stepfather, two door knocking ladies from my grandmother's hall, Jennifer, the hermit's mother, the missing minister, the pianist, and three of Mabel's sons that she had thought were running from the law and just not calling her. Gordy was a sociopath rapist who preyed on young women. My grandmother was a sociopath killer who honed her skills in her parent's chicken processing plant as she was growing up.

My grandmother loved only one person, Gordy Gardenia. Whatever he told her, or asked her to do, she went along with it for a lifetime. In devotion to Gordy, my grandmother had killed anyone that she thought was a threat to her becoming Gordy's queen. Many of the young women found in the metal building had been beheaded by my grandmother. Gordy loved no one but baby Gracie. Gordy was a rapist with a taste for very young women. My grandmother killed all of his victims, except Jennifer. Gordy killed her.

I wish I had listened to Gracie on the day I walked up to her door to chat and ask about what was going on between my grandmother and Gordy. She had told me that she had peeked behind a locked door and saw something that could get her killed. I now realize that she must have somehow got a key and unlocked the door in Gordy's bedroom that opened out into the metal building. She had runaway in fear for her life. I was lucky to have gotten the newspaper clipping from her. The police tested DNA on a hairbrush belonging to Gracie. She turned out to be a missing newborn belonging to a teen that had disappeared two counties over about nineteen years prior. No one knows why Gordy chose to keep Gracie. Her mother's skeleton was found in an unmarked grave in the little family cemetery inside the metal building. She was one of Gordy's early victims. Her head and body were together in her grave. Why Gordy chose to tell the story about him having a young wife in the city that had left him with a baby is unknown. He took a lot of secrets to the grave with him.

I did not attend the spring semester at the university in California. I spent January and part of February in a psych hospital due to a mental collapse over Key, Tank, and Tag's horrific deaths. Snuff and I helped law enforcement piece all of the tragedies together. Rosa visited me every day in the hospital and held me in her arms, when my tears fell like rain. Snuff never left my side. He held himself together for me.

Mabel had the three heads of her sons cremated. She buried them next to her trash hauler husband in their family cemetery. She threw one heck of a shine party afterwards and all of Rosa's drivers attended. There was no one sober enough to drive Rosa's trucks the next day. Even Rosa tied one on in respect of Mabel's sons. After all, Mabel was Marshall of Gardenia and deserved the respect. Not only that, she was a hero. She had saved the former Mayor Chester Holly's life, and that of his father.

Rosa became the mayor of Gardenia, the murder capital of our state. When she took office, Gardenia was home to ten citizens and 107 murders. I was in a psych ward when she took office.

Also found in the metal building were the white feathers of at least a hundred or more white turkeys. My grandmother had taken their feathers and made angel wings. She had glued the feathers on the back of the little, full skeletons of the children that sat at the base of the white chair. Granny Mabel had complained to me that my grandmother had been throwing turkey heads to her dogs, to get past them and steal shine. It is believed, she got some of her victims drunk, before she chopped off their heads with her antique military sword. No one knows where the sword came from.

The original twenty vaults and caskets in Heaven's Gate Cemetery were dug up by law enforcement to make sure there weren't extra bodies in them.

On the first day of June, I rented a van in preparation to kiss Gardenia goodbye. I had three semesters of college left, and would complete them at the university in California.

When I was seventeen, I wanted to kiss Gardenia and its citizens goodbye. Now, I was a few days away from turning twenty and my feelings had changed. I was not going to California alone. My father, Snuff, sold his trailer and acreage. He was going with me to start over in California. We both were reeling from the horrific, tragic deaths of the women we loved. We needed each other. A third person was going with us to California, and at my request. Granny Mabel's three older sons were dead and her two younger sons were slightly touched and not capable of watching out for her. I owed Mabel a debt that I could never repay. She had saved Snuff's life the day my grandmother was swinging her sword around in the metal building. I told Mabel that I was going to need a house keeper as well as someone to watch my backside in California. She gave her Pit Bulls away and seemed relieved to have someone want her. She was going on eighty years old. I couldn't leave her behind. Besides, every good detective needs someone who can throw a rock and protect his backside in a pinch.

In the very back of the van, secured safely in a shipping box, were four urns containing the ashes of Jennifer, Key, Tank, and Tag.

There is one unexplainable thing concerning the solving of the Heaven's Gate murders. One of the original tombstones in Heaven's Gate Cemetery marked the grave of a Dr. Melvin Mayo. He had been buried in the cemetery two years before Gordy Gardenia bought the huge farm to build his dump on. His tombstone did not have a religious or medical inscription on it. Instead, there were the simple words: I DARED TO TEST THE GODS.

When Dr. Mayo's casket was dug up, to see if there were extra bodies in it, what was found instead were multiple love letters from different nurses, and at least sixteen pieces of dried up, molded, banana crème pie that had been buried with him.

I returned to the hospital where I had met Dr. Mayo, after I got out of the psych ward. The head nurse on my grandfather's floor told me that Dr. Mayo had been dead for at least forty years and that her mother, a former head nurse had once worked for him. He had died from complications from a simple surgery for hemorrhoids.

Dr. Mayo reached back from the grave and chose to push my buttons. His admonition, telling me to test the gods, has shaped my life. Not only is he my hero, I think he has chosen to be my spirit guide.

Have you encountered your SPIRIT GUIDE or ANGEL IN HUMAN FORM somewhere on your journey? They walk all around us. I was oblivious to Dr. Mayo being a ghost, the day I encountered him as I sat with my ill grandfather.

Test the Gods!

Zeke's Feet Detective Series

Available at Amazon.com

SILENT WINGS

TEST THE GODS

Coming Soon...

Christmas Comes Knocking

www.ingramcontent.com/pod-product-compliance
Lightning Source LLC
Chambersburg PA
CBHW070853250626

47159CB00003B/1045